THE ARK OF TIME

BOOK ONE OF THE ARK TRILOGY

by PETER A. KERR

An A DEO LUMEN publication.

The Ark of Time

Copyright © 2014 Peter A. Kerr

All rights reserved.

An A DEO LUMEN publication

www.ArkTrilogy.com

Library of Congress Cataloging-in-Publication Data

Kerr, Peter A.

 Ark of Time / Peter A. Kerr m—First Edition

"An A DEO LUMEN publication."

ISBN-13: 978-0-9899698-9-5 (Softcover and e-book)
    1.   Space Warfare—Fiction.

A DEO LUMEN books are available at Amazon.com in print and Kindle format

Second Edition: May 2015

Printed in the United States of America

Cover images by ©iStockphoto.com/Sylphe_7 and NASA

Revised cover design by Peter A. Kerr

DEDICATION

To my loving wife Rebecca—in appreciation for the past and in anticipation of enjoying your company for all time.

Contents

ACKNOWLEDGMENTS

The *Ark of Time* is the first book in the Ark Trilogy and represents many years of plotting and planning. I wish to thank all those who supported me and sacrificed to bring this book into reality. First and foremost I am grateful to my wife Rebecca and my children Asriel, Mikiah, Zachary, and Saraya. I hope your sacrifice of my time and attention reaps dividends of both in the future, as I truly love your presence in my life. Thereafter I wish to thank my editor and former student Rebecca Frazer for her countless hours making this book better—thanks also for having a heart to make everything around you better. The errors that may linger in this book are most certainly all mine. Thanks also to my mother Mary Ann Kerr, who is an excellent author of historic fiction, and my father Philip N. Kerr, who taught me what it means to be a strong father and a loving daddy. Thanks to John Jeffers for reading the first draft and offering excellent suggestions, as well as to all my students and friends who have encouraged me to complete the book so they could read it. Finally, thanks to you readers—I hope you'll enjoy this book and check out my other books at ArkTrilogy.com, and that we'll be partners in reading for many years to come.

Peter A. Kerr
May 2015 A.D.

THE ARK
OF TIME

CHAPTER 1

Last Stand

"That's a suicide mission." Admiral Bill Haarkonan delivered the comment in his typical deadpan fashion, as if the fact that he was being ordered to face his own death were no more important than ordering something to eat for lunch. United Earth High Command undoubtedly realized what a futile action it would be to make a full frontal assault with the pittance of a fleet at his command.

"I know," said the United Earth Secretary of Defense, looking genuinely miserable. "I can't tell you how hard it is even just to ask you to do it."

"Then don't ask." Haarkonan couldn't help feeling slightly amused by the look of bewilderment crossing his old friend's face. As if he would let his old Academy roommate down at a time like this. "Because, sir, we volunteer."

Both men grew silent, recognizing a depth of mutual respect seldom found outside the military, where acts of heroism were often counted in lives lost as much as in medals gained.

"Thanks," said the Secretary lamely.

"It's been a pleasure serving with you, sir. Keep the pride, class of 2295. Haarkonan out."

The admiral punched off the connection and then stared for a second at the blank viz-screen, thinking how appropriate it was that his last words to his commander and friend was their Academy class slogan. The fires of that hell-of-an-education had forged a lifelong friendship worth every drop of sweat and blood the Academy had squeezed from him.

But that was a long time ago, and he didn't have time for memories. All memories these days led him back to Elise. His dear Elise, wife for 32 years whom he had left in their home on Lunar One when the first aliens had arrived...

He didn't have time for memories; he only had time to die. And God-willing, he'd take some of the invaders with him.

Haarkonan stood and turned briskly, striding out of his private quarters toward the command bridge, his mind trying desperately to find a tactic that could hurt the enemy and make his fleet's sacrifice count. He had risen in the ranks due not only to hard work, but also because of his reputation as a creative problem-solver. In fact, he was generally acknowledged as the best tactician in Earth's small military. Sadly, most of his tactics had been employed against terrorist organizations rather than true militaries. And in this case, no tactic could prevent his certain defeat.

"Admiral on the bridge!" announced Lieutenant Frida Beroni, quickly dodging out of his way as he stalked toward his place on the battle deck. The "command chair" looked like a small plastic lounge chair that had been mixed with a computer bank. It had been recently added, and Haarkonan's huge six-foot-five, lanky frame made him look like an adult precariously balancing on a child's rocking chair. Indeed, the *Valkyrie* itself was actually the latest large colony ship, recently refitted and launched to head the small "armada" in defense of Earth. No real military spaceships had ever been built. Humanity had never encountered any type of foreign sentience. No one had thought of needing warships in space, and Earth had maintained its ban on all nuclear weapons since the Great Nuclear War of 2040. After all, humanity's greatest enemy was humanity. Or so Haarkonan had once believed.

The admiral settled himself before looking up at the large frontal view screen. Though he had a standard head DataPort behind his left ear that could connect with the space craft or interface with other information sources, on this ship only the pilot needed the enhanced reflexes jacking-in delivered. The earth calmly rotated in the view screen, making Haarkonan realize viscerally what he already accepted intellectually: Earth was doomed, and he was about to die.

"Those who are about to die salute you," he muttered wryly under his breath, looking for the last time at the peaceful image with swirling white clouds and scattered patches of green strewn across the sea of blue. The words would be just as true for his armada as it had been for the gladiators of ancient Rome. He hit a button to change the view. Looming large and getting larger was a swarm of objects racing toward his mother planet with reckless abandon.

Haarkonan knew this would be the first and last stand against these beings. The first encounter humans had with them could hardly be called a fight, much less a stand, though it had crippled Earth's ship-building facilities. Just a few weeks earlier the earth was shocked as hundreds of alien craft sprung from the Kuiper Belt heading toward Earth. Even more disturbing, craft had erupted from the depths of Mars and quickly swarmed toward the moon.

Admiral Haarkonan would never forget the horrifying visuals, as it was one of the few times he had ever experienced the cliché of his skin crawling. In Lunar One's sparkling three-dimensional viz he had seen the red planet erupting with hard-shell creatures that blended perfectly with the dusky-red sand of Mars. At first scientists had hypothesized that the creatures were wearing some sort of space suits, as they clearly gave off a metallic sheen in the thin atmosphere of the fourth planet from Sol. And how could anyone live on that planet without protective equipment? Scientists were no longer certain. The beings moved as if completely unencumbered by external suits or machinery, with many leg-like tentacles fluidly coordinated to produce speeds far in excess of any Earth creature. There seemed to be many body types, with some of them even sprouting wings at will. Still, everyone was surprised when the first alien "launched" into the sky, seemingly tossed by another creature that had been dubbed "Mother." The small craft-beings broke Mars' atmosphere like rocket ships, but never spewed a plume of fire or any other recognizable trailing indications of propulsion.

That was scary enough. But then light-radar had confirmed that the full storm of aliens were approaching Earth from the Kuiper Belt at speeds approaching half the speed of light—much faster than humans had ever been able to achieve. That force had decelerated significantly and now lit up the admiral's view screen as it neared the earth.

"Arm nukes one and two," Haarkonan bellowed, flipping his wild blonde bangs back and away from his slate-blue eyes. Though most of his hair was neatly clipped short, his longish bangs were barely within regulation, making a subtle statement to the establishment that you didn't have to be a blockhead robot-type to serve in the military.

"Weapons armed," came the clipped reply from the tactical weapons officer. Only the gentle hum of computers and occasional keystrokes could be heard, as the *Valkyrie*'s crew each tried to swallow their own fear and despair. Haarkonan let the silence linger, knowing his crew had to win their inner battles and make their peace with death.

Looking at the battle screen, Haarkonan couldn't understand how all the explorations of Mars had missed the hundred or so aliens that had been buried there, or had failed to detect the approaching armada. The enemy's vanguard must have been deep below the red planet's surface and dwelled there for centuries if not millennia. Humanity had long thought water and life were once possible on Mars, but the vanguard of aliens was never suspected. As the first swarm had quickly approached the moon, manned and unmanned probes had been sent to gather data but were summarily destroyed. In fact, from the video captured by powerful telescopes orbiting Earth and anchored on the moon, it seemed as if the foreign craft had simply rammed into Earth's welcoming messengers, potentially by accident.

Haarkonan smiled grimly as he remembered the Liberal Dove Party leaders eat their words of peace as the alien "reconnaissance" force turned into the vanguard of an all-out assault. There was no stealth, and no attempt to parley with humanity. Their intent was clear from the beginning, but humanity had controlled its impulses, firing on the massed aliens only after the first hideous creature slammed into a moon transport and devoured its hull. With seeming ease they had destroyed Lunar One, crushing titanium and steal in what looked like pinchers that protruded from their….mouths? Haarkonan was one of only a few hundred survivors who had once called the moon home.

"Sir, the vanguard force that originally arose from Mars has now been completely integrated with the main body of aggressors," reported Lt. Beroni. "Their fleet will arrive at Earth in under four hours."

Haarkonan grunted acknowledgement as a humorous thought fluttered through his mind. He may be the military leader who failed to protect Earth, but at least he didn't need to fear history. This menace would ensure there would be no subsequent history. What a time for such vainglorious pride! But he was certain these creatures were vastly superior, and he expected they would have little trouble destroying Earth's land defenses. They could also easily discover the three colonies and few dozen outposts and labs humanity possessed scattered throughout the Milky Way. Those wouldn't really even need to be found—all of them would be doomed in under a decade without Earth's support anyway.

If only humanity had taken to the stars a few centuries earlier! Then there might have been enough time to build self-sustaining colonies, in essence having a redundant system to keep humanity from extinction. But that would only have been possible had humanity given up its selfish tendencies and united as one people earlier. In a way, it was fierce determination and selfishness that made humanity strong and ingenious, but those qualities also had cost the lives of half the planet's population in the GNW of 2040.

What he wouldn't give for a fraction of the nuclear capability Earth possessed back then! While nuclear technology was still harnessed for energy and propulsion, all weapons-grade fissile materials were banned. The knowledge to build nuclear missiles

13

existed, but humanity's frantic efforts to create a defense for Earth had only resulted in the *Valkyrie*'s two weapons, which were actually found in storage and refurbished. The rest of the spacecraft under Haarkonan's command had a miscellany of mining lasers and other construction energy beams that had been hastily modified for the upcoming combat.

Haarkonan rubbed his eyes with fatigue. He had been up for what felt like the whole week planning and pulling together the defense force, and his usually clear gray-blue eyes showed the bloodshot red of extreme weariness. If these over-grown lobsters thought Earth was just going to surrender, they were in for a surprise. He may have no hope of winning, but he sure as Heaven and Hell was going to make this battle count for something.

Valkyrie's display filled with the images of the advancing fleet. It was like a wall of huge metal ants, stretching miles long and wide and deep. The swarm advanced in roughly a cube-shaped formation, with no discernible tactical intent. Enemy vessel sizes ranged from just about two meters to large "mother" ships easily the size of a small city. There were five Motherships, spaced equally at the front of the moving mass. These "mothers" were like the one that had tossed the smaller creatures/craft into space from Mars, before it somehow sprang from Mars' surface to join the main body of invaders. Haarkonan had targeted two of the mothers with nukes, hoping they were valuable assets. Their dull-reddish hulls seemed to soak in the sun's rays, not letting any light escape like the tell-tale gleam of most metals—if they were hulls of ships and not exoskeletons. The mothers also had huge tentacles sprouting from their sides, and Haarkonan thought the fronts of the things sported eyes instead of command centers.

"Power up all engines, ahead at half. Tactical, confirm targeting nuke one at Mothership Bravo, and nuke two at Mothership Delta."

"Confirmed."

Haarkonan mentally activated his interspace communicator via his DataPort. "Sorry guys, but I can't think of a better plan, so we'll do this as we discussed. Captain Raygar's flotilla will guard our left flank, Commander Spatzy has the right. We'll lead the charge at the center mass. Any questions?"

It wasn't much of a plan. Spread the two nukes out, divide the enemy into three sections, and then storm into the center section at full speed with weapons raging. The aliens had shown in their attack on the moon that their plan was simply to attach to anything in space, then bore holes until the vessels lost too much atmosphere or exploded.

"No questions then," Haarkonan said into the com silence. "We'll engage at full speed so as to make ourselves more difficult targets. Make them get out of our way. If we ram them, at least there will be fewer of them." He paused and looked both subordinates in the eye through the view screens. "It has been a pleasure serving with you."

Haarkonan barely heard the acknowledging traditional reply "and also with you" from his subordinates, as his attention turned to the upcoming fight. It wasn't much of a last stand. It wasn't really a "stand" at all. It seemed fitting that humanity's last space battle should be a blaze of charging glory. Of course, it was also their first space battle.

"They are now in nuclear range," reported the tactical officer, with only professionalism left in his voice. It was past the time for fear—now was the time for action.

"Fire nukes, ahead to full—let's do it!" Haarkonan growled.

The wedge of human ships jumped forward, crushing crews deep into their acceleration chairs. Two nuclear missiles launched smoothly and blazed toward separate targets. Everyone on the bridge seemed to hold their breath as the missiles tracked their targets and raced ahead of the small human fleet. A few minutes later the view screens showed two direct hits, with the missiles evaporating into incandescent clouds of fiery fury. Even the massive alien Motherships couldn't bear the explosive impact of several hundred megatons. The huge craft halted their acceleration and rolled slightly under the primordial plumes which engulfed the ships then quickly sputtered out as the vacuum of space and voracious fire soaked up all the oxygen. Smaller craft behind the Motherships failed to avoid the wounded vessels, adding their minor explosions to the quickly cooling infernos.

The human formation closed in on the enemy during the confusion, attacking the massed ships between the wounded Motherships. The core of the alien ships didn't attempt to avoid the charge, but instead embraced it. Responding with extreme velocities of their own, they headed on collision courses with the human wedge.

Laser cannons began etching the human wedge's way into the oncoming alien formation. Though not made for military purposes, the high-powered mining rays cut the smaller enemy ships/bodies in half and seared holes through multiple alien craft simultaneously. The larger alien ships must have been better armored, as they shrugged the mining lasers aside without effect.

Undaunted by the paltry human weapons, the larger alien vessels plowed straight into the web of beams, attempting to fasten themselves to the human fleet hulls. The extreme velocities hindered their interception, and the *Valkyrie* raced into the middle of the enemy swarm without picking up boarders. Many of the smaller alien vessels somehow were able to quickly reverse direction and were now chasing his fleet even while the humans plummeted deeper into the enemy formation. Admiral Haarkonan glowered at the display as it registered an alien attaching itself to Raygar's command ship *Starblazer*.

"Tactical—fire aft lasers at the enemy attached to *Starblazer*. Minimum lumens."

Lt. Col. Kip Johnson looked up briefly from his tactical display. "Yes, sir. That'll still damage her." It was not so much a protest as simply relaying information. Johnson quickly targeted center mass on the alien that had affixed itself to *Starblazer's* hull. At these velocities, with both ships jerking and weaving their way through the enemy, there was no other way to get a hit, and there was no possibility of a finesse angle shot that would burn the alien off without hitting *Starblazer*. Johnson winced even as he worked. A miss would mean hitting a friendly ship with the full force of the blast. "Firing now," he reported.

The aft laser cannon spat its focused light, and despite the frantic pace and against incredible odds, the beam flashed perfectly on center mass of the enemy, piercing a hole through it and damaging *Starblazer's* hull beneath it. The enemy exterior shattered and floated away like pieces of a crushed egg shell. The hole in *Starblazer's* hull appeared minimal, and Haarkonan hoped it was not deep enough to penetrate to the interior.

"Nice shooting," Haarkonan complimented absently, his main attention already refocusing on the strategic view of the battle in his display. Two human ships had been destroyed so far. It looked like the aliens had eaten through their hulls, with frontal pinchers ripping through titanium like so much Styrofoam. Haarkonan had no doubt that the humans had sent dozens of the enemy to whatever afterlife they deserved, but he also knew it would not be enough.

The admiral noted with admiration that the rest of his fleet had seen how he had handled the alien on *Starblazer* and were now similarly dusting off aliens that attached to adjacent ships. Even at minimal lumens the human lasers would eventually make so many holes in each other that they would commit fratricide. Still, small holes and slow death were a lot better than allowing the aliens to tear up external armor and quickly penetrate into a ship's interior.

The human formation held together until they entered the enemy formation's center. Then the last of Commander Spatzy's flotilla evaporated, and Captain Raygar didn't have enough ships to spread out and cover *Valkyrie's* entire flank. The formation began to drift apart, and without coordinated attack and defensive cooperation they were picked apart like a flock of birds consuming a thin trail of bread crumbs.

Haarkonan never expected to get this far, but that wasn't much consolation as he saw his fleet disappearing rapidly from the display screen. There were simply too many aliens, and his ships didn't have the kind of armor nor armaments that would have allowed them to survive. Haarkonan felt a lump in his throat as he felt the full-force of the loss. Those were his comrades in arms, his friends—and Earth's last hope.

"Shields are down," reported Lt. Col. Staci Minker, the defensive measures operator. Only *Valkyrie* even had a shield, which had been a prototype hastily modified for his command ship. The electro luminous shield had taken a beating as it repelled dozens of aliens, but the creatures just continued hurling themselves against it. Haarkonan knew the *Valkyrie's* end was in sight, but still his iron determination forced him to scan his display to see if he could assist any other human craft. Only the *Starblazer* was left on the viz. The rest of the fleet—all of them—had been pulverized by these strange lobster-looking aliens.

"Four boarders," shouted Minker, an uncharacteristic note of hysteria in her voice. Haarkonan watched in amazement as the hull began to be chewed through like pizza. His display showed *Starblazer* had taken on eight of the aliens and so was in no position to assist. The aliens clearly had no problem catching up to his craft from behind, even traveling at 0.1 light speed which was about 30,000 kilometers per second. Haarkonan's mind wondered what kind of drives and inertial dampeners they used, then realized it didn't matter. Soon nothing but the final destination of his soul would matter.

Suddenly Haarkonan's communicator came alive with Raygar's voice. "Pleasure serving with you admiral—give 'em hell." Haarkonan's right eyebrow shot up in curiosity. Did Raygar really think *Valkyrie* would be around any longer than *Starblazer*?

Then a blaze of light knocked out the displays, and *Valkyrie* shuddered and cantered to a strange angle as its thrusters failed but forward momentum accelerated. *Starblazer* lit space like a third nuclear weapon, consuming dozens of enemies. Its blast created a ball of fire that even spread out to engulf *Valkyrie*. Haarkonan's eyes narrowed as he realized it was no simple explosion. It was a deliberate overheating of *Starblazer's* nuclear reactor drive.

Haarkonan quickly determined to mirror his subordinate's brilliant death. "Nyko, overheat the drive core," he commanded his pilot.

"Wait--belay that order," he added hesitantly, looking with surprise at his viz-screen as it came back online. The creatures that had been on *Valkyrie's* hull were no longer there. They must have been seared off by Raygar's sacrifice. Furthermore, *Valkyrie* had been pushed to nearly 0.12 the speed of light. The inertial dampeners finally stopped screaming in protest as the *Valkyrie* burst out of the rear of the dense cloud of alien vessels. They were now heading away from Earth and the aliens weren't even attempting pursuit, possibly thinking they were wreckage rather than a target.

"Turn us around," he ordered grimly.

"No can do," replied Captain Nyko Masako, the ship's current pilot who was formerly the *Valkyrie's* commander when it was designated as a colony ship. "We've lost all thruster power. Life support back-ups are on-line, but we can't maneuver at all. Even if we could, we don't have enough energy to fire the lasers more than once or twice. We're out of the action."

It was quite strange, thought Haarkonan as he gazed at the increasing distance between his ship and his beloved home world. He had intended to go out in a blaze of glory, and now all that awaited him was a slow whimpering death as his craft hurled itself out of the solar system. He wiped the mist that began to form below his eyes as he realized he had failed not only his planet but also his family. His wife Elise had died in the attack on Lunar One and could never be sufficiently avenged. Now his three daughters and two grandchildren would have to meet the enemy not in space, but in their homes just south of New Denver.

CHAPTER 2

Hope on the *Horizon*

Over the next week, between the frantic repairs trying to stabilize vital systems, all Haarkonan and his crew could do was watch the viz-screen reports of the enemy chewing through Earth's defenses and landing en masse. Whole cities were consumed in pitched battles, and a few more nuclear weapons flared like angry volcanoes, consuming some of Earth's enemies at the price of scorching Earth's fertile surface. Before leaving effective sensor range Haarkonan noted that two of the Motherships had stayed in orbit, but the third and final surviving Mothership had eased its way to the surface to finalize the subjugation and exploitation of the planet.

Haarkonan didn't have the heart to "pull the plug" and just die. Some of the other officers had suggested they just let life-support run out. But Haarkonan was a fighter. He would fight for every last bit of life.

"We don't need thrust yet," he explained to his chief engineer for what seemed like the thousandth time. "Yes, I'm asking for a miracle, but only a *small* miracle. We just need an engine to run so we can prolong life support and buy more time. I don't care if it produces thrust. We need energy!"

Chief Engineer Sandra Hiromoto gulped, then smiled slyly. "Alrighty, Admiral. I'll give you engines that don't produce much thrust in order to stabilize electric generators that don't make much energy so that some military types who can't do much fighting can live a little longer. Did I get that right?"

The barely 5-foot tall chief engineer was a very comely girl of Asian descent, with what Haarkonan considered a rare combination of beauty and spunk as well as a knack for everything mechanical. Indeed, her ability to consistently out-perform men in the male-dominated engineering world made her a rarity, and was probably the reason she was still single at 28. Too many men took getting beaten by a woman very hard on their egos and simply didn't have the maturity to be in a relationship with a woman with so much talent. Haarkonan smiled, his eyes narrowing and happy crow's feet wrinkling at their edges. He knew if the repairs could be done, they would be done, and he was vaguely surprised at the human spirit. Even after seeing Earth assaulted, and knowing they were on a voyage that was sure to end in death, somehow humor remained.

He thanked God for the hundredth time that he was on a colony ship. The thing had been made with so many redundant features to support life that even with six holes and a roasted aft section the ship was carefully cradling and nourishing the life within it. He had an active hydroponics room and a suitable amount of solar sails deployed gathering energy to fuel the backup oxygen and waste filtration systems for some time. But he needed more energy.

Hiromoto started to leave, but then turned back. "You know, sir," she said hesitantly, then plowed on. "Even if I do get the drives running, there's nowhere to go. Alpha Centauri's human colony is 1500 Earth-days at light speed, and we'd be lucky to get a quarter of that moving in the correct direction. That means we're 16 years away, and what's left of this tub, in my professional opinion, isn't going to make it that long. Not to mention we haven't heard from Alpha Centauri for two decades, strongly suggesting the aliens have been there already."

The admiral wanted to lash out at her to contain the despair before it spread, but a quick glance around told him she was merely vocalizing what they all knew to be true. If the Alpha Centauri colony were still functioning, it would most likely be the next target for the aliens anyway. If he wanted to be safe, he'd have to go to the next large galaxy, which would be Andromeda and another 44,000 years at light speed. So while he battled to hold his ship together, he knew there was no place for them to go. Humanity was simply too fragile. The Universe mocked a species that had so many requirements for survival. Earth was truly one in a billion, if not a billion billion.

He looked at Hiromoto and knew he couldn't allow the crew's hope to slip away just yet, even if his own hope had died with his wife. "I know. But there are other planets, Chief. Get us that energy."

Repairs continued unabated for the next week, with the occasional system failure crisis breaking into the monotony of round-the-clock shift work that was needed to nurse *Valkyrie* back to a stable condition. The colony ship contained many spare parts, but often repair crews had to cannibalize redundant features to ensure just a single system was operative. Admiral Haarkonan had been especially surprised by Hiromoto's ability to deliver not just energy, but a workable fusion engine after dismantling the other three for parts.

With an engine came the possibility to maneuver and even slow down. Maneuvering was especially important seeing as how the shield was partially down and the smallest particles were proving very damaging to the forward armor at such extreme speeds. Haarkonan had immediately ordered deceleration, though he knew it would take some time to implement. They had been traveling faster than their damaged scanners and lasers could effectively sweep in front of them, making it a perilous flight. Though decelerating was prudent, it was also costly. It would take a long time to be able to obtain speeds even close to a quarter of light speed with just one engine.

The admiral grumbled to himself as he futilely searched the star charts again. He had to decide which solar system in front of them they should head toward, or if he should return to Earth and certain, pointless death. His ruse about "other planets" had made people hopeful, thinking he knew what he was doing and had a plan.

Now he had to formulate a plan, despite there being no good options. Haarkonan knew the one thing the crew couldn't lose was hope.

Still, every time Haarkonan tried to formulate a plan, his mind wandered to those he had led to their deaths. He was supposed to be a "tactical genius," but there was nothing he could think of to stop the enemy. His head-long strike had inflicted some casualties, but it was nowhere near damaging enough to stop the invaders. Now would he lie to his people to keep up a false hope and lead them to a slow but certain destruction? He shifted uncomfortably in his command chair and finally made a decision. They would return to Earth and accept their fate. There was simply nowhere else to go.

"I don't believe it!" yelped Lieutenant Neil LeMoray, breaking the admiral's reverie. The Lieutenant was everything to be expected in a communications officer. He was well-built, square-jawed, just under six-foot tall, and extroverted to a fault. The man loved to talk, and Admiral Haarkonan often had to cut him off in mid-report and ask him to simply get to the bottom line. Haarkonan was also used to LeMoray's muttering to himself on the bridge while monitoring com traffic, and found LeMoray's exuberant attitude to be often misdirected. Still, he was curious about what could so surprise the young officer this far from civilization.

"Sir, you're not gonna believe this!" LeMoray exclaimed with his typical enthusiasm. "We're getting a signal over the viz, and it's in standard Anglisk via hyper wire. What's more, it's not coming from Earth, but from in front of us!"

"Could it just be an echo?" Haarkonan asked, knowing strange things happened when both signals and ships traveled even at just a tenth of light speed.

"It could be. It *is* a rather dim signal. But it's getting stronger, and I expect we'll be able to receive it clearly in a minute."

"Put it on main," ordered Haarkonan, allowing the entire bridge to hear. He hardly expected the signal to be anything but an echo, but he recognized the entire bridge had quieted with suspended hope. He didn't want to be the one to tell them the disappointing news that it was really nothing. It was better to let them hear it for themselves.

"SSSSkkk. Do you copy? Over ssssK." The audio was fuzzy, and there was as yet no visual. The voice was that of a human male, who was indeed speaking in Anglisk, the standard language that everyone on Earth learned either as a native speaker or at least as a second fluent language. The viz blurred and then a figure came into view, still with a bit of static.

"ShhhhSSkk-peat. This is *Horizon Patrol Three* to *Valkyrie*. Is anyone there? Do you copy? Over."

"Open channel," Haarkonan said, filled with wonder. He calmed his excitement and was proud of himself when he said with a level voice "This is *Valkyrie*, we copy."

"Welcome to *Horizon*, Admiral! This is *Horizon Patrol Three*. Do you have thrust to further decelerate? At your current speed you will overshoot our position in minutes and be out of com range and well on your way out of the solar system. Where are you going in such a hurry, anyway?"

"We weren't going anywhere in particular," answered Haarkonan with his typical dry humor. "Kind of just out for a stroll," he added.

"Some stroll—I didn't know we'd built a ship that goes as fast as you were going. It was real tricky trying to intercept your course."

"Let's just say we got a push. And yes, we have a thruster online, and will further decelerate immediately," Haarkonan nodded to Captain Masako to make it so as he continued. "Do you have beds for a crew our size?"

"Call us the Motel 66, sir. You bet we do. You're now passing my position. After deceleration return to InterSolar coordinates 5638 by 5657 on chart 401. I'll meet you there and show you to your rooms." The signal was already starting to break up.

"Who are you?" the admiral demanded, baffled. He was in command of Earth's defense forces and hadn't heard a word about human outposts a week and a half beyond Pluto's orbit. There was nothing out here but a few asteroids, at best. Certainly nothing warranting an outpost.

"Like I said, we are *Horizon*. I'll tell you all shhhsssk- it when you get back shhsskkk." The viz-screen went blank again.

"Sorry sir, we lost the feed," commented LeMoray needlessly.

"Full deceleration," commanded Haarkonan. "Plug those coordinates into the computer. Let's see who our saviors are. And why they didn't help save Earth."

***

It took another week to decelerate and be guided by escorts to a dwarf planet that seemed invisible to both sensors *and* sight. It was simply a deeper black than the surrounding black, with only small glints of grey. While there had been much speculation from the crew that they would find either a trap from the aggressive aliens, or perhaps another alien intelligence, Admiral Haarkonan's guess at a small human research outpost turned out to be most accurate. The *Valkyrie* thruster-landed on what was clearly a human-built external landing pad. With the damaged systems, the landing was anything but soft, and the near-crash ensured the ship would require extensive repairs if not outright scrapping.

"Since we're not lifting back off this rock anytime soon, we better go see what we've gotten ourselves into," said Haarkonan, standing up from his command chair. "LeMoray, you're with me. Everyone else stays here and starts preparing for a general egress. Captain Masako—you have the command."

Haarkonan was in a foul mood as he donned his space battle suit and stepped off his precious ship into the 0.7 Newton gravity. So many people had died. So little hope remained, and now his ship was grounded, making the fortunate rendezvous with these people seem only as bright as a single candle in a baseball park of darkness. And the candle seemed to be flickering toward extinction. Haarkonan wished he had died in battle. Now he would have to live knowing his planet, his friends, his family—everyone he knew—were being killed or harvested or whatever the aliens were doing to them.

As he slow-jumped down the ramp, Haarkonan noticed beneath his ship was a thin black circle of what looked like rock. LeMoray reached the bottom of the ramp first and tried to kneel to inspect the black substance, only to have his feet flip from under him and land on his derriere. Haarkonan figured the low gravity would ensure the L.T. landed lightly enough, so he decided to go easy on LeMoray's ego by ignoring the spill. He knelt at the base of the ramp to inspect the black substance himself.

It didn't take much time to discover why the L.T. had fallen. The black stuff wasn't rock, but a thin layer of water on top of ice. The ice had probably been melted by the *Valkyrie's* landing thruster, and it was obviously wasting no time to refreeze as the thrusters cooled. Ice on this rock would be very useful, Haarkonan mused.

Lieutenant LeMoray picked himself off the ground, and the two carefully low-gravity hopped toward a blast door not far from the landing pad. Within a meter of the ramp the water had frozen so cold that it was no longer slippery. It reminded Haarkonan of his trips to McMurdo Bay at the Antarctic where they had used the same icy area for a seaport in the summer and as a landing strip in the winter.

Surprisingly, no humans were in sight. Instead, a small "automaton" wheeled robot designed for simple services zipped up to them, blinked its "follow me" lights, and led them the rest of the way to the portal. Haarkonan was disappointed, as a welcoming party would have been able to start answering his questions. Communications silence had been maintained for the past three weeks, other than to transmit coordinates and confirm the landing pad, so that this *"Horizon"* base would be kept well-hidden from the alien invasion force.

"Sending an automaton seems a bit rude, doesn't it, sir?" LeMoray complained over his intercom, striding to the left of his superior officer. "They have us travel for weeks, then just send this little tin can to show us in. This level of disrespect would never have occurred on a military installation. Not with a flag officer, that's for sure."

"I doubt this *is* the military," Haarkonan said, not at all concerned with protocol issues. "And you know how these scientist types are. They may not know the proper protocol. Or, more likely, they got distracted and forgot we were landing a 100 megaton spaceship on their pad."

Both men chuckled as the automaton led them through the outer portal and into a large decontamination/depressurization chamber. The room was clearly a standard "double D" chamber, equipped to service dozens of people at a time, so both men simply entered the nearest stall and awaited decon. In seconds, as Haarkonan expected, various nozzles shot out hot water and other chemicals along with ultrasound pulses to clean off the space suits. What he didn't expect, however, was that the entire room started to descend, nearly toppling both men with the initial jolt. After that the ride was very smooth, and clearly it saved time to decon and depressurize while traveling to the base below. Still, Haarkonan thought it was a strange sensation, kind of like taking a shower in an elevator.

After a few minutes the nozzles stopped spraying decontamination goo and switched to hot air, quickly blow-drying both men. The room stopped its brisk descent, jolting to a complete stop as the shower doors opened and a flashing green light on the floor reported that all was well. Both men removed their helmets. The automaton had waited for them outside the showers and now whistled for their attention before leading them out of the elevator area.

Doors parted into the walls, and Haarkonan was reminded of a sports stadium locker room as he and LeMoray found themselves in a room with small cabinets and various kinds of space suits lining the walls. There were even benches to help people who needed to suit up, but right now there were no other humans in sight.

Lt. LeMoray and Admiral Haarkonan helped each other remove their space suits before resuming their parade behind the automaton. The little machine clearly had no semi-sentience chip, so it simply led them without conversation. After a few minutes of winding through various corridors, they stopped in front of large blast doors, and the little droid flashed a red light before veering off to another task.

Haarkonan spotted the entry pad and palmed it. The pad read his hand print and blinked green, initializing motors that rolled the heavy doors efficiently into the sides of the wall. Haarkonan felt a small gust of wind as he strode through the portal, causing him to reflexively hold his breath. After a small sniff he realized the cause of the wind was a slightly higher pressurization and significantly higher oxygen content. Lt. LeMoray entered and the door closed quickly behind him. The admiral smiled and took in a large breath that made him feel slightly invigorated. Elevated oxygen levels was a common practice in large research institutes, as a higher oxygen content seemed to better stimulate thinking and assist in sustained mental concentration.

Haarkonan looked around at what appeared to be a standard command center, with white metallic walls enclosing a great open space which was home to dozens of computers and flat monitors as well as 3D holographs. They were entering from the left side, as the front wall was made obvious by the three large viz-screen panels that stretched at least 15 meters wide and 10 meters tall. There were at least 40 people busily going about what seemed routine duties, and a tall man in a white lab coat looked up at them and then left his glass-enclosed office at the back center of the room.

The man seemed to be in his sixties, but his gait suggested he was still full of vigor if not athleticism. His skin looked pale, even beside the white lab coat, and his hair was a bright mop of white with silver highlights, carefully but practically combed straight back with a part to the left side. As he approached, the admiral saw he was a bit over six feet tall and of medium to thin build.

Admiral Haarkonan had always been a good judge of character and found his first impressions were typically quite accurate. This man's light green eyes seemed to exude both intelligence and somehow the burden of leadership. There was also some kind of glint in his eyes that suggested he was smiling inside, as if he alone understood some sort of cosmic joke that the Universe perpetually told.

Haarkonan extended his hand to the scientist. "I'm Admiral Haarkonan, commander of what was Earth's defense force, and of what is left of the *Valkyrie*, a B3 colony ship we modified to be our command vessel. This is my communications officer, Lieutenant Neil LeMoray."

"Yes, yes," the man shook Haarkonan's hand with a grip a bit shy of the typical military shake. "We know who you are, and we welcome you and your crew. I'm Dr. Ian Plexar." The scientist shifted his weight slightly and lightly rubbed his nose with his index finger. "Let's see, titles. You military types like your titles. I guess you may call me the chief scientist here on *Horizon*, though I spend more time doing administrative functions."

"*Horizon*," the admiral repeated, looking around at the command center. "What is this place? I didn't know it existed, and I can assure you I have top clearances."

"*This* is *Horizon*," Dr. Plexar announced, spreading out his hands to indicate their surroundings. "It's perfectly normal that you didn't know about us. We're a need-to-know only location. In fact, all the people here, before your ship arrived of course, agreed to give up their homes on Earth and live here instead. That helped keep it a secret location. While I'm quite sure you have a top secret clearance with various other compartmental clearances beyond that, *Horizon* was intentionally kept from all military officers. But I doubt any of that is relevant now."

"So what do you do here?" the Admiral asked, looking around and wondering what other gaping holes existed in his intelligence reports.

"We were commissioned by the World Congress through the United Earth Space Administration to continue research into temporal dialysis and transport."

"Time travel," exclaimed LeMoray. "But that's illegal!"

The admiral gave him a quick but menacing glance. LeMoray understood the implied threat and fell silent.

"Yes, time travel. And yes, it was determined illegal on Earth," Plexar resumed. "It was also nearly impossible on Earth, because of psychic interference, but that's another matter altogether.

We were granted special authorization to conduct large-scale, localized time dilation experiments. And the military was specifically excluded because the World Congress didn't want our work turned into a weapon. They understood the danger of some ambitious soul going back in time to tamper with history for political purposes. It would certainly be tempting to reverse a battle here or there, or introduce a technology, but that'd be unfair to the side that won fair and square the first time, wouldn't it?"

Haarkonan grunted assent. Such a time-weapon would be too tempting to resist. And it made sense that such research be conducted far from Earth in order to minimize any potential time rifts.

"In any case, now our survival depends to some degree on the extent of our past secrecy," continued Plexar. "Even if the Narcoid—that's what people here are starting to call the aliens—even if they fail to discover evidence of us on Earth, they're bound to discover us eventually with patrols. That's why we've banned transmissions and insisted on the communications silence."

"Yes, that of course makes sense," replied Haarkonan.

"But why didn't you send out a welcoming party?" blurted LeMoray, curiosity having overcome his recent chastisement. "Surely that wouldn't have endangered your location."

"No, no, of course not," replied Dr. Plexar. "I apologize for any inconvenience or breech of protocol there, but we're dismally undermanned. That's why we're so excited about your arrival. With you there just might be a chance that our plan will work..."

"Let's not get ahead of ourselves," interrupted Haarkonan. "Essential things first. I noticed you have some water supply here. Is this place self-sustaining? More to the point, can you handle another 500 people?"

Haarkonan locked onto Dr. Plexar's eyes as if to wrangle from them the truth, even if it were unpleasant, before continuing. "Our hydroponics farm is still functional, but it would be overtaxed to care for more people than just my crew for any significant duration."

"Oh yes, we've plenty of life-support resources, rest assured about that," Plexar waved as if batting aside an inconsequential issue. "Indeed, we have facilities to house dozens of thousands more, and *Horizon* has underground frozen water reservoirs capable of serving millions for many centuries. It's not perpetual, mind you, but proper resource management could extend our supplies for a long time. We've also tapped into this planetoid's core, which supplies us with heat and a wonderful source of energy. Our fear is more of being discovered."

"Being discovered? You're practically invisible," inserted LeMoray. "What is this dwarf planet made from? It's too large to be artificial, but we could hardly see it on entry, until we were practically on top of it."

"We're on what is called a 'dark asteroid,' which means an asteroid that reflects less than 5% of the light that hits it," replied Plexar in a tone suggesting this was a well-practiced lecture. "Ours is a particularly dark asteroid, reflecting less than 1% of the light that hits it, because its surface is mostly black metal, which is a new element we found here. We call the asteroid "Centaur", and it operates on its own, even spinning while it circles the sun."

"How big is it?" LeMoray asked.

"We're almost the size of Pluto. We figure Centaur was formerly either a moon of Jupiter or part of one of the current moons of Jupiter. In any case, it must have collided with something huge, sending it clear out here instead of being absorbed into the Kuiper Belt like most asteroids around Sol."

Dr. Plexar motioned for the newcomers to follow him back to his glass-walled office, and Lt. LeMoray fell in beside the scientist as the admiral took up the rear inspecting his surroundings. "How many people do you have here now?" Haarkonan asked, noting a few dozen empty chairs in the command room.

"We have only a few thousand right now, but we hope to acquire more people in time. Or maybe I should say from time. We're quite glad to accommodate you and your crew, and we have plenty for you all to do. You're not going to be a burden. You may even be part of our long-term salvation—"

The admiral cut him short, his dismal temperament returning. "I don't see how any of us will survive long-term if you cannot indefinitely hold and support the human race on *Horizon*. We'll eventually run out of supplies and die. Wouldn't it have been better to reveal yourselves and help us in the defense of Earth?" The admiral practically growled the last bit of his question. He found cowardice disgusting, and stick-your-head-in-the-ground academics and politicians were infuriating.

Dr. Plexar didn't take offense from the tone, but his eyes saddened. "We could have sent a dozen small ships, but surely nothing that would have acted as a real deterrent or even much assistance to your force. We don't think of ourselves as the continuance of the human race, as we realize what you said is true, and we'll inevitably run out of life-space and resources here. No, we're considering far more drastic measures." The doctor entered his glass-walled office and walked around his dark wooden desk that seemed incongruous with all the other metal and plastic furnishings of the installation.

LeMoray paused at the doorway and pulled the admiral aside before they entered the office. "I know this guy," LeMoray whispered excitedly. "I knew I'd heard his name before. Plexar was the world's best quantum-time scientist about a decade ago. He practically wrote the book on theoretical time travel and dialysis. Actually, he did write my textbook. That's why I remember him; we all thought it strange that we were using his textbook when the newspapers reported his death."

"I hope I look that spry ten years after I die," replied Haarkonan with a wry smile. He entered Plexar's office and took a seat facing Plexar's desk.

Dr. Plexar smiled too, both in welcoming them to his office and because he'd overheard the end of their conversation. As LeMoray was seated, Plexar pushed a button on a thin silver remote control device. Gradually the glass walls swirled into an opaque white and purple color, offering them some privacy.

"Do you really think the human race even has a chance to survive?" LeMoray blurted out, then looked uncomfortable for having voiced his real fear.

"No, right now we don't," replied Plexar smoothly. "But I say we work to give us a chance. As I said, we have a rather ambitious plan. With you here, it just might work."

"More ambitious than continuing the human race by surviving out here?" LeMoray asked incredulously. "I'd have thought that was ambitious enough."

"Yes—that would be ambitious, but it'd also be impossible. Indeed, we started making a colony ship to try to restart elsewhere, but then decided with the silence from Alpha Centauri that there is really nowhere else to go. So we've been redesigning our ship, fondly dubbed the *Ark of Time*, for another purpose. I don't want to find another home: I want our home back. And that may just be possible, now that we have made time travel a reality."

CHAPTER 3

Romans to the Rescue

Senior Centurion and *Primus Pilus* Valerius Feronae braced himself for the next violent assault of waves, flailing to get a good hold on the slippery wooden rail. But he was too late. The cresting water broke violently over the trireme's bow and blew him off his feet, tossing him over the edge of the ship like a piece of flotsam. He cried out helplessly as he flew down in leather cuirass and body armor toward the ocean, which opened its maw to invite its latest victim. As he tumbled toward the frothing abyss, all he could picture in his mind was the surreal image of Lilah, his daughter, the most precious person he would leave behind as he journeyed to Hades below.

But he didn't splash into the freezing oblivion. Something held his ankle like an iron vice, wrenching it painfully but halting his plummet into the sea. His body jerked back and slammed hard against the hull of the ship. A hand grasped the back of his knee and started hauling him back into the large Roman vessel. And so back into the land of the living.

Breathless, he saw his savior was his old friend Otho, a mountain of a man who had stood by his side for the last 15 years of military service. Valerius was quickly and unceremoniously dumped toward the center of the ship, where he just had time to grab a hold of the nearest mast pole before another onslaught of the waves drove all other considerations from his mind. He held on tenaciously, refusing to listen to his body's complaints of exhaustion.

Otho clapped him on the back with one hand, the other thick arm wrapped around the pole above Valerius' grip. "Thought you'd go for a swim at a time like this, did ya?" he asked with a big grin. His brown eyes sparkled as he looked down at his long time commander and friend. "You know, you may not be a sea commander, but I think you are still suppose' to go down with the ship, not before it!"

"I owe you one," Valerius managed to gasp out as he caught his breath and straightened a bit. He was not afraid to die, but he would have been disappointed to undergo such an ignoble death at the hands of mere water. Being lost at sea also boded poorly for a decent afterlife. One more reason to avoid ships at all cost in the future. If he had a future.

"Naw, I just owe you one less, sir," shouted Otho over the roar of the waves, with ocean spray matting his thick curly black hair and trickling down his bearded face as he looked down at Valerius. "That means I'm down to what, owing you 22 lives?" His big wet grin made him look like a bear who had just succeeded in raiding a honey pot.

Before Valerius could answer, another bout of the ocean's wrath rocked the boat, making timbers creak with the strain. Many of the men on deck had hacked the mast ropes and tied themselves to whatever looked sturdy. Others joined Valerius and Otho, trusting their own strength to hold them to the ship that was their only chance of salvation this far out in the Mediterranean.

Valerius thought it was just like Otho to be smiling at death's threshold. Well why not? No better way to die than the way they had lived.

Deep thunder rolled and reverberated across the churning sea, like a million bass drums pounding a dirge. Lightning streaked across the pitch-dark sky, and Valerius could see the ship's crew clinging to other portions of the trireme's exterior. While most of the people above deck were sailors by trade, Valerius' men were all ground soldiers, and not at all used to the sea's powerful gales. But it didn't take a trained eye to realize this would be their last voyage. Rain and seawater sloshed over the deck, making the footing difficult for the few who braved letting go of the superstructure.

"We have to let the slaves out!" he shouted at Otho, again letting go of the mast to go back to trying to accomplish that task. Otho grabbed Valerius' belt, and despite his big hands he deftly passed a rope through Valerius' belt, then secured it to his own belt. If his leader were blown overboard again, he would be better prepared to haul him back.

Valerius winced slightly as his wrenched ankle buckled under his weight, but he continued forward. If the ship capsized or sunk, all the slave rowers below deck wouldn't have a chance to escape. Not that there was much of a chance even above deck. While most commanders preferred their slaves to go down with the ship rather than increase the chaos on the deck in the midst of a storm, Valerius strongly believed everyone had the right to at least a chance for life. He honestly didn't expect anyone on board to live past the next hour anyway.

The winds and sweeping sheets of water pushed and pulled him, but Valerius was determined to reach the hatch leading down to the galley. As he approached, the terrified screams of people below drowned out even the fierce wind's noise, and hands thrust up through the grated hatch begging to be set free. Peering down, Valerius saw that the prisoners were now up to their shoulders in water. The lower decks were filling and the ship would soon sink into the sea.

Valerius threw himself down on the deck, grabbing the mesh wooden hatch so that he wouldn't wash away as another wave crashed on deck. He propped himself up on his knees, and because he didn't have the key, drew his Spanish-made *spatha* and began hacking at the wood that held the lock in place. While the longer cavalry sword was less suited to the current task than the typical Roman short sword, his switch for the extra range had served him well in many past battles where discipline had melted into a melee of every man for himself.

Suddenly the dark that had engulfed them for the past hour lit up, as if the sun had decided to end its dismal hiatus with a spectacular return to the sky's stage. Only the light was somehow eerie, like light at sunset diffused by a mist, with more red in it than Valerius had ever seen. The storm immediately around them started dispersing, and the ship lurched upwards as the waters directly beneath it calmed unnaturally. Somehow even the wind's growl softened to a distant purr.

Valerius said a quick prayer to his patron goddess Athena as he looked up, shielding his eyes that weren't able to adjust to such a stark change of luminosity. He then stood up, noticing only the air and waters closest to the ship had stilled. It was as if they were in the center of an arena of calm, while just beyond the storm continued churning the waves.

Had he already died and was now on his way to the Elysian fields? People always said it was ultimately peaceful. He stamped his left foot and winced as he felt the sting of his hurt ankle sending needles of pain up his leg. Not in the afterlife yet, he thought with a wry grin.

Then all his attention was focused on the light. A huge flying metal bird the size of a small coliseum was descending toward their position. The red light they were in emanated from what looked like a 10 foot diameter mirror that protruded from the vessel and pointed their way. He heard Otho behind him gasp, confirming it wasn't just his imagination.

The object was slowly drifting toward them, tilting back and forth slightly, like a leaf slowly descending to the ground. Valerius never put much stock in mythology, but the thought flew through his mind that this might be Helios's chariot, finally ending his voyage across the sky to come crashing to Earth. But though it was bright like the sun, it didn't look like a chariot, and it certainly wasn't being pulled by four horses. Maybe the swift Pyrois, Eos, Aethon and Phlegon steeds had abandoned their master's unusual-looking chariot?

The red light continued to dance across the whole scene as the airborne vessel ceased descending and hovered 50 feet above the trireme. A head-splitting whine ripped through the air. Men fell to their knees, clenching their ears and screaming in terror. Valerius stumbled several steps backward, gripping his ears to shield them from the sound. The squeal still penetrated his head and felt like it was bouncing back and forth in his skull. A second shrill noise sounded and Valerius vaguely noticed a second beam of light arching out from another protruding mirror before he fell back on the deck of the ship, unconscious.

***

When Valerius awoke, his head was swimming. Better his head than his whole body, he thought grimly, remembering the storm and how he had been certain he would be one more soldier swallowed by the sea. Startled by the memory, his light-blue eyes jerked open only to find himself questioning if he had indeed survived the waters. Maybe death was so peaceful you simply didn't feel it coming.

He certainly was no longer on the Mediterranean Sea. He and his men had been on the way to replace the Egyptian guard who ruled Rome's bread basket as a protectorate directly under the Emperor. It was the normal annual rotation, delayed slightly due to poor weather. The fleet admiral had reassured Valerius the bad weather had passed, and that it was in their best interest to cross quickly. He had deferred to the seaman's experience and allowed his cohort to board the ships and cross. Next time he would consider the long march *around* the Mediterranean.

Now he lay in a large white room that somehow was light without being open to the sun. The light wasn't a stark bright light like he was used to from the forum's gleaming white marble at noon. Instead, this light somehow emanated from the walls, but with a warm, full, golden glow.

Hundreds of his men, mixed with the sailors and slaves, were strewn about the room unconscious. But there was something strange about them. Valerius realized they were all wearing identical white robes. He looked down feeling the softness of his own robe, and wondered what manner of material was so smooth and warm. The weaving used threads so thin and tightly spun that no human hand could have woven the garment. So he was with the gods then. Looking around, he saw that the few men who had apparently awakened before him were just sitting in a dazed stupor. By reflex his hand went to his upper thigh, searching for his dagger, only to find he was indeed naked under the robe.

Valerius didn't know what to do, but decided he would do something. He stood up, rising unsteadily at first, then straightening with more confidence to his full five-foot-nine inches height. His handsome face was slightly weathered by a life of soldiering, but still looked slightly younger than his real age of 38. High cheek bones and a strong Italian nose blended naturally on his tanned face and told of his Roman aristocratic heritage. He was of slightly thinner than average build, but as many enemies of Rome had discovered, his frame supported much more than average strength. His raven-black hair had just begun to get dustings of grey. Otho moaned beside him, swearing as he too saw their new surroundings.

"By the gods, where are we?" Otho exclaimed, sitting up quickly and then clutching his head in obvious pain. His voice seemed to lose all its energy, probably only carrying a few feet, which was unusual for a man who could bellow orders over several hundred meters. The room seemed to swallow noise, bathing the men in silence.

"This isn't the Elysian fields," Otho continued. "Do the gods hate us so much that after all our fighting glory they steal away our prize just because Pluto and Poseidon conspired against us?"

"Let us not blame the gods just yet." As an afterthought Valerius added, "And if this *is* their abode, let us also not blaspheme them."

Otho just grunted agreement. He too had little faith in the fables about the gods and had seldom avoided verbally offending them in the past. But this turn of events was fast making him an agnostic, if not an actual believer.

"Our first priority is finding out how many of us remain. Otho, give me a count of how many soldiers and how many sailors from our fleet survived." Valerius knew it would be no small task given that the usual garments that separated soldier from sailor were missing. Even the slaves would be difficult to differentiate. He continued organizing and directing those who were awake to help the others in various ways. A type of water fountain was discovered recessed into one of the walls, and Valerius asked that the more alert people assist to give the groggy a drink.

After a little over an hour the tally was in. Of the more than 6,000 legionnaires that had sailed from Ostia, 400 were contained in this rectangular room with glowing walls. Another hundred sailors and an additional 70 slaves had also congregated together, cowering in the back corner. With one action accomplished, Valerius started to feel a little more in control of the situation. All such feelings fled as he heard a slight hum and three of the four walls slowly lowered *into* the floor, disappearing completely and leaving a barely-discernable crack.

Now he and his men were in a fourth of a much larger room, with a stage at the center. A low murmur swept the great hall. In the other quadrants that had just been revealed were all manner of people, the clear majority of them being Romans. But these were apparently people from all corners of the empire, as one legion looked to have originated on the Persian front whereas in another he recognized a tribune who should have been in Britannia engaged with the Celts.

Like a stage prop in the Coliseum, a figure was elevated from below to appear on the central platform. It looked like a man, but wore a fabric spun out of pure copper and had a stunted scabbard with a small black device unlike any sword or dagger Valerius had ever seen. Most of the men prostrated themselves or fell to their knees in worship.

Valerius felt more compelled to rebellion than adoration. What was going on? Where were they, and would they be returned so that they could do their duty? He had received an excellent education and knew of neither poet nor philosopher who had even hinted at such an afterlife.

The copper man spoke, or at least Valerius assumed it was the man on the platform. The actual voice seemed to boom from somewhere overhead, so that it seemed no matter where one was in the huge room the voice always sounded at the same ominous level.

"You are not dead, and we mean you no harm," said the deep voice in a strangely accented Latin. The voice had a metallic sound that matched well with the copper appearance of the speaker. "I am no god. Please stand as men and as friends."

Some men simply ignored the command. Most looked around, and then slowly rose to their feet. They looked unsure of themselves, with expressions that were a mix of surprise and mild embarrassment. The voice continued, but though Valerius had a keen ear, he failed to detect any colloquialisms that could be used to better pinpoint the speaker's geographic origin in the vast Roman Empire.

"You have been snatched from death to be recruited for the most glorious battle of all time—the fight for Mother Earth. While you did not die, your lives as you knew them are over. You were all about to die due to one circumstance or another. Some of you will be recorded in history as having drowned, others as being lost to a sand storm or whatever deadly plight we rescued you from. There is much to tell you, and all will be revealed in due time. First, we request the leaders among you to step forward so that we can further discuss the proper care of your men. Again, we are friends, you are guests, and we will not harm you."

Valerius began to step forward when Otho threw out a stout arm barring his path. "May be a trap, sir," he whispered, glancing around.

"Yes. It might be. But if they meant us harm they could simply have refused to rescue us from the sea. I also do not doubt they have superior forces to harm us now, if they wished. We owe these rescuers at least the time to understand their purposes. I will meet with them."

Otho lowered his arm pensively, still looking around with suspicion as Valerius marched toward the center stage. Valerius brushed past his men, reading mixed reactions in their faces. Some were clearly still scared, and others just mumbled in surprise and disbelief. The men seemed slightly heartened as they saw him, and reverently cleared a path. Even those who did not recognize him made way, understanding who he was by his air of command and confident strides. Otho's hulking form behind him didn't hurt either. Those who did recognize his face smiled slightly, nodding their heads. These men trusted him and knew he would not do anything to disgrace Rome. And he knew he could count on them no matter what the three fates spun in his tapestry of destiny.

***

Valerius was seated directly across from "Doctor" Niger White, a man who had introduced himself as a "scientist," which as far as Valerius was concerned really meant "practical philosopher." That designation seemed like an oxymoron of the most confusing kind. With just a glance, one could see that this man did not have the physical capacity for anything but mild labor, so he must be an educator. He certainly liked to caveat all of his sentences just as the sophists used to do during his childhood education. The other four men seated around the table in white robes that matched his own looked perplexed. They seemed content for now to let Valerius speak for all the captured Romans, seeing as how he was a *Primus Pilus* and the most experienced military officer.

"So you see," Doctor White continued, "We need you to come with us back to the future in order to save the world. While we have a place that can sustain life, we must have people to build weapons and eventually to retake our planet."

"Why us?" asked Valerius, voicing a question others around the table also clearly wanted answered. "Why abduct us?"

"Because you were about to die and be lost to history. It's important that we only take people who will not be missed. We can't afford to interfere with the way time was meant to progress. Though the time stream is resilient, it can be ripped, and we really don't know what would happen then. That's why all our tests were conducted on a distant asteroid station called *Horizon*. That's where we're going now. We were being cautious and slowly learning about the consequences of time travel, but then Earth was invaded and the stakes were raised. We decided that we'd rather risk destroying all time-dependent reality than allow the alien predators to do as they wish with our home planet."

"So you took us just before we died, hoping our absence in the world would not be missed? And you're worried about what the effects will be on the future? By Zeus, or whatever gods there may be, this is all too confusing." There were simply too many new concepts for Valerius to grasp. He never knew the heavens were so vast, the stars were actually big enough for men to walk upon, and somehow it was possible not only to fly but to travel through time just like one traveled on a boat. His stomach roiled at the thought of being on something like a boat again. Only if he understood correctly, instead of water, they were traveling through air and space. What a comforting thought.

"Centurion," the scientist began again slowly, "We don't expect you to understand everything. We don't even understand everything. But we have run tests and developed temporal mathematics to help us understand some of the issues associated with time travel.

"Here's what's best evidenced by the data. If we go back in time, everything we touch, from the microscopic to the macroscopic, changes. Those changes are inserted into the past and have the potential to cascade into the future, like ripples on water that are increased and magnified by other ripples. At first we thought time would simply split into two, based on assumptions from quantum mechanics which suggested there may be an infinite number of universes reflecting an infinite number of variables that could change. But that theory was produced more out of ignorance than science, and may have been influenced by the 20th century's bias to eliminate mystery and have a natural origin theory rather than believe in a deity. But I digress."

Valerius was glad it was a digression, as he had hardly understood any of it. The man's Latin was atrocious! Did the philosopher mean that people from one time era honestly had tried to say there was nothing beyond themselves? No gods? Just a natural beginning? Such people were called atheists in his day and were often punished for such folly. Without a higher being, no morality was stable, no person would be trustworthy, and no faith could be put into anything. Indeed, all of society would be fragmented, as religion brought unity and purpose. Atheism was for the cowardly, cynical, ungrateful, and scoffers—not for the mighty Romans who recognized the hands of the gods at work throughout the earth propelling them to victory.

The "scientist" must have recognized the distant look in Valerius' eyes, as he cleared his throat and waited for his audience to mentally return before proceeding. "Anyway, we now believe ours is possibly the only fragile reality and that altering the past in any significant way may hasten the end of the time continuum."

Valerius felt lost. The words were Latin but they were also incomprehensible. This physical philosopher sounded just as hard to pin down as prophets and oracles in his own time. Or world. Or whatever he had just left. Doctor White seemed full of words like "possibly" and "maybe," yet he spoke in a tone of complete confidence and authority.

"Time travel protocol demands no one in the past be touched who will be missed, as we believe time will not split but will actually change at the point of insertion, forcing a new timeline and eradicating the old. Therefore insertion teams must be VERY careful to not substantially alter the timeline. Despite our precautions, it's possible that we're still creating incongruities by these temporal interventions, and each flaw in the fabric of time may eventually add up and curtail the duration of all space-time."

The doctor fidgeted as he saw the blank faces. "Think of it this way. Time is like a line stretching from the moment of creation to an end we call eternity. We can put stitches in time, but even they make bundles that may result in instability. The more we tamper with time, the more the line buckles and knots, creating paradoxes which result in speeding eternity's approach for everyone."

Doctor White paused again and sighed as he saw the blank stares around the table were not dissipating. "Never mind all that. I really wish Captain Masako were healthy, as this is his job. I'm just supposed to provide clone bodies. Anyway, I suppose the details aren't important. Here's what you need to know. We're here to ask you to join us in a battle, not just for a great country like Rome, but for the human race as a whole. We've saved you from certain death. Now we ask that you arise to a new life that will undoubtedly be foreign, difficult, and full of surprises but is noble, as you will be the people who rescue humanity. Are you with us?"

Though these words were much easier to comprehend, no one around the table responded immediately. Valerius decided to cut to the chase. "I speak for us all to say we are grateful for the rescue, though it would seem we live only to die again shortly. I do not pretend to understand what you have shared, but I ask this one question: Is what we are to join going to shame Rome or bring her glory?"

Doctor White scratched his head, then swallowed. "It will not shame Rome. In fact, these aliens have invaded and now hold the Rome of the present day. We will liberate Rome from her oppressors, in point of fact."

"A foreign power controls Rome? Why did you not simply say it was so? Of course we will liberate the Eternal City! We have sworn to protect her. That must include fighting her enemies now, wherever…or *whenever* we are."

The other commanders around the table all grunted their assent. Now came the real impossible task; how would he address his men about the current circumstances? It was probably best to keep it simple…and ensure Otho was around to discourage revolts by the sailors and slaves.

***

Valerius chuckled as he watched Otho duck his head reflexively and paw the air above him. The flying ship that had rescued them from the Mediterranean had traveled for a fortnight and had just swung under a docking bar and into an enormous underground landing bay. Otho was obviously relieved they had avoided collision and was a little embarrassed by his reflexive reaction. A big man like him was probably used to ducking his head in small places, thought Valerius.

"Don't fear, good friend. These sailors of the sky seem to have precision in their craft. They also do not have the wind and waves to push them off course. It seems we soon will be docked at this fabled fortress *Horizon*."

"Aye," Otho replied, straightening to regain his dignity. "But having no wind and waves also begs the question of why we move at all."

Both men returned to looking out the forward "viz-screen." Most of the ancients, those picked up from the past, were aligned behind their leaders, enthralled by the large viz-screen as it filled with the interior of *Horizon's* docking bay.

The ship stopped its forward momentum and then hovered for a few seconds before lowering onto a landing pad. A slight shudder let them know the ship had landed, and within a few minutes a ramp that could fit 20 men shoulder-to-shoulder lowered like a tongue from the front of the *Ark of Time*. The bay had been hyper-pumped with atmosphere to welcome the ancients to their new home. Valerius listened as the omnipresent voice called "speaker" instructed them to head down the ramp. Deciding forward was the only real option, he strode boldly down the ramp, and his men followed closely behind him.

"Commander Valerius Feronae. Welcome to *Horizon*." An incredibly tall man with a lanky build extended his hand as if to take something from him. Valerius gave him a quixotic look, trying but failing to think of what gift was customary to offer when greeted in this strange fashion. He didn't really have anything to give, as his clothes and equipment had never been returned.

The tall man let his hand fall to his side with a look of mild embarrassment. "Well, hello. My name is Dr. Ian Plexar. I'm what serves as the director of *Horizon*. That is, I am in charge until we decide how to structure our leadership. Well, in charge is a bit strong. Let me just say I represent all of us here in welcoming you and wishing you the best as you make our home your home."

Valerius choked back a laugh at how the man was so timid about explaining his position of leadership. No true leader could be so timid in claiming his rightful position. Valerius would have thought it a ruse had he not learned a little over the past two weeks about *Horizon* and the place of prominence given to practical philosophers in this new place...or time...or both. Over the past few weeks he and his men had been consulting an oracle called "computer" to learn of relevant historic, cultural and situational details. They had also all been receiving a crash course in the Anglisk language, augmented by their new DataPort emplacements at the base of their skulls that served to interface minds and machines. While the DP knowledge gave them all a full vocabulary, accent and speaking skills still had to be learned, and practice was needed for full fluency.

Valerius had been pleasantly surprised that Anglisk had significant similarities with Latin and was clearly designed for ease of learning. Having learned four ancient tongues, his language skills were still serving him well as he learned Anglisk pronunciations.

"Thank you, Doctor Plexar," he replied in hesitant Anglisk. "I am not knowing what all is for our future, but I pledge that we will unite with you to free Rome and the barbarian provinces from the foreign invaders. Until this task is completed, my sword is yours."

The rest of the day was spent in-processing, with a fairly smooth system that impressed Valerius. Whatever other leadership failures might exist, attention to detail in logistics wasn't one of them. Soldiers were given attire and spacious quarters that housed four men to a room, with private quarters for upper-ranking officers and senior enlisted men. The sailors and slaves were given similar quarters, which may have caused some consternation in the ranks had the new rooms not been far superior to that which was expected in Egypt. Valerius declined having a room to himself, but eventually agreed to share a four-man room with just Otho since that also gave him a small meeting area where he could assemble his sub-leaders.

On his first night aboard *Horizon*, Valerius lay awake in his bunk for hours pondering his plight. The silence was incredible, and almost eerie. He had always lived with the noise of a city or encampment, or the splashing of the sea, or at least the sounds of nature at night. Even on the *Ark of Time* you could hear people talking and a low hum of activity. Here there was only silence. In a way, his past life was now just silence, or at best background noise. Everything here was new, and Valerius would have to make a new life for himself. He vowed his new life would not be a quiet one.

CHAPTER 4

Life on the *Horizon*

Temporal mechanics made no sense. Valerius rubbed his blurry eyes, trying once again not to catch some much-needed sleep during the lecture. Doctor Emil Ztsvistion continued his lecture as if everyone were rapt with attention. In fact, Dr. Z always delivered his talks without any regard for the audience, lost in his own excitement for the subject.

"There are many theories about how the time stream handles temporal paradox, or would handle a temporal paradox. For instance, if you go back in time and kill your father before you are born, you could not have been born, and hence could never have killed your father, thus you are in a paradox. The truth is, we don't know what would happen. We can't even be certain if one has ever happened or not." Dr. Z turned from the e-board waving his modern stylus like an orchestral baton, his German accent thickening with his growing excitement. "Ve probably don't vant to know what would happen!"

"Why not?" asked Rachel Rais, her light-green eyes sparkling with curiosity. She was fairly tall and had long raven-black hair that shimmered when she moved her head. Her skin was white like porcelain, suggesting she was from the past, as most of the moderns had permanently tanned skin much like Valerius' own skin tone. Valerius was impressed enough with her looks to be inquisitive about her personality as well. Surprisingly, Dr. Z heard the question and shook his head once as if startled awake from a good dream before looking at her and answering.

"It's too dangerous, or at least ve think it would be. If time were altered ve'd be a part of the alteration, and have no way of knowing anything occurred. In the past, the idea was that temporal paradox could never occur because the one perpetrating the paradox would actually just split off a new reality. If you imagine infinite universes in which all possible actions or particle movements are taken, then creating a paradox just pushes you into a new universe."

"But that's not just a new universe of possibility," Rachel said in a contemplative tone, as if trying to figure the question out even while she was asking it. "It's actually a universe that includes a paradox—so it's an impossible universe. Are we to imagine that there are not only infinite universes of all possibilities but also of all impossible possibilities? Isn't that just nonsense at some point?"

"Exactly true. Dealing with a paradox using a multiverse paradigm may seem like an easy solution, but you end up postulating the existence of an infinite amount of both possible and impossible universes. Such a theory gets you nowhere. Indeed, we have never found anything to be infinite. Infinity only exists in religion. In the real world, in physics, infinity is merely a marker that says you don't understand something."

Rachel seemed satisfied, and Dr. Z clearly decided that was enough digression from his well-memorized lecture.

"So that is one reason we now believe in a time theory called Conservation of Reality, or COR. Most of the leading COR theories are conservative, suggesting the time stream is very difficult to interfere with. COR is backed by several lines of mathematical evidence. We believe that the time stream cannot be altered. If you went back in time and tried to kill your father, the instant before you acted you would disappear from realty, and time would progress as if you died at the instant you attempted to change the time line."

"That seems rather fantastic," Valerius heard Rachel mutter under her breath. Dr. Z took no notice of her but continued his lecture.

"Many of you may think this is not possible, and you wonder what happens to this person. Remember, time and space are similar things—they are simply dimensions. But if time gets upset, it compensates by moving individuals in space. Hence, the person who tries to interfere is given a space of digressing quantity that moves toward zero at infinity. That is to say, they cease taking up space, or in common vernacular, they disappear. In fact, I believe they are unwittingly using their wills to disappear similar to how we use the human will to travel through time. This suggests that one day we may be able to use psycho-kinesics techniques to travel through space and not just time."

Rachel interrupted again. "But you said infinity doesn't exist in physics."

"Yes, but in this case I was extrapolating toward infinity, not invoking it. You would simply continue to shrink for as long as time lasts, and we now know that time has an ending. Remember Newton's laws? One action here makes equal and opposite reaction there. What we know with certainty is that interfering with time impacts reality by creating a bunching or knotting in the time stream, hastening the conclusion of time throughout the Universe. Time is actually a terminal rather than an unlimited variable, but its ubiquity means there is no such thing as an isolated alteration. What we do here to damage the time stream damages the time stream everywhere."

Valerius didn't want to believe a word of it, but he really could hardly believe anything that had happened to him in the last few months. The fact that he was here listening to such nonsense almost proved the nonsense correct. The very *tabcomp* in front of him, actively transcribing notes for him, proved these people were serious about education and that it was not just a twisted joke. He was also now in charge of missions to the past, which brought up an obvious practical question.

Valerius raised his hand and caught Dr. Z's attention before asking, "What happens if we make a mistake and create a paradox on one of our temporal insertion missions?"

"Ah, well, no one is certain. Under COR you would not be able to interfere but would disappear even while you were creating the paradox. We have had some people missing from time missions, but we don't know if that verifies COR or is from simple desertion. People may have thought staying in the past is a better life than fighting here in the present."

"What do other theories suggest?" asked Valerius, wanting to know as much as possible about what could happen should his temporal missions fail.

"In general, less conservative theories suggest that time is less resilient rather than unchangeable. When you make a change in the past other events change to cover the initial alteration and nullify its effects. It's kind of like walking on a spider web, where each strand is a choice. You make many choices, but you end up in the same place on the other side of the web."

Dr. Z cleared his throat and screwed up his face as if he were broaching into an area he thought was a tad distasteful. "There are also less conservative views, but they're unsupported in the math. The least conservative view is that a single significant change in time will create a paradox of such magnitude that it will immediately collapse the entire Universe, bringing us to the end of all time-space. We're pretty sure that doesn't happen; after all, we are still here. But it does hint at the magnitude of our responsibility, and it's the reason why it's imperative that our time-snatches are 'snagless temporal interpositions.' We even leave behind cloned bodies when we think those are needed, so that there is no evidence we were there."

"But if you can clone people, why not just clone an army here," asked Rachel.

"You must be from a more recent time period, yes?"

"The early 21st century," replied Rachel.

"Well then, at that time some animals had been cloned. It would be another century or so before humans started being cloned. What we initially thought to be a defect in our technology eventually turned out to be a defect in our understanding of humanity. Every time we cloned a person, they came out like a zombie in a coma, with no mind and no will of their own. And that was if they even had any life in them at all. Then we discovered what people have always known—that the human mind is more than merely a brain. There is some soul-force involved, something beyond the physical. We cannot clone live people, but we can replicate DNA and create whole human bodies—but that's Dr. Entwater's specialty. What you should know here is that it was this discovery of the human soul-force that is how we stumbled upon temporal transition.

"How's that?" broke in Rachel again. "How does the discovery of a 'soul' lead to the ability to transit time?"

"We are already past time for class, so I shall be brief. Temporal mechanics is really a bridge between Einstein's general relativity and its bastard offspring quantum mechanics, plus the newer psychodynamics field. Once the first two philosophies were thought diametrically opposed because one suggests that light is a constant and the other suggests all things are random at the subatomic levels. Since 'random' cannot coexist with 'constant,' we had a paradox there.

"In truth, the uniting factor is the relative time-space position of the human mind. It has long been speculated in quantum mechanics that nothing happens unless it is observed—that somehow the observation makes the thing real. What we have done is learned that time-space is porous, and the 'holes' are quantum level patterns we call quark-waves. Really, these are what brainwaves affect and why observation constitutes reality. Our brain waves interact at the quantum level to shape reality, or at least to confirm it.

"Our own Dr. Plexar discovered that this also applies to temporal direction. With the right equipment, we can set our minds to believing backward time travel and then make it happen. People can travel through time because in a real sense we set our own realities. The old saying that if you set your mind to it, you can do anything, is true. In fact, time progresses because that is the general setting of the human mind, but we have found that doesn't preclude strong enough minds blended with the right technology from being able to break away and go backward, taking large masses with them as needed. It is a matter of belief. One of the real benefits of *Horizon* is that it is so far from the human mind collective, with all of its doubts. No one on Earth could ever haul a large mass back in time—there is too much mental temporal inertia resisting time's direction change. With so many people now here, we must do our temporal transitions en-route to our destinations."

Dr. Z rubbed the bridge of his nose where his glasses had left small indentations before continuing. "We were free to experiment out here at *Horizon* because nothing we did in any time period would upset someone on earth. Our quark-waves would not be contrasting, and so no temporal crisis would occur. The lack of human presence in *Horizon's* past ensured we would not adversely affect the time stream. Strangely, now every time we bring more people to *Horizon* it gets a little harder to go back in time.

"But if you do have such control of time, why not just go to the future and see what happens?" asked Rachel.

"We cannot conceptualize our future to a sufficient degree to travel there. So for us, we can travel anywhere back in time, but we can only travel ahead to the point where our pilot was once alive. But we must end here for the day."

Dr. Z looked at his watch again and huffed at having violated his typically punctilious class conclusion. "I know many of you have not understood most of this, and that's fine. What you must know is that we strive to make snagless temporal interpositions that do not affect the time stream. You are being trained to go back in time to abduct people just prior to death so that we can create a force to retake the earth, and you must do it without creating temporal paradox which would endanger you and possibly all of reality. You can read more about all of these things on your own. For now, thank you for the extra class time—have a good lunch."

Valerius funneled out of class with the rest of the students, and headed toward the John Glenn Cafeteria. It was strange to travel through the pristine white corridors, and though he was told the walls were not marble, he couldn't help but be reminded of glorious Rome.

Even the colorful illumination beacons on the walls and occasional sliding doors didn't stop his comparison.

Valerius went through the line and grabbed a drink, then put his plate under the Food Compiler's spigot. "Steak, potatoes, and corn. Hot. Two-thousand calories total," he commanded the FoodComp. Three thick globs of grayish mash drizzled onto his plate. Valerius smiled as he turned from the machine and surveyed the cafeteria, looking for a table. These moderns thought their food unappetizing due to its color and consistency, but it tasted fabulous. Compared with most of the food he had eaten, in the field and at home, this stuff was wonderful. It always came at the right temperature, with a grand variety of flavors and interesting spices that he'd never had before. And this new vegetable called sweet corn was spectacular. He grabbed a fresh apple and a melon slice grown in the hydroponics farm, then spotted Otho and sat across from him at a lunch table near the back of the large room.

"Hey, commander, make any sense of all that philosopher prattle?" asked Otho, a hearty smile on his face and a large chunk of FoodComp-steak stuck to his fork. "You officers should be enjoying it, seeing as how you specialize in nonsense anyway."

Valerius grunted assent and bit into the fruit called "watermelon." He slurped the juices before replying to Otho's taunt. "If by 'nonsense' for officers you mean honor and principles, then I ask you to refrain from criticizing what you don't understand. On that very same advice, I will refrain from recounting to you the day's lesson, for I just as surely do not understand *it*."

"Good," said Otho, plopping the steak-like morsel into his mouth and chasing it down with what the moderns called "beer" though it didn't taste anything like the mead they were used to. It also seemed to never create inebriation, no matter how hard Otho tried to evoke the state.

"If I had met anyone on Earth, even Aristotle himself, blathering ideas like we are being taught, I'd have been sure of his insanity," Valerius continued. "But I can't deny that we are here, and that they brought us here, so how can I reject their explanation for how it all works? Today Dr. Z explained a theory called COR that suggests time itself is like a string that can be knotted, thereby shortening it and hastening the end of time, not just for us but for the whole Universe. Can you believe—"

"I thought you said you'd spare me the lesson!" growled Otho, only partly in jest.

Valerius was going to respond with yet another friendly verbal barb when Rachel from temporal mechanics class strolled over with her plate of food and slid into a chair beside him. Every man at the table looked up to watch beauty in motion, then quickly turned back to their food to pretend they were unaffected by it. Valerius smiled at her.

"Welcome," he said, briefly wondering if he should extend a hand to be shaken or if that was too formal for this occasion. He decided against it since she had her hands busy putting a napkin in her lap and picking up the eating utensils.

"Thanks," she said in perfect Anglisk. Those from the post-computer age all seemed to get Anglisk quickly since it was very similar to something called "English" which he learned originated from Britannia. How strange that such an inconsequential island should someday bequeath its tongue to the world, while the clearly superior Latin would be relegated to the history books and called a "dead language"!

"So, did you buy that stuff about disappearing or did you think one of the other theories made more sense?" she asked with a wry smile.

"Why ask me?" Valerius asked, putting another piece of the excellent potato-tasting mash into his mouth.

"Because you actually ask questions and seem to think about what's being said. I think most people in those classes just swallow everything they're told, or maybe they don't even get it. From what I understand, COR suggests that if you or I make a mistake on one of the time-snatches, we simply disappear and no one ever sees us again. We better get hazardous duty pay for that!"

"Hazardous duty what?" asked Valerius, trying to follow the discussion but constantly being distracted by the way her big green eyes contrasted with her dark hair and porcelain skin. And how did she have teeth that white? Valerius was baffled by this woman who could rival Venus herself in beauty but who chose to use her mind instead of play the coy flirtatious games he expected from pretty ladies.

"Hazardous duty pay. That's extra pay for a dangerous mission."

"Oh. Wish we had that in my time."

"It'd have made even Rome bankrupt!" interjected Otho from across the table with a big smile. "Every mission's dangerous—otherwise it isn't a mission, it's a vacation. I didn't even know we were getting paid at all. Are we getting paid now?"

"No, Otho, we're not mercenaries who have to get paid to do a job," replied Valerius good-naturedly. "Isn't getting our lives back and our needs met enough?"

"I suppose so," replied Otho grudgingly before turning back to wolfing down his food.

Valerius looked back at Rachel, who had started eating as well. "So you think COR may not be correct? What makes you a credible critic? I know I fall far short of conceiving most of the concepts in class, so I certainly don't feel I could have a basis for disagreeing with their practical philosophies."

"I just think it's too convenient for them. Maybe it's a scare tactic or something. What better way to make us not run away or interfere with things than to tell us that doing so erases us from existence."

"What's a 'scare tactic'?" Valerius asked, once again intrigued by the descriptiveness of an Anglisk term. As it had been explained to him, Anglisk had no unbroken rules, all words were spelled exactly as they sounded, there were no conjugations but instead a single word was added and modified to denote tense and aspect for a full sentence, and there were no masculine/feminine forms and no definite articles. The creator of this language even included an intentional rhyme scheme, excluded all homonyms and true synonyms, and ensured all words were easy to pronounce. Valerius had to begrudgingly agree that this may indeed be an improvement upon his native Latin—it certainly was a lot easier to learn. He scratched the back of his head where the DataPort had been inserted as he pondered the new term.

"You don't know what a scare tactic is? You can figure that one out—you're an ancient Roman, right?" asked Rachel with a smile. "Why did you put red plumes on your helmets?"

"So that the enemy would cower when they observed a sea of red marching to send them to Hades. In fact, I once saw an entire battle won before a single *pilum* was thrown. The enemy saw us coming and were so afraid that they started fighting against themselves and began to dissolve. All we had to do was show up to plunder the routed army."

"Then the red plume was a 'scare tactic'—you scared people to get them to do what you wanted," said Rachel.

"Oh. So maybe COR is scaring us to make us behave. That's possible, though I've not noticed any other form of duplicity here. In fact, these people seem almost too open and honest and sincere. It makes one nervous how they demonstrate their feelings in the open or discuss intimate details with strangers."

"You get used to it," said Rachel. "Public display of affection was even worse in my time period."

"It was discouraged among well-bred people of my time period," said Valerius. "And I do not know why it's tolerated here."

"What I don't know," interjected Otho with an uncharacteristically thoughtful expression on his face, "Is why we can't just go back in time and change things so that humanity's prepared for the arrival of the Narcoid."

Valerius looked at his friend and smiled. "So you do want to know what we talked about in class! I'll spare you the details. It seems that creating paradoxes in the past curtails the length of space-time and hastens all reality toward the end of time."

"Right," said Otho, slowly nodding his head in mock seriousness. "Shortening space time and making paradoxes. Well...I say we do it anyway!"

"Otho!" said Rachel in mock surprise. "Who are you to decide to shorten the length of the Universe simply to repel aliens from a single planet among the billion-billion known planets? That would be the epitome of selfishness."

"I am a Roman," said Otho proudly, "And the Universe should recognize that Romans are just that important."

Valerius chuckled at Otho's defiance. "Look, I'm with you old friend. Maybe as a last resort we just decide to violate the time stream thing. But for now it seems prudent to follow the rules and not make any ripples in the past. I'm having drinks with Dr. Plexar tonight—maybe I can ask him about the consequences of time travel incongruities. He always seems to be able to put complex issues into simple words that can be properly digested."

"Sounds like a good idea—can I come too?" asked Rachel.

"Sure—we'd be happy to have your lovely company," replied Valerius with a salacious smile.

Otho rolled his eyes in disgust at the flirting but thankfully remained silent.

***

Valerius showed up early, as was his custom when meeting with a superior officer. Of course, Dr. Plexar only vaguely fit that description, but after six months on-station Valerius understood that Dr. Plexar was an honorable and affable man worthy of respect, which was more than he could say for some of his previous commanders from the Roman Senate. Many of them were spoiled whelps in command because of birth right instead of capability. Valerius had experienced first-hand the organizational ability of Dr. Plexar, and now he knew the man to be not only a genius, but also a man of integrity and ability.

The room was large, illuminated by a mix of soft white and blue lighting, with plenty of darker spaces for those who wanted to be alone or possibly alone with a friend. Many people had strange-colored liquids in front of them, often bubbling in elaborate glasses that snaked in thin and fat coils. The light music in the background was some sort of electronic version of classical music but was mostly drowned out by the purr of people speaking in lowered tones. Many people simply sat and enjoyed their beverages. There was a small stage tucked in one corner, but it was barren for the moment. Off in another corner were a few entertainment DeathDare machines, but they also looked abandoned right now.

Valerius had to fight hard to keep his jaw from dropping as Rachel entered the room. By the gods she was gorgeous! She wore a simple white silk blouse that perfectly accentuated her ample bosom and thin waist without being ostentatious or tasteless, and had on a white skirt with a blue-flower pattern that made him remember spring in Tuscany. Her oval face with distinct, thin jaw line and high cheekbones made her look youthful, betrayed only by the obvious wisdom gleaming from those green eyes. She graced him with a warm smile and wave as she crossed the room to join him.

Dr. Plexar showed up shortly thereafter and they all enjoyed pleasantries while ordering drinks. Rachel had met Plexar briefly before but did not have weekly meetings with him like Valerius did. Valerius actually saw quite a bit of Plexar since he'd been given command of *Horizon's* temporal corps and had to attend staff meetings. The conversation quickly turned to Dr. Z's classes and Rachel got Plexar caught up on their lunchtime musings.

"I quite agree with you, Rachel," said Plexar, leaning back as he always did when he talked about topics that interested him most and deserved time for contemplation. "I'm a proponent of the Resetting Theory myself—in fact, it's my theory. But Dr. Z's quite correct to say most scientists believe in COR—there's no ruse there. In the end, we simply don't know."

"What's Resetting Theory?" asked Rachel.

Plexar smiled, clearly enjoying the chance to explain his theory. "It's rather simple. I think one person's future can take place in another person's past. Just as time bends to maintain the speed of light as a constant, maybe causality bends to maintain reality. Maybe if you go back in time and kill your father before you're born, time simply continues from that point on as if it were the present and not the past. All that would have been in your timeline existed, but only as a history for you. You are caused by that history, but everything else goes on as if it never existed. It's kind of like resetting reality."

"What do you find appealing about that theory?" asked Rachel.

"I think it starts to explain miracles, or those inexplicable portions of history. Maybe some of the miraculous occurrences are really just the outcome of time travelers? It's not that they don't have explanation, just that they can only be explained by the intervention of a future that no longer exists."

"But how's Resetting Theory different than the multi-universe paradigm we don't believe in anymore?" Rachel asked.

"Its results are similar, and that's why it's nearly impossible to determine exactly what's happening, but the premises are very different. Rather than having an infinite number of universes out there just waiting for us to create a paradox and leap from one to another, my theory says there is only one time stream, and that paradoxes can be folded into that stream. The problem is, every time a paradox is folded in, it may have the ultimate effect of folding all of time-space, shortening it not only for us, but for everyone and everything in the Universe."

"Under that paradigm, what would happen if I create a paradox while in the past?" asked Valerius, still obsessed with the dilemma.

"While you could live just fine in the past even after creating the paradox, when you transitioned to the future you would either cease to exist, as Dr. Z likes to explain, or you would simply fail to transition and be stuck in your past. Your interference creates a new future that cannot be pictured by your psycho-temporal transition pilot, just as our future now is not accessible to us. That's why it's paramount that we do not substantially alter the time stream, since we wish to return to our own futures."

"So if I mess up the time stream in the past, I probably won't know it until I try to transition back to the future?"

"That's what I believe," said Plexar with a small smile. "So don't mess up."

"I'm a practical man," said Valerius after a short silence. "So it seems to me that the answer to this question has very real implications. If you're right, and time simply resets, why shouldn't we just go back and prepare humanity for the alien invasion? We could go back to my time and introduce your technology and scientific method, and by the time the aliens arrived they'd find a humanity united, armed to the teeth, and prepared to take its place in the Universe."

"If it were up to you they'd find a *Roman* world armed to the teeth," laughed Plexar good humoredly. "But I still don't think we can chance it."

"Surely it could be a fallback position, then," said Valerius, always putting things into his military perspective. "If the aliens discover *Horizon* and all is lost, we might be able to salvage the situation by making a last-minute gamble on which theory is correct and sending someone back to change history."

"I've also thought about what we should do as a last resort, so I'm glad you're thinking of it," replied Plexar gravely. "But let me be clear: I'd never allow us to intentionally alter the time stream. To go back and alter something means everything thereafter changes. Either time *for the whole Universe* ends because of the paradox that is created, or at the very least, most of the people who have lived since that change will most likely be eradicated as the new circumstances change copulation habits, times, etc. That would be tantamount to mass murder. Not to mention the shortening of the time line for all creatures in the Universe."

"I understand your concern about collapsing all of space-time," said Valerius, a puzzled look wrinkling his face. "But your concern about people who will never exist escapes me. It can't be murder to stop people from ever living."

"You're talking about influencing time thousands of years before the alien attack. That would mean hundreds of generations destroyed—a type of global genocide. Everyone you know—your wife, your daughter, your friends—would be deleted from existence. As the discoverer of time travel, I'd be responsible for the worst atrocity in human history."

"What do you mean?" asked Rachel. "We're talking about the end of the human race. You'd rather protect a few hundred generations than save our species?"

"Yes, actually, their lives mean more to me than future lives that as yet have not been created. The future does not exist, or at least cannot be accessed by us. Look, I know you both mean well, but our scientists confirmed back in the 21st century that just because someone is unborn, doesn't mean killing them is not murder. At that time the controversial issues of abortion and cloning reached a peak, and we discovered that you cannot clone a human life. It turns out dead on arrival—without a soul. We also discovered that the soul is implanted in a human fetus far before birth. Indeed, it was that revelation that finally eradicated abortion from the earth and led to my area of temporal psycho-mechanics, as we started discovering exactly what the human soul can do."

"That's how we go through time, right, by someone willing it to happen?" asked Valerius.

"Exactly. Human life is truly a deeper mystery than we realized, being equipped not just to adjust physical matter with other physical matter but also able to manipulate reality from psycho-energy. Life doesn't begin at birth, or even at the age of viability outside the womb. It seems life begins at conception—somehow our procreative act is injected with a living soul that cannot be duplicated in clones and defies all observation, similar to dark matter and dark energy in that respect."

"In my time," Rachel said thoughtfully, "at the very beginning of the third millennium, we were still experimenting with cloning. The abortion debate was mostly between feminists and religionists rather than between scientists dedicated to knowing when life begins."

"I know," said Plexar. "But even in your time the scientists were able to keep pushing back the date of viability, and it was ideology not science that allowed abortion to continue even on fetuses that were viable outside the womb. We eventually decided we could not play God and change our morals to fit our circumstances; we realized the soul of a human is precious, and if there is even a chance that it is human life, then it must have the right to live."

"I was always against abortion beyond 22 days after conception," said Rachel introspectively. "It seemed to me that if death is lack of brainwaves and lack of heartbeat, then we'd be hypocritical to say presence of brainwaves and presence of heartbeat is not life."

"Yes...that's a good deduction, and probably the best intellectual decision you could have made in your time period. In any case, the belief in preserving human life carried over into the legal issues of temporal transition, though not many cases ever reached the courts since we simply banned all time travel except experiments far off in space that would have little effect on Earth. To go back in time and change history would be to kill the billions of people who *would* have existed without our intervention. We also are certain that such a blatant intervention would have an impact upon the time-space duration, though we can't understand the divergence enough to calculate the exact shortening of the Universe's existence."

Valerius stared at his beer, thinking of the implications of what was being said. He decided to break the awkward silence with another question. "Do you suppose the Narcoid have a life that is also worth protecting?"

"Ah, now there's a hard question. Who are we to kill them in order to preserve ourselves? I certainly don't think humanity has some sort of intrinsic value that makes us superior to other sentient creatures. But we know so little about them—are they indeed sentient or are they destroying by instinct...maybe even an instinct for self-preservation? I don't know. What I do know is that they attack without forethought for others, and while humanity has many failings, respecting others seems to be a quality the Universe may need more of."

"So you're willing to plot against the aliens but unwilling to alter time to do it?" Rachel asked.

"Right. We can't change the past, but we can plunder it to give us a future. In a way, our salvation is our history, and our heroes are the unsung heroes of the past who 'died' ignoble and seemingly meaningless deaths. There is great paradox there. Our future rests on our past, and time itself will be the ark that carries us past the present crisis and into a brighter tomorrow."

CHAPTER 5

Fallen Nature

Admiral Bill Haarkonan looked across the staff meeting table with cool reserve. "This recent raiding of the fresh food storage area was unexpected, but I promise we won't be caught unprepared like this again. I've detailed guards for all our food storage and hydroponics farms. It's unfortunate that we have to waste manpower guarding food, but I see no other way forward with the influx of such diverse populations from the past. We were lucky the Vikings didn't really like fruit and vegetables."

That got a small chuckle from Dr. Plexar who sat to his immediate left and at the head of the large oak conference table. Ever since Dr. Plexar had appointed Haarkonan the head of operations for *Horizon* he'd been busy planning the efficient use of their scarce resources, but he hadn't spent too much time on internal security matters. Now, with more and more people coming from the past, there had been an increasing number of altercations and even some battery and theft crimes. There were simply too many diverse groups trying to get along with too few resources to keep everyone satisfied.

"We may need to think again about time-snatching Vikings," said Dr. Plexar with a smile. "Clearly their raiding tendencies are not easy even for us to retrain. Exactly who we should be looking to snatch is actually what I wanted to discuss today. You've all seen the lists of mass snatches that we're planning, based on historic research into occasions where many people were lost and no discovery of bodies is reported. However, it seems to me that we could use more leaders and talented minds from the past. I'd like to brainstorm a list of humanity's best people who fit in with our mission. Any nominations?"

"Are we talking war heroes, philosophers, or artists and the like?" asked Valerius.

Haarkonan looked at the former Roman with respect, thinking that Valerius had proven a very good leader thus far, even possessing a flexible enough mind to bridge the gap between the ancient peoples and the moderns. Dr. Plexar had appointed Valerius Commander of Temporal Insertions, so he now sat immediately to Haarkonan's right at the staff conference table.

"I think we mostly need military men who think at a strategic level," said Haarkonan. "We certainly don't need artists. By philosophers, do you mean scientists?"

"Yes," said Valerius slowly. "It seems to me that fighting the Narcoid today is almost like a modern army with machine guns fighting a legion from my time. We must work to even the weapons technology divide, and only then will it make sense to strategize about how to use those weapons to retake Earth."

Haarkonan nodded agreement. "That makes good sense. I'd like to add that I believe many of history's generals will prove unsuitable, as they were rather hard to get along with. The last thing I need is Attila the Hun, Adolf Hitler, or Stalin on board plotting a takeover or another communist revolution."

"I agree," said Plexar. "We probably need to set some standards on both military leaders and scientists. For example, I don't see how even the greatest ancient scientific minds will do us much good today. Really, any scientist before Isaac Newton would probably be too hard to train. "

"But there were some fantastic minds before Newton," protested Dr. Gary Entwater from further down the table. He was a short swarthy man, in charge of the cloning operations needed for replacing bodies in the past. It would be his job to clone the bodies of famous people so that their corpses wouldn't be missed. Haarkonan didn't like the man. He always seemed in dissent and was short-tempered with people, projecting an air that his time was too important to be bothered by mere average minds. "You're leaving out all the ancient Greeks who first developed science, and even Galileo," Entwater whined.

Dr. Plexar shrugged. "Fine. Keep Galileo in mind, but I still feel any earlier than that and you'd have to teach the whole scientific method and debunk magic before going into quantum theory, and I really don't think we have enough time for that level of education. What do you think Valerius?"

"I know the Greeks were far more clever than I, but as one who has experienced the shock of trying to learn modern science, I'd agree with you. I really don't grasp the science behind things, and I couldn't fathom the task of furthering scientific knowledge in this age. It seems to me that more modern scientists would be best."

The group then got to the serious business of proposing who should be considered for snatching. After an hour of discussion the list included many well-known scientists. Einstein from the 20th century and Isaac Newton from the 18th century topped the list. Einstein had discovered the theories of general and specific relativity and was generally considered the most brilliant mind of all time. Newton was said to be the last man who knew everything that could be known. An English scientist and theologian, it was he who postulated the foundational laws of physics and the movement of planets.

Following such great minds were other superb scientists, including Serbian engineer Nikola Tesla (1856-1943) who had pioneered the fields of electricity and magnetism, Polish physicist and chemist Marie Curie (1867-1934) who had studied radioactivity, and Danish physicist Niels Bohr (1885-1962) who made fundamental contributions to the understanding of atomic structure and quantum mechanics. Other notables included Max Planck (1858-1947) a German physicist considered to be the founder of quantum theory, and Jens Andersen (2018-2080), the Norwegian entrepreneur and mathematician who got the closest to creating a Grand Unified Theory (GUT) of physics before then proving it was impossible. He had also discovered the dampening field used by *Horizon*'s insertion teams to calm storms during abductions, and the same technology was being looked at to create a *repulsar* field to protect spacecraft from the Narcoid. The most recent scientist on the list was Carl Fuo (2092-2146), an American astrophysicist who discovered some of the properties of dark energy and formulated the equations for matter to energy transmutation which had in turn laid the ground work for temporal transition.

Dr. Plexar smiled as he reviewed the list. "Good work. In many ways that was the easy part. Now we'll need to see who on the list can be missing from their graves. I know for a fact that Einstein will be difficult, as they preserved his brain for extra study. Dr. Entwater, can your clones duplicate the brain so as to fool an intense 21st century dissection?"

"Not a chance," replied Entwater rubbing his nose. "The brain shape is too affected by learning. I'm afraid we'll have to skip on Mr. Einstein."

"Wasn't Einstein also a doctor?" asked Haarkonan with curiosity. He had noticed that Dr. Entwater was persnickety about titles, never dropping a "doctor" when it was applicable.

"Actually, he wasn't," explained Entwater with a wry smile. "Einstein said there was no one qualified to grant him a doctorate. He was certainly far beyond his contemporaries. Now we teach his ideas to 12-year-olds. I personally would much rather have a modern 12-year-old than an ancient mind that is clouded by superstitions and incapable of grasping simple physics concepts."

Valerius started to take umbrage from the suggestion that people from the past were stupid when Plexar smoothly intervened.

"Missing out on Mr. Einstein is indeed a shame. Nothing to help that," said Plexar. "Get me a list by tomorrow of anyone else who you think we should consider snatching, and I'll send it through the historians.

"It looks like we have a solid scientist list, so let's look at military leaders. There've been many brutes that history recognizes with success, but those must be avoided so as to create the least amount of interpersonal friction. I propose we restrict our military commander acquisitions to those who were known to be wise or educated for their time, and who were not known for being brutal. If we need the brutes for the actual ground combat, we'll get them last. In front of you is a list of the top 100 commanders throughout all time based solely on their accomplishments. Any suggestions?"

Haarkonan cleared his throat to get people's attention. "It seems to me that we should also not expend resources getting generals who were great due to being in the right place at the right time or because they had superior weaponry. From this list I'd say we should consider Alexander the Great, maybe Genghis Khan, Napoleon, Hannibal Barca, Timur, Julius Caesar, Belisarius, and General Antonio Scalerio from the Great Nuclear War."

"Hannibal was brutal," interjected Valerius. "I would not serve under him."

"Are you sure that's not just your Roman pride talking?" sneered Entwater.

"No. I'm not sure. But in my day we remember Hannibal Barca as an evil man."

"History today suggests otherwise, my Roman friend," broke in Haarkonan. "Hannibal was well educated, and a brilliant tactician. I think he's worthy of consideration."

"Scipio beat him," said Valerius with a little pride.

"Yes, and Scipio should be on the list. But I think Hannibal should also be considered," said Haarkonan gently.

Valerius remained silent, clearly trying to swallow the idea of resurrecting Rome's worst enemy.

"We're just brainstorming here," said Dr. Plexar. "We'll be certain to send the names back through the historians before we make the final selections. Any other nominations?"

The group worked another hour before adding Robert E. Lee, Thomas "Stonewall" Jackson, Adolf Gustav from Sweden, Erwin Rommel from Germany, Scipio Africanus, William the

Conqueror, Cyrus the Great, Richard the Lionheart, Saladin, and Pyrrhus of Epirus. Ramses the Great, Mao Zedong, Georgy Zhukov, George Patton, Douglas MacArthur, and Zven Kirkland were all rejected due to having reputations for being difficult personalities.

It seemed to Haarkonan somehow fitting that many great military leaders would miss the chance for a second go on life because they exhibited major personality failings and huge egos. War should make a man humble, he reflected, as it all too clearly illuminates death's gateway to the next realm of existence. And in that realm, life's deeds are not judged by accomplishments but by intent and proven character.

"If we're satisfied with this list of military leaders, I'd like to take a moment for us to consider my replacement," said Dr. Plexar.

The room grew quiet in anticipation, as everyone liked working with Plexar and wondered who could take his place. Haarkonan started to think of objections for why he couldn't step into Plexar's position. He certainly didn't want that burden.

"All this talk of historic leaders got me thinking that we also should get the best minds available to lead *Horizon*," said Plexar. "I need to get back to research, and we'd be wise to employ someone more qualified than myself to lead our diverse coalition. At the top of my list is Julius Caesar because he had political, administrative, and military experience, but I understand the way he died makes his time-snatch difficult."

Haarkonan smiled at the understatement. Caesar had been murdered in public, stabbed 23 times by senators, though only one wound proved ultimately fatal. His dead body and cremation ceremony were then used as propaganda, but that would be handled easily enough by a cloned corpse.

Plexar continued. "Even if we can discover a way to recruit Caesar, his skills would probably be best employed with Valerius' Earth invasion strategy team. What we need is a civilian leader who knows how to lead during wartime, and who can administrate and create resolve. I propose we recruit Sir Winston Churchill."

"A good choice," said Haarkonan thoughtfully. "Of course, he'd need some time to orient to the 24th century, and we'd have to give him some new organs to prolong his lifespan. He died older, didn't he?"

"Yes, I think he was almost 90," said Entwater. "While we couldn't get him up to a 300 year lifespan that we consider standard, I'm sure we could clone some organs, modify some genes, and clean his blood to extend his life another 30-50 years."

Others also voiced their support for the idea, and Valerius was instructed to add Sir Winston Churchill to his list of potential time-snatches.

The meeting then continued with Lieutenant Neil LeMoray delivering a brief report on what was happening to the earth. While no communications were allowed with Earth, passive observations were interpreted to try to understand the big picture. It seemed that the Narcoid had destroyed most military targets, raided major cities, then just left the countryside alone. The aliens were clearly after mineral resources of some sort and had begun to burrow into the earth seeking precious metals at many locations around the world. The largest Narcoid population seemed to be in South Africa, and LeMoray guessed that Africa was their primary target because it had more unexploited resources.

Humanity had indeed tried to defend itself, but the Narcoid simply destroyed anything that got in their way. No communication with the aliens had been established, though it was clear the Narcoid knew what nuclear weapons were since they quickly occupied or destroyed all locations that had radioactive materials, ranging from power plants to waste storage facilities. The enemy was not mindless, but also clearly did not think in ways humans could predict.

Dr. Plexar concluded the meeting by reporting on the status of the larger space ships. "We're putting the *Valkyrie's* repairs on hold for now—there simply is too much damage there. Instead, we're refitting the *Ark of Time* with new technology so that it can colonize, as it was originally designed to do. Its sister ship the *Time Raider* will be doing all of the temporal insertion missions for a while. The *Ark of Time's* refit is coming along nicely, thanks in large part to the work of *Horizon's* scientific community. Pretty much everyone on my original staff who is not needed with weapons development has been spending time working on it. I think they know it might well be their home someday, so they're taking special care of it. Soon we'll have to decide if we want to send it to Alpha Centauri or if we should hold it back as an escape ship should we be spotted."

Haarkonan felt a sting of disappointment as he was reminded that the *Valkyrie* had been found too damaged to deserve immediate repairs. "I thought Alpha Centauri was dead," he interjected a bit more grumpily than he had intended. "I considered going there before I knew *Horizon* existed, but I didn't see the point. Is there something at Alpha Centauri that was also kept from the military?"

"No," Plexar responded patiently. "We lost all contact with our outpost there 20 years ago. We don't know anything more about that than you do. However, the outpost was established about the same time as *Horizon*, just over 40 years ago. It was made to be completely self-sustaining, since even communications would take more than four years one way at the speed of light. It had many redundant systems and its own manufacturing abilities. Who knows, there may still be remnants to pick up or people to rescue? At the very least, the scrap refined metals and liquid water are worth targeting. Alpha Centauri One is still the closest planet we know of that can support human life."

"We know it *used* to support human life," Haarkonan corrected sadly. "But I'm glad to hear you're not hiding anything else from us military types. And it's good to hear that the *Ark of Time* is ahead of schedule."

"Yes, that's a bright spot. You should check it out sometime—you'll find it has quite a few surprises onboard," said Plexar with a smile.

"I'll do that."

"Speaking of surprises, the *Ark of Time* is being used as a test bed for innovative projects, and we'll be conducting a full run of all its systems during tonight's shift. You should check that out too. I'm especially excited to see how Dr. Cua's *repulsar* field works. Testing will involve more than 500 people on two short missions, concluding early tomorrow morning. If the first test shows that the ship is functioning well, the second short mission will include families onboard to give them an idea of what we've been working on, and to test out some of the colonization comforts we've installed."

When the meeting ended Haarkonan quickly left the room so as to avoid unnecessary social conversations. He had a lot to do before his rest cycle, and he wanted to get ahead of things so that he'd have time the next day to see the *Ark of Time* return and possibly make a quick nostalgic visit to his beloved *Valkyrie*.

***

Haarkonan awoke to the shrill sound of his communicator. He sat up in bed, quickly cleared his throat, and then pressed the wall button to open a communication channel. "Haarkonan here," he answered, surprising himself that he didn't sound groggier. He certainly felt tired and knew he was nowhere near the end of his sleep cycle.

"Sorry to disturb you, sir. This is Lt. Haroldson from the Operations Center. We just got a report from security that I think you'd want to know about as soon as possible."

"Yes, go ahead," said Haarkonan, wondering what could be so important that it couldn't wait until morning.

"Scientist First Class Hosheema Cua was just found dead in his room, and security thinks it was murder."

Haarkonan was shocked speechless for a few seconds. He remembered meeting Cua a few times, and had liked the scientist's warm personality. Cua was also the leading scientist attempting to improve force field technology and so would be a serious loss to the scientific community. "I'll be right there," he said, sliding out of bed and quickly getting dressed.

The scientists' habitation wing was just below his level, and as he strode toward Cua's door he had to disperse many onlookers who crowded the hall trying to get a glimpse into the room. People peeled back as they recognized their operations officer.

"That's enough gawking people," he announced with a stern voice. "We'll look into this and figure out what's going on. Please return to your rooms and wait for the official report before spreading rumors. Anyone who actually has information that might help us please stay around to give your statements to the detectives."

As he stepped into Cua's room he smelled the hint of iron and salt that indicated human blood. Sure enough, Cua lay on the floor with a crushed skull, his blood pooling on the spongy blue plastic carpet. A security detective was examining the body and collecting samples, while his partner photographed the room.

"What happened here?" Haarkonan demanded, his stomach slightly twisting at the graphic nature of the death.

"He didn't bump his head, if that's what you're askin'," replied the detective. "Looks like someone bumped it for him. We need to do an analysis, but I'd guess he was struck on the head several times with a blunt object."

Haarkonan looked around the small room. It looked tidy enough, with books nicely aligned and clothing neatly folded in drawers. The place could have passed a military inspection. "I'd say the 'blunt object' isn't here anymore. And there doesn't seem to be any signs of a struggle. With our sound-proof walls no one would hear a struggle anyway."

"Looks that way, sir," the detective said kneeling over the body and taking DNA samples.

"No struggle may suggest familiarity with the murderer. I want this to be your highest priority. Find out who didn't like Cuo, and who may benefit from his death. We have enough tension around here trying to force people to get along without having a murderer loose too. If you need any resources, just request them through me."

"Yes, sir," the detective replied, then turned back to his work. Haarkonan knew when he was more in the way than being helpful, so he quickly withdrew from the room. Striding back to his own room he couldn't help feeling the human race had a death wish. How could anyone kill a fellow human being when the whole race faced extinction? Whoever did this would be found and made to serve as an example.

After lying down for an hour he decided he wasn't going back to sleep and so might as well just get up. While he wasn't very hungry, he decided breakfast might calm his stomach, and in the past he had found eating more helped compensate for sleeping less. Few people were in the John Glenn cafeteria at this early hour, so he quickly got some oatmeal and fruit and found a table.

The John Glenn served food around the clock, and people worked various shifts so as to spread out the waking hours and not overtax common areas such as eating facilities and weight rooms. All personnel were required to work out for a minimum of an hour each day, because even though *Horizon* had some mass and rotational gravity, it was well-below Earth standard, and calcium loss was a real concern.

Having failed to come up with an idea about how to proceed to investigate the night's murder, Haarkonan remembered that the *Ark of Time's* first test voyage was probably completed and decided it would be fun to see her take off for the second test mission. He liked the idea of seeing the families and was glad they could get a break from being stuck in the all-too-familiar confinements of *Horizon*.

He quickly cleaned up his place, scraped the apple core and a banana peel into a recycling vat, and strode down the white halls toward the lifts that stretched up to the surface. After seeing the *Ark of Time* takeoff he planned to inspect his old ship the *Valkyrie*, more out of nostalgia than really needing to see how extensive the damage still was. Seeing spacecraft was just the thing he needed to get his mind off the murder and lift his spirit after the depressing night.

Haarkonan entered the lift to the command observation tower that gave an excellent view of the landing pad where the *Ark of Time* would rest on the surface of *Horizon*. He punched the top button and waited a few seconds as the doors closed. A minor jolt of motion preceded the extreme acceleration as the lift pulled him briskly to the surface of the planet.

As the elevator began to decelerate, everything shuddered violently, jerking Haarkonan to the floor and twisting his ankle in the process. Haarkonan recognized the effects of a large explosion. Had the Narcoid invasion of *Horizon* begun? If they'd just had six more months to prepare, maybe the technologies would have been in place to fight the Narcoid! And how had the lobsters avoided detection?

He was still pulling himself upright when the elevator arrived at its destination. As the doors slid open his combat-trained body pumped him with adrenaline. He expected to see the chaos of battle, but instead the tower was filled with silence, as everyone stood slack-jawed staring out the viewports. So maybe it wasn't the Narcoid?

His relief that the tower was still intact and the Narcoid were nowhere in sight was short-lived, as he followed the tower crew's gaze down to the landing pad. Down on the surface of *Horizon* there were numerous small fires quickly igniting and being snuffed out without an atmosphere to sustain them. A dark explosion stain was formed on the landing pad surface, and parts of the surrounding soil looked scorched as if a minor sun had exploded there.

"What happened," he demanded, quickly taking charge of the situation and wresting the tower crew's attention away from the viz-screens.

"Sir. Um, hello sir. The *Ark of Time,* sir. She just exploded," stammered one of the tower controllers. "She was taking off for her final test flight, and then she disappeared in a ball of fire. One second she was there, then she was gone. I've never seen anything like it."

"How many people were onboard?"

"Nearly 600, sir. There were women and children too. All…gone."

"I thought this flight called for just under 500 people."

"That's correct, sir; that was the original plan. But the *Ark of Time* had a successful first short flight, so it landed and added extra researchers. All the families also boarded, you know, to thank them for supporting their spouses who've been working so hard on the ship."

"What experiments were they conducting on the second flight?"

"Dr. Cua's force field screen was the main one, sir. They're calling it the repulsar. It performed admirably on the first voyage, but Dr. Cua got sick and there was some doubt as to whether or not he'd make the second flight. Even if they decided to go ahead with the test, there's no way it would be initiated on takeoff. It should have waited until the *Ark of Time* was well away from here."

"Well, something went wrong," Haarkonan growled. Then the name hit him. "You're sure it was Dr. Cua's project?"

"Yes, sir."

"Then why wasn't Dr. Cua onboard?"

"I thought he was, sir. He authorized the testing. I have the authorization for it here on my tabcomp."

Haarkonan looked over the files on the viz-screen, quickly scanning through the official documents. It was indeed Dr. Cua's project and team that had been aboard the *Ark of Time*, and Dr. Cua was listed as being on the second voyage too, though that could have been an error.

Just over 600 souls gone in an instant. Did Cua know something wasn't right and so avoided the mission? And who killed Cua? Were these events connected? There were too many unanswered questions, but Haarkonan knew he had to get to the bottom of it all before more people were harmed and the very existence of humanity further threatened.

CHAPTER 6

Defense of Earth

"What are you hiding from me?" growled Stephen Stone with a menacing glare. "And don't give me that crap about classification again. I'm the acting United Earth President, and we're in a state of war! How can there possibly be something I should not know that will affect the outcome of this war?"

"Are you sure you're the President?" asked James Steele with a wry smile. "We never found the bodies of the six cabinet members who were ahead of you in the line of succession."

"You're not gonna find 'em either, 'cause they were turned to powder by the first strikes that pounded the United Earth capitals of London and Beijing. To tell you the truth, no, I'm not certain. I don't even want the job. Do you know someone else who can take it?"

Most men would have shrunk away from the former Secretary of Defense's tempestuous anger, but Steele had felt it before when he headed up the special forces under Stone. He knew the man lit fast but also cooled fast.

"No sir. And to tell you the truth, I can't think of someone as qualified as you for the job anyway. Who better to be President during war than the former Secretary of Defense?"

Acting President Stone took a deep breath, then regretted it as he caught the faint smell of Freon from the stale air that was churned in by the air conditioning unit. Eagle's Nest Air Force Base was a misnamed location if ever there were one, located as it was 20 stories below the Colorado mountains rather than high above them. With tunnels that laced through the mountains in every direction, Eagle's Nest was the planned safe haven for United Earth's government, as well as for the Air Force Academy, Peterson Air Force Base, and Falcon Air Force Base. It had been one of the only installations in America to survive the Great Nuclear War, and so far it remained hidden from the Narcoid. Stone had luckily already been at Eagle's Nest directing the space war when the assault on Earth began. Unfortunately, no other person higher up in the government chain had made it to Eagle's Nest.

"Have you heard anything from China? Maybe the Vice President survived."

"Again, no sir. My guess is that she died almost the same time as the President, seeing as how Beijing's Earth capital two was hit with a Mothership at the same time as London."

"It seems like the Narcoid were very sophisticated in their initial choice of targets, taking out our command and control. But if they know so much about us, why not acknowledge our attempts to communicate with them?"

"We don't know, sir."

"You're the intel guy—so give me some intelligence! I'm open to best guesses at this point."

"Sir, as far as we can tell, they simply hit the cities that had the most nuclear activity and have been following basically the same pattern ever since. All Earth locations with nuclear materials have been pulverized, to include power plants and dumps, and all major military installations above ground. Now the Narcoid have started their burrowing projects in South Africa, Arizona, and the Dead Sea, and they seem to be ignoring anyone who ignores them."

"So back to my original question. Do we have any assets in space that may still bring some power to bear on the enemy?" Stone's glare made it clear that he would not be denied the information this time.

"Mr. President, what I'm about to tell you is not just classified Top Secret, but was compartmentalized so that no member of Earth's military could ever know about it. Since you're no longer the Secretary of Defense, I feel you're warranted access, but the fewer people who know this information the better. We do indeed have an installation beyond Pluto that may still be intact. It was called project *Horizon*, and that's also the name of the installation."

"What are they doing way out there, and why wasn't I allowed to know about it?" demanded Stone. He was a relentless seeker of information, which had gotten him elected twice as a Congressman before being appointed as the Secretary of Defense.

"*Horizon's* been conducting research into temporal transition," Steele said flatly. "They were based out there so that whatever happened to 'em would not interfere with Earth's history, and no military personnel were briefed because that was in the deal Congress made when they decided to fund the project."

"I guess time travel could pose a problem in the wrong hands, but I hardly think we needed to fear our own military. How many people are out there?"

"Last I heard they had about 4,000 people, mostly scientists and support personnel. But *Horizon* was built to house tens of thousands. All those who went out there were never expected to return. We even made special conditions for them, allowing them to take or create families there."

"So we have about 4,000 white coat types on a huge installation out past Pluto. Did they have any military hardware?"

"They were designed to be self-sustaining, and have their own ship docks and engineering crews. They only had a few smaller-sized mining vessels and shuttles, plus two cruiser class sister ships when we cut their umbilical cord. That was a few years ago, so while they could have made some ships on their own, I wouldn't expect much."

"And as far as we know they're still alive?"

Steele paused to consider the question. After years in the special forces and then serving as the lead civilian military adviser to the President, he knew the value of accurate data and the importance of not saying anything he didn't know.

"As far as we know they're still there. Our radar didn't detect any Narcoid activity near where we estimate *Horizon* is located, and it's on a dark asteroid that's very hard to find. On the other hand, we've not heard anything from them since the Narcoid entered the system, but transmission silence would be expected if they don't want the Narcoid to pay them a visit."

"Let's assume they're alive. What can they do for us?"

"Not much. Certainly not much without revealing their location. The only thing I can think of is that one of the reasons we spent so much to make that installation so large was to have a backup location should the earth meet some kind of catastrophic end. If we lose it all here, we could still hope humanity continues aboard *Horizon*. That's why I think it's so important that we keep this under wraps."

"Under wraps, yes," Stone said in deep thought. "But do nothing with the information, no. We need to feed them everything we can about the Narcoid and what's happening here. Just because we can't imagine any way they can help us doesn't mean we can't help them should they have to face the Narcoid someday."

"Sir, we can't risk communicating with them. Even tight beam can be intercepted, and we have no way of knowing how Narcoid signal detection works. They almost seem to be natives of space itself—we'd be foolish to think they can't detect signals.

"I know that. What if we bounce it off the moon? If they detect that, they might just think it's a broken transmission intended to talk to Lunar One…when we still had a Lunar One."

"That's not a bad idea. We'd have to correct for the moon's location and be very precise with the tight beam, and weather might interfere with things, but I think it could be done. Since the albedo of the moon is very low, maybe reflecting 10% of the light that hits it, we'd have to use some serious watts, but I think we could do it."

"If we did want two-way communications, what would be the delay?" Stone asked.

"From here to Pluto is about four minutes at light speed, so a bit more than that to *Horizon*...if they're listening. But I still think one way is all we should risk." Steele said.

"I agree. Let's do it. Feed 'em whatever we can, starting with a message that explains what we're doing every hour on the hour, then just give 'em whatever radio news you can find. I want *Horizon* to know what we're facing in case they have to face it in the future."

"Yes, sir. If there's nothing else, I need to be getting ready for tonight's mission."

"You leading it?"

"Yes, sir. I don't get out in the field too often, but this one's important."

"I know. Yes, that's all. And Steele—good luck."

***

"You're sure that's it?" asked James Steele in hushed tones. He was lying on the top of a muddy hill covered with patches of grass observing a large warehouse-like dome structure. He shifted his weight slightly to look back down the hill at his scout and felt one of the grenades on his belt press into his side. It felt great to be back in his special forces urban infiltration uniform, though the black paint smeared across his face still tickled irritatingly.

"That's it," replied Jo McNeal, a recent recruit into Earth's defense force. "I've been watching it for two weeks. They go in a lot, and send in sphere-shaped containers every so often, and then every 28 hours a line of five or six Narcoid emerge. I think it's some kind of tank factory or hatching ground, or something."

"The creatures that emerge—are they the huge ones or the smaller two-meter size?"

"I'd say they're all right about two-meter sized, sir. Maybe they're birthed here and eventually grow into the larger ones?"

"Maybe, but their body shapes are so different it's hard to imagine. Right now we don't think that's the case. There are at least 10 different sizes, and their outer armor seems too hard to allow growth...unless they shed their skin like snakes, but then we'd see empty shells lying around. I wish that were the case so we could pick some of it up and study it. Maybe we can retrieve some shell fragments tonight."

Steele raised his night-vision goggles and surveyed the area again. All was quiet. "I don't see sentries or even passive defenses. Have you noticed anything like that?"

"No, sir," replied Jo, brushing away her red bangs from the front of her face that was also smeared with black face paint. "Nothing like that. These guys don't seem to think we're a threat. They sure aren't very security conscious."

"We'll show them the error of their ways. Did you have a plan to get us inside?"

"Not really. About a quarter turn clockwise from our position is the main door, and it's big—at least three stories high and at least that distance long. It seems to open automatically for them, since I noticed it always starts opening when they are about 10 meters away from it. Other than that, I haven't seen anything suggesting an entrance. I thought we could try sneaking in with a convoy, but as you see, there's too much open ground. I don't see any way to sneak up and get in. I thought you had a plan."

"I'd like to knock politely and rely on their good hosting skills," Steele said sarcastically. "But I don't think that'd work. Don't worry, we brought some hardware along. We're going to blast through the shell, see what we can see, take what we can take, and get out of here before reinforcements show up."

"Do you want me to go in with you?" asked Jo, clearly afraid.

"No, you're fine right here. You aren't trained for this, and my guys are. You just stay here and observe, and when you see us either dying or running out of here, you run too. Can you do that?"

"Yes, sir. I'm not much in a fight, but I can observe all you want."

"That's all I want from you. You've done well." Steele turned back around to look at the dome. It was oval-shaped, almost like a huge tortoise shell, stretching at least as long as a football field and as high as a four-story building. In some ways it resembled a big egg that was more than half buried below ground level, with its cream-colored surface interspersed with mottled bits of darker brown.

Deciding it was time to put the plan into action, he waved up the rest of his strike team, who had been waiting at the base of the hill. They quickly slithered up the hill and waited on his left and right. Jo crawled the last few feet up to join him as well.

"When you going in?" she asked.

"Right after they leave. You said Narcoid emerge every 28 hours, right? I figure after they ship out there will be fewer in there for us to deal with should things go hot. And I'm expecting things will go hot."

"That's right. Like I reported, you could set your clock to their timing, if you had a 28 hour clock. The next outbound shipment will be in about 20 minutes."

Ten minutes later Steele was pleased to spot a small convoy approaching the sphere where Jo had indicated the main entrance lay. He was glad to be able to observe the resupply first hand. Sure enough, when the first Narcoid pulling a large container sphere was about 10 meters away from the structure a huge door started opening. Steele was surprised that he couldn't hear any gears turning, and noticed that the huge door simply slid into the shell wall.

About 10 minutes after the delivery the outer door opened again, and five Narcoid marched out in perfect synchronization. Steele pointed his night vision goggles their way to get a better look. This was the closest he had ever come to seeing the enemy in person.

He clearly made out their ant-like bodies, walking upright and towering to about two meters high. Their torsos consisted of two oval-like structures melded together, with a third smaller oval-shaped structure on top that seemed like a head. Many appendages stuck out of the bottom two oval areas, and the head seemed to have pinchers for cheeks and small antenna sticking straight out from where ears would be on a human. The head also had a strong brow ridge above two eye turrets that reminded Steele of wearing a helmet. No analogue to a nose could be detected.

From the lowest oval sprouted four legs, two on each side, that seemed flexible, flipping to the ground in symmetric fashion to propel the body forward with a gait that looked more like rolling than the pumping up and down motion human legs made. Plenty more appendages came out of the torso, at least six of which were longer and could be considered arms.

As soon as the convoy cleared the dome the large door started sliding shut. The speed and efficiency of the door confirmed to Steele that he couldn't sneak in that way. After the convoy had left visual range, he motioned his men forward.

His platoon quickly jogged to the base of the huge hangar then crouched down as one specialist carrying a modified welding torch took a stance about a meter from the structure. Shutting his face guard, he pumped his torch to full, aimed it, and began burning a small door into the structure. The hangar's material at first absorbed the heat, but eventually it began to melt where it was directly under fire. With admirable skill, the infantryman melted a line up from the ground, across, back down, and across again to his starting point, creating a small door about a meter square. He shut down the torch, waited a few seconds, then advanced to gauge the residual heat.

"She's cool," he announced under his breath, stepping to the side to secure his torch while the rest of the platoon started infiltrating the structure.

It only took a minute to get the eight men inside. Glancing around, Steele realized they had not gained access to a smaller room on the outside wall but had instead burned their way into the main hangar room. Most of the wall to his left and right had machinery or large containers close by, and he realized his team had been lucky to burn through a section that was not blocked by equipment. Instead, straight ahead was a kind of corridor formed by piles of junk and shelves holding metal and ceramic boxes of various sizes. The lighting was a strange bluish color that seemed to originate from the walls and ceiling. Probably a fluorescent or even phosphorescent paint or coating, Steele decided. A low hum permeated the building, but other than that he couldn't hear any sounds.

Steele directed his men to spread out in pairs and take samples of whatever they could open or grab. He then joined his partner who had already begun to go down the corridor, establishing a perimeter for the others. Steele let the burly SSgt. Jones take point as they advanced. He had worked with Jones on previous missions, and while Steele was not without skills himself, he knew no one on the team matched Jones for weapon accuracy and sheer strength. Jones also carried a heavy Small Arms Rocket (SAR) launcher which could destroy a Narcoid outright, whereas Steele's Advanced Infantry Rifle (AIR) would need many hits to take down the well-armored beings.

Jones stealthily moved down the corridor, like a panther stalking its prey, looking everywhere with all his senses fully alert. Steele admired Jones' speed, even heavy-laden with the SAR launcher, and tried to match it while cautiously casting furtive glances in all directions. The corridor was about four meters wide, formed by shelving that contained thick cylinder tubes that were a bit over two meters long and one meter in diameter. The shelves rose to about five meters high. Far above those he could see the ceiling, slightly glowing with a pale blue color that pervaded the whole hanger-like structure.

Jones stopped abruptly, raising his fist in the signal to halt and take cover as he crouched close to the right shelving. Steele tried to melt into the shadows, about four meters behind Jones. He looked at Jones to try to discover what was happening.

Jones stared further down the corridor, clearly searching for something. Steele couldn't see anything but more of the same bland shelving. Jones then cocked his head as if intent on listening. Then Steele heard it too. Somewhere ahead was a human voice, crying out in pain. It was not a cry for help, but more a shrill utterance of hurt and despair. Jones threw back a questioning look. Steele knew he had to decide to try to find the source of the cry, or stick to the original plan of just creating a perimeter in which the rest of his men could operate.

Steele was not squeamish. In his business he had seen much suffering, and he had often had to make decisions that led to people being neglected or killed. His priority was always the mission first, then keeping his people alive, and only if those two objectives were not in danger could he devote resources to other causes. He didn't want to deviate from the original plan—his team was counting on him and Jones to establish a safe zone and defend their sample acquisition efforts. Still, the real mission was to gather intelligence. What better way to discover what was happening in the building than to bring a person out of it?

All these thoughts flashed through his mind in a matter of seconds, and he quickly waved two fingers forward indicating to Jones that they would explore the sound's source. Jones quickly sprang into action, trotting ahead at a quick jog and using fewer active observation techniques. Steele hurried after him, hoping he'd made the right decision.

As they proceeded, the screams grew louder and began to be mixed with some metallic clicking and scraping noises. Steele wondered what was going on. None of his intelligence reports had even suggested humans were in the building. Unless they were being transported in via the spherical containers, he couldn't imagine how they had gotten here. Maybe the sounds were a trap, set up to attract and then kill humans who got through the hangar's skin? No, that would be paranoid even for a human foe, and the Narcoid seemed nothing if not cool and in control.

After a few minutes of rapid advance, Jones reached an open area and crouched down at the end of the shelving. As Steele reached him, Jones darted his head around the corner of the structure for a quick peek, then quickly retracted his head. Terror filled his eyes as they swiveled toward Steele.

Steele couldn't imagine what would scare the burly veteran. He gave Jones a look that asked for information, but Jones shook his head and signaled that there was an enemy close by preventing verbal communication. Jones instead switched positions with Steele to allow him to take a turn peering around the corner.

Steele stuck his head out and involuntarily gasped. Six humans were in the center of the clearing, somehow perched on Narcoid bodies. Some were screaming in agony while others just stared ahead with blank gazes. Streaks of blood and human body parts were strewn across the floor, mixed with what looked like ample amounts of fecal matter and urine. His eyes followed the streaking to glance at the far back right of the clearing. There a pile of human body parts caught his eye. It seemed that humans had been dismembered and cut into 20 cm cube sections, then stacked and were waiting to be stuffed into cylindrical containers like the ones on the shelving. The whole place stank of fear and feces, tinged with the metallic-raw taste of fresh blood. It was a human slaughterhouse.

Another cry of pain ripped through the air, jerking his attention back to the center of the clearing. There the real horror was taking place. Steele saw what may have once been a very attractive woman being pulled into a Narcoid body. Her torso was sticking out of a small Narcoid shell that had arms pulling her into itself. Though her arms were somehow secured behind her back, her whole torso writhed in pain and fought in a desperate attempt to break free. At first Steele thought the Narcoid must be trying to swallow the human whole, somewhat similar to a snake's eating its prey by dislocating its jaw and swallowing. Then the truth hit him. The human was not being eaten—she was being cocooned. The human body was being inserted into a Narcoid shell. The Narcoid shell's arms were holding the woman in place and stuffing her down into its torso, while slimy tubes snaked up and were injecting themselves into her body near the kidneys and belly button.

Steele was a hard man, but something in him snapped. He couldn't leave these people to this fate, even if it meant compromising the mission or even getting himself killed. That woman needed help, and he was the only one who could give it. Without stopping to signal Jones he just leapt up and ran toward the center of the room, shooting his Advanced Infantry Rifle at the base of the Narcoid bodies that were cocooning their human hosts. He skidded to a halt and his eyes went wide as he realized his mistake. There were Narcoid supervising the cocooning process, but they had been further to the left in the clearing and he had been too intent on saving the human victims to see them. His peripheral vision picked up at least two of the creatures, quickly closing in on him from his left back side. One of the Narcoid must have reacted very quickly to his assault, as it now loomed to his left within pincher range. In fact, it already had its claw raised to strike down at Steele's head. As he tried to duck and swing his AIR to aim at the new target, he realized he wouldn't make it in time, and that even if he did his AIR would not have the stopping power to interrupt a Narcoid death swing.

His life didn't flash before his eyes, but time did seem to stand still. The Narcoid's death swipe seemed to freeze, as Steele's body pumped him full of his final dose of adrenalin. Then the creature's head exploded, covering Steele in goo and casting globs of it throughout the clearing space.

Jones had launched a Small Arms Rocket and hit the creature right in what could be thought of as an eye socket. The small concussion knocked Steele off his feet and sent him to the floor sliding a few meters through the human offal and feces. Steele's face was covered in blackish slime from the Narcoid's death, some of which had hit him so hard that it drew blood. Wiping the goo and blood from his eyes, Steele noted that Jones was now fully engaged, pumping out two more SARs with deadly accuracy, destroying two more Narcoid in the clearing space.

There was no time to even thank Jones. Knowing Jones had his back, Steele switched his full attention once again to the cocooning humans, and grasped his AIR's trigger. Hollow point slugs spit out and riddled the Narcoid bases with dozens of holes. The bases must have had some sentience in them, as they tottered and then tipped over, a few of them spilling out some of the humans who were in the process of being cocooned. Steele grabbed the arms of the woman he had first seen, and not being able to think of a better plan, applied brute force to try to dislodge her from the Narcoid base.

She started to come out with a squishy sound, as small tubes from the Narcoid base slushed out of her body and began casting about all the while ejecting some kind of dull greenish slime. Some of the slime hit Steele but he ignored it as he concentrated on pulling. The woman's left foot seemed to be stuck in the Narcoid base. Steele realized he needed more leverage, so he put one foot on the Narcoid base and hugged the woman's torso before straining to pull her out. She was covered in Narcoid slime, so he had to tighten his grip, and she screamed in pain as he put all his strength into pulling her free.

More explosions added to the chaotic scene. Jones had arrived in the clearing and yelled something incomprehensible into Steele's ringing ears, then tossed his SAR launcher and reached out to take Steele's AIR. Steele interpreted that to mean Jones was out of rockets. He glanced over to see where the last explosions had erupted and noticed reinforcement Narcoid had begun to appear on the far back right of the clearing area near the pile of human meat. The alien defenders were being slowed down by burning shelves, but Steele knew if his team didn't leave soon they wouldn't be leaving at all.

With a final tug of desperation he jerked the woman free of the Narcoid base, and probably pulled her ankle out of its socket. A bone-wrenching *crunch* noise erupted as he fell backwards, slamming into the floor and sliding across it. This time the woman came with him, so he hit the floor hard, shooting pain through his left shoulder which took the brunt of the fall. Steele pushed the woman's body to the side and rolled over, in the process glancing down at her foot and seeing that instead of a left foot there was only a stump that was dripping Narcoid goo. The woman was unconscious and bleeding out of various holes that had been recently made to interface her with the Narcoid body.

Jones' rough hands pulled Steele to his feet and thrust the AIR back into his hands in one smooth motion. Before he could protest, Jones stooped down and grabbed the woman in a fireman's carry, coming up to hold one leg and one arm in front of his thick neck. Jones started running down the corridor from which they had first come with the woman riding sideways on his back. The two of them almost fell as they slid and lumbered desperately across the wet floor.

Steele looked up to assess the situation. The Narcoid were pushing past some of the damaged shelves Jones must have destroyed with his last rocket, and would be in the clearing area in seconds. Two human bodies still writhed in pain, sticking partly out from the tipped-over Narcoid bases. He took a few steps back toward the corridor, then made up his mind. He turned, took aim, and shot the remaining humans before sprinting after Jones.

It took a minute or two to catch up with the SSgt. and his passenger. Steele could never have run that fast with another person on his back. Instead of passing them by, he swiveled around to spray more rounds at the Narcoid, firing more by instinct than because he actually thought the bullets would prove effective. He could hear the tell-tale slapping sound further down the corridor and knew the Narcoid defenders were indeed following them.

The two men ran as fast as they could, ragged breath heaving as they exerted all their energy toward survival. After another minute or two they met up with four men from their platoon who were hurrying toward them. As per their training, two men had already left the hanger with all the samples. If they deemed it safe enough, they would already be establishing an escape route. If there were hostiles outside, their primary job was to survive and return to Eagle's Nest with the samples. One of the platoon members relieved Jones of his burden, also assuming a fireman's carry hold, and the six of them continued running toward the small hole they had burned through the hangar skin.

As they reached the entrance, Steele pivoted and saw the Narcoid far down the corridor in fast pursuit. He sprayed some bullets at them and was not surprised to see his direct hits were hardly slowing them down. The first soldier slipped through the hole, reached back, and dragged the woman through after him. With admirable haste the rest of them scurried through the hole. Steele was the last man through, leaping outside just as the first Narcoid slammed into the wall where he had been standing.

The good news was that the Narcoid were too big to fit through the hole. The bad news was that as he emerged from the hangar, Steele realized his men were already in a pitched battle with Narcoid reinforcements outside the dome. A torrent of the metal shards the Narcoid flung in place of bullets ripped into the ground just a few meters from Steele's feet and continued to shoot through one of his sergeants a few meters away.

"Don't fight—just run!" he yelled over the din, trying to mobilize his platoon who had taken defensive positions beside the hangar. Just then an explosive roar and flash of heat came from the direction of the hangar entrance where the Narcoid forces had been advancing on their position. Steele scooped up his wounded sergeant and saw a muzzle flash from another SAR launcher on the hill. Someone up there was providing them cover, and he didn't plan to waste it. He blessed good old Jo or whoever it was, and started following his men who had already begun running toward the relative safety of the small rolling hills.

Steele tried to account for his platoon. He knew two men had left early and were possibly with Jo covering their escape. Ahead of him he counted the remaining four men, and it looked like Jones had once again taken responsibility to carry the woman they had been trying to rescue. At least one man was still unaccounted for. He searched in vain as he scurried up the hill. He wanted to go back, but he knew that would be suicide. He hoped against all reason that the other team member was ahead and not left behind for the Narcoid to kill.

As they skittered over the crest and down the far side of the hill toward safety, Steele hoped he'd never have to go back to that place of death. If he did return, he vowed, he would not be there just to gather information, but to blow it off the face of the earth.

***

Acting United Earth President Stephen Stone looked up as James Steele entered his office deep inside the Rocky Mountains. Steele moved slowly, still in pain from his many minor wounds. He noticed his report from yesterday's infiltration lay on the President's desk.

"Have you had time to read that?" he asked with a wry smile that quickly faded as his cheek muscles pulled at the scabs on his face. He'd been lucky and expected just a few minor facial scars from the mission. While he might regret looking in a mirror, one of his men would never have the opportunity to look anywhere ever again.

"Yes. Well, I skimmed it. I don't have time to actually read anything. I'm surprised you had time to write it."

"Not much else to do in the hospital," Steele replied absently, still dwelling on his fallen platoon member. He kept wondering if he could have moved faster, given better orders, done *something* to prevent the loss.

Stone read his mind. "Honestly, with the kind of firepower you faced, you were lucky to have anyone escape that place. You did well."

"Thank you, sir," Steele said, still not consoled but forcing himself to the task at hand. "The good news is that we not only recovered some excellent Narcoid specimens that are being studied right now, but we also rescued a young lady. Her name is Susan Haarkonan. From her—"

"Haarkonan you say?" questioned Stone. "Any relation to the former Admiral Haarkonan?"

"I don't know. I can ask. She's too young to be his wife."

"Maybe a daughter or niece? I don't know, but look into it. Bill was a good friend."

"Yes, sir." Steele noticed the pain and distant look in his superior's eyes. He paused a second before continuing. "As I was saying, from her we learned that the Narcoid are indeed using humans both as a food source and as a basis for expanding their army."

"Expanding their army?" replied Stone, shocked enough to awaken from his distant thoughts. "You think people are joining them?"

"Not willingly, no sir. But it's my preliminary analysis that the Narcoid are growing their numbers by cocooning living beings. I think people are brought alive into those processing centers, and then the most physically fit are chosen to be cocooned and become part of the Narcoid military."

The President shook his head with incredulity. "That's grotesque. That also means I need to read your report more carefully. What else did I miss?"

"It's just conjecture right now, but having interviewed Susan extensively, I think we've something else to worry about. She said the Narcoid started out acting very dumb about humans, but that they then quickly became more sophisticated in their understanding about how humans are resisting their dominion. It seems that they're learning about humanity at an incredible rate."

"So they're quick learners?" asked the President, not quite seeing the point.

"Yes…at least that. Sir, there's no easy way to say this. I now believe that the assimilation process not only gives the Narcoid more troops, but it also gives them intelligence on their prey."

"You mean they not only get the body of the human that is assimilated, but they get the mind too?"

"Something like that. There's just too much evidence that they're somehow gaining a lot of specific information. It could be obtained through interrogation, or drugs, or by some other highly effective means, but from what we've been able to discover, no one has ever been interrogated by the Narcoid. You either get assimilated or eaten. That's why I think the assimilation process also involves acquiring intel."

Stone was quiet for a minute thinking about the implications. "If you're right, then we need some new rules of engagement. Specifically, we can't allow anyone with sensitive knowledge to be captured."

"That's what I decided too, sir. Anyone who's captured who knows about Eagle's Nest would potentially compromise our location. We have to keep secrets not just from the Narcoid directly, but also from humans who may be captured and assimilated. This war just became much more complicated."

"True. It's not just Eagle's Nest I'm worried about. We have to protect *Horizon* at all cost. We can't jeopardize what may be the last hope for humanity's survival. Please ensure that in your communication efforts the fewest possible number of people actually know about *Horizon*. Also, draft up a list of people who know about *Horizon* already and any other similarly critical information. I'll be issuing an order to everyone on the list that they aren't authorized to be captured alive. That means they'll have to carry a death pill 24/7. This is more important than our lives—we're talking the survival of our species."

CHAPTER 7

Discord on the *Horizon*

Haarkonan looked through the *Ark of Time's* manifest. Some of *Horizon's* best minds had been on board. No swear word was strong enough to contain his disgust, so he simply grunted as if taking a blow to the solar plexus. First their leading Electro Repulse Web scientist Dr. Cua died, then this catastrophe. He looked up and gave his chosen inspector a harsh glare before controlling himself enough to ask "So what do you think? Was it sabotage or an accident?"

Detective Staff Sergeant Eada McNealy cleared her throat and brushed her brown bangs with golden highlights to one side of her face. She had been sitting politely on the other side of Haarkonan's desk, waiting for his questions about her preliminary report. Her face was cute if not beautiful, with round cheeks and a ski-slope like small nose. Her five-foot tall petite athletic frame completed her cute exterior that belied her quick wits and the fact that she held black belts in two martial arts.

She was also an outstanding investigator, knowing how to bat her eyes and look innocent while asking the critical questions. Now it was Haarkonan asking the important question.

"Sir, there's simply not enough evidence to know. Whatever caused the explosion, it was hotter than anything I've ever seen, and it left nearly no evidence."

"I saw that in here," Haarkonan said tapping the tabcomp on his desk. "It must have been hot as a nuclear bomb, but without the radiation. What could cause that?"

"I think it was Dr. Cua's machine, sir. Remember he was working on a "cold nuke" that delivered precise effects with no radiation before his research on *Horizon*. Maybe his project incorporated similar technology to power his Electro Repulse Web. I've yet to see the details on that thing because it was compartmentally classified."

"I'll get you access to that," growled Haarkonan. "What about suspects? Who could possibly want this to happen?"

"That's just it, sir. I can't think of anyone on station with a motive to murder 600 people, unless they are somehow communicating with the Narcoid and being bribed. But there's no evidence of that. Why even bother sabotaging if they were in contact with the Narcoid? All they'd need to do is tell them where we are and we'd be finished."

"I know. It just doesn't make sense. How about we take another angle? Instead of looking for motive, let's start looking for ability. Who had access to the *Ark of Time* and has scientific knowledge enough to sabotage her…and is still alive on *Horizon*?"

"At the top of that list would certainly be Dr. Cua. Given his death, maybe it was someone working through Cua who then killed him to erase the trail."

"Good point. So make a list of the people who could have done this and look into Cua's life to see if someone may have been working through him. We've got to get to the bottom of this. Are there any angles I'm missing?"

"Sir, I think we should stick with motive a bit longer. As you saw on page three of my report, it's possible that some of the new recruits hold some kind of religious or philosophical value that would make them wish for humanity's destruction."

"Yes, I was glad to see you thinking out of the box there. I just don't think that happened, since we have historians look through every people group thoroughly before we snatch them. I'd think suicidal tendencies would be a disqualifying variable. Let's hold on to the ideological angle and stick with the capabilities line of investigation."

"Yes, sir."

"Good. Sergeant Eada, if this was not an accident, then we've not only got a murderer on this station, but a terrorist who is threatening the future of humanity. You'll get whatever you need to complete this investigation."

"Thank you sir. Will that be all?"

"Yes—dismissed."

Haarkonan couldn't help but watch the young lady with mild pleasure as she did an about face and exited the door. Excellent military bearing, and a sharp mind on that one. He also noticed that while she might be rather small, she had curves in all the right spots. He shook his head slightly bemused by such a thought. Here the future of the human race was in the balance and his male instincts refused to admit the gravity of the situation. He guessed that was also a good thing. If *Horizon* were successful, and the human race were to continue, they'd have to get all those instincts going full tilt to replenish the people already lost on Earth. From the reports that had started coming in from a transmission bouncing off the moon, he now had a much clearer picture of what was happening on Earth, and it wasn't good.

"Com, call the communications center," the admiral ordered his communicator. He heard the slight purring sound for just a second or two before the communications center accepted his call.

"LeMoray here, Admiral. What can I do for you?"

"I know we've a briefing tomorrow morning, but I wanted to know if you have gleaned anything else from that Earth transmission."

"Yes, sir. You're not the only one wanting frequent updates. We're learning a lot, and I think some of it will be useful for our counter-attack."

"Good—just give me the highlights now."

"As you know, yesterday we started receiving transmissions, and it's clear that Earth has some resistance forces that are quickly organizing and have begun infiltration and guerilla warfare missions. You'll remember that yesterday we learned about how United Earth's initial resistance included detonating three nuclear bombs on Narcoid strongholds. Now we know they ran out of nuclear weapons and that all of UE's sites with nuclear abilities, including storage areas and even dumps, have been entirely destroyed, spreading radiation. While radiation doesn't seem to have as devastating an effect on Narcoid as it does on humans, it's clear that they fear nuclear power. Since then, the Narcoid seem to be exploiting Earth's natural resources as well as using its human population as food and as host bodies to replenish their army."

"Using humans as food and what?" asked Haarkonan incredulously.

"As host bodies, sir. Earth intel believes the Narcoid abduct people, place them in spherical transportation containers, and eventually use their bodies as the core of a cocooning process that slowly builds armor around them. As humans are assimilated, the aliens gain not only our bodies but also learn from our thoughts."

"So we now have Narcoid with human cores?"

"Yes, sir. And it's not good for counterintelligence. The Narcoid seem to be learning about humans fast. We're learning about them too. For instance, given their vastly different sizes, it's possible that they are actually many different alien species also cocooned."

"There must be some original Narcoid species."

"Yes sir. Right now we think it might be the Motherships, but we really don't know."

Haarkonan smiled to himself, thinking that maybe he did *something* right when leading the space armada. At least the Narcoid would have two or three fewer Motherships. "Do you know anything else about this cocooning?"

"At least one report suggests that the cocooning process can be resisted by humans feeling intense pain and hatred, which irritates the Narcoid host shells and prevents successful cocooning. The downside is it seems to result in human death as well. Earth resistance is trying to gather resources and a plan, but right now they have little hope other than hiding and conducting small skirmishes. The Narcoid own the skies and strike targets with impunity once they are identified."

"Who's in charge of Earth's government? Yesterday you said you thought the communication feed is coming from Eagle's Nest…" Haarkonan couldn't hide the hope in his voice. Yesterday he'd asked the same question but without result. Eagle's Nest was where the Secretary of Defense should have gone in time of war, and the Secretary of Defense was his longtime friend and Academy roommate.

"That's right. We're now certain the signal originates at Eagle's Nest, then bounces off the moon, probably in an attempt to hide both the source's and our location. It sounds like former Secretary of Defense Stone is at Eagle's Nest and is now leading the resistance as acting President."

"Stone!" Haarkonan couldn't help exclaiming. "That's good news. Great news! A few nukes couldn't keep him down. At least the resistance is in good hands."

"If the quality of intel is any indication, I agree with you there. I'll forever be in the debt of whoever thought to keep us informed."

"Anything else?"

"There're many less important details. I guess one last interesting bit I plan to brief tomorrow is that the Narcoid appear to be building some sort of deep mining project at the Dead Sea. We don't know exactly what they're looking for. It may be minerals that are buried deep, or maybe they like the high saline content…it's just too   early   to   tell."

"Thanks L.T. Good work—I look forward to your full briefing in the morning."

"Yes, sir."

"Haarkonan out."

***

Staff Sergeant Eada McNealy was on to something. She had already interviewed various people trying to see if there were any detectable abnormalities with the *Ark of Time* before the explosion. Just about everything checked out except one passenger who was on the *Ark of Time* for its first flight test but got off it before it took off for its continued testing, even though he was scheduled to continue on board. That sounded suspicious, and she was going to get to the bottom of it. SSgt. Eada paused outside an office door, took a breath, then knocked and entered without waiting for a response.

"SSgt. Eada," Dr. Entwater acknowledged irritably, looking up from his desk as she entered the room. Eada took time to briefly look around the room before establishing eye contact with Entwater. The room was fairly small, with no pictures on the walls, and only a small metal book shelf and large metal desk for furnishings. Even the desk was void of personal memorabilia, and the only decoration breaking up the monotony of gray metal and dull white walls were stacks of paper festooned throughout the office.

Eada looked at Entwater before asking, "May I sit down?"

"As you wish," Entwater said, waving his hand dismissively to indicate she should sit in the chair opposite his desk.

"Thank you. As you know, I've been tasked with investigating the *Ark of Time*'s explosion, and I have a few questions for you…"

"This is a waste of time," interrupted Entwater forcefully. "It was an accident. Let it go at that." Entwater sighed, visibly struggling to reign in his irritation. "Look. I'm very busy right now, trying to construct a second cloning device using mostly parts on hand, and the *Ark of Time*'s explosion took with it some of my best engineers. I'm willing to give you a few minutes, but please just get to the point."

"Of course," Eada said, trying to keep her own irritation from being heard in her voice. "I understand you should have been on the *Ark of Time* when it exploded. In fact, you're the only person who was on the first flight who got off the ship while it changed over for its second experiment. Why did you get off?"

"Is it a crime to get off a ship when it lands at your home station?" sneered Entwater.

"No, of course not. I just wondered why you did it."

"I had a headache and was running on too little sleep," said Entwater. "I typically work days and that whole mess of a flight test happened on the night shift. I had to be on the maiden voyage because I was involved with some of the tech we were testing. After everything seemed to be working I turned the testing over to Dr. Lyman."

SSgt. Eada just looked at him patiently, making Dr. Entwater squirm.

"Honestly, that second flight was as much a joyride with the families as it was a serious test flight. I was tired, I don't like being around kids, and they didn't need me!"

"Did you notice anything unusual while on the first flight?"

"Yes, I was in a space ship. That's unusual. We ran tests on experimental equipment. By definition, that's unusual."

Eada chose to ignore his mockery. "I mean, did you notice anything that was dangerous, or anyone acting suspicious?"

"No, nothing. I caught Dr. Lyman smoking in the space ship, but he put it out when I confronted him. That's nothing new for him—he grows his own tobacco and probably just forgot the ship has stricter rules than we do here at *Horizon*. On the other hand, he probably knew exactly what he was doing and didn't care—that's just the way he is."

"Was," said Eada.

"Yes, was. But he'd never endanger the ship. I'm sorry, but I can't help you."

Eada made a few notes on her tabcomp before resuming her questioning. "Where were you when the *Ark of Time* exploded?"

"What kind of question is that!" Entwater exploded. "What do you think I was doing, trying to activate a remote bomb? I had a headache. I was sleeping. You can check my room logs if you don't believe me. I was in my room and didn't find out about the explosion until I was phoned by the Com section who were verifying I was still among the living. Not a pleasant way to get awakened, I might add."

Eada detected that Entwater was uncomfortable and hiding something, but she couldn't pin it down. Why would he need to be deceptive? Entwater seemed to be saying the right things, and she would indeed verify his story, but he was far too upset at everything. He also seemed to display almost no emotion for his deceased colleagues. Maybe anger was his way of dealing with loss?

Entwater interrupted her thinking. "Look, I'm very busy doing real work and not chasing after some conspiracy theory. If there're no more questions I'll ask you to leave me alone."

"OK, sir" Eada said putting on her professional exterior to hide her inner anger. "That will be all for now. I'd thank you for your cooperation, but that may seem like sarcasm. I'll be contacting you if I have any further need of your time for this investigation."

"By all means. Good day, SSgt. Eada," Entwater said, emphasizing the rank like it was an insult.

"Good day," Eada said, getting up and walking out of the office. She was a bit disappointed the interview hadn't yielded more information. Entwater had been belligerent, but if he were guilty he was wise enough not to drop clues she could readily chase down.

Checking the computer logs confirmed Entwater's story. He had debarked the *Ark of Time* and gone first to his lab, then a few minutes later to his quarters where he remained until after the Com desk had informed him of the explosion. Eada frowned at the computer screen. Something didn't seem right, but she couldn't quite pin it down.

Then it struck her. She cross checked her guess with the video time log of the *Ark of Time* explosion. Since going into restricted doors required computer verification of identity, she had exact times for when Entwater entered *Horizon* from the *Ark of Time*, when he went into his lab, when he exited it, and when he entered his own room. Entwater had left the *Ark of Time* at exactly 7:00 am *Horizon* Standard Time (HST). After spending just a few minutes in his lab, maybe dropping something off or checking on something, he left his lab at exactly 7:10 am. The guy was nothing if not meticulous. His walk took about two minutes to get to his own room. The *Ark of Time* then exploded at exactly 7:15 am. What were the chances that three time stamps would all be exactly on the minute? It was possible that it was all coincidence, but it was also possible that someone had tampered with the time logs. Whatever had happened, she was determined to get to the bottom of it.

***

"We must continue the back-up plan of colonization," insisted Haarkonan, getting uncharacteristically upset that such a point would even be debated. He took a big breath and tried to bridle his temper before continuing. It would not do anyone at the specially-called command briefing any good if he lost his temper. In fact, he needed the large gathering to leave feeling comfortable about how their command team operated and didn't want them thinking members were being bullied against their wills.

Haarkonan looked straight at Entwater and started again with a calmer voice. "I don't know if our temporal abduction and retaking Earth strategy is even viable—I'd say that it's actually the back-up plan and colonization should be thought of as the primary plan. If the human race is going to continue, it must get off this cold rock and find a planet worth settling."

Entwater wasn't trying to hide his anger. "And I say the colonization project simply squanders resources from our main plan to retake Earth! We don't know if there's a suitable planet out there. If we continue to pursue both goals simultaneously, especially after the *Ark of Time* explosion, we're guaranteed to fail at them both. We must concentrate our resources on one goal: retaking our ancestral planet and freeing Earth's people from the clutches of the Narcoid."

Before Haarkonan could respond, Plexar interrupted with his typical calm reserve. "We all agree we must fight the Narcoid, but many of us also believe that it would be imprudent to not have a back-up plan of colonization. I think we've spent enough time clarifying all sides of the issue, so I propose we put this to a vote. That's why we called this special meeting in the first place, and one reason we asked for representatives from each people-group on the station. This decision affects us all. Please use your tabcomps to vote now. I can assure you that you'll have complete anonymity—no one will know how you voted."

Two minutes later all the votes were in and tabulated by Plexar's tabcomp. He wrinkled his nose a little as he scrutinized the graphs and data scrolling across his tabcomp. "It looks like two thirds of us feel colonization must remain an objective," he announced. Haarkonan breathed a sigh of relief, even while he failed to suppress his surprise that colonization had not garnered even more votes.

Plexar continued in his patient voice, "We therefore will continue to hold the *Valkyrie* back as our last resort colonization ship. Our temporal insertion efforts will have to be scaled down since we lost *Ark of Time*, but I'm glad many of you could see past our shared desire to return to Earth and were willing to think about the need for a back-up plan.

"Now to the other business of temporal insertion planning. In the past we just used our command team—those gathered around this table—to make decisions, but I'm given to believe there have arisen some complaints." Plexar scanned the chairs filled with people lining all four walls. The command meeting room was filled beyond capacity for this meeting.

"We'd like to hear those complaints now and hopefully address them as best we can for future missions," he continued. "I therefore open the floor to discuss the process of deciding temporal insertion missions."

Haarkonan could barely keep quiet as leader after leader around the room shared how they thought the temporal insertion system was biased, how the future should have equal amounts of their various ethnic groups as Earth at present, or as in Earth's past, or even the idea that they should balance missions so as to populate *Horizon* with exactly equal proportions of ethnic groups. Such bickering on the whole seemed like nonsense to Haarkonan.

He marveled at the way Plexar seemed to listen intently and take notes. Had their roles been reversed, Haarkonan would have been hard-pressed not to simply laugh in the various leaders' faces. *We're trying to save the human race, and these people are trying to make temporal insertions into a political correctness exercise!* he thought with exasperation.

As far as he could tell, the only good point made was the concern about how far too many men were being taken as opposed to equal amounts of men and women. This was of course not the intent, but naturally arose from the fact that most temporal abduction missions targeted wars that only involved men. It was easy, however, for Haarkonan to see how a mostly male *Horizon* was undesirable. He remembered from history how China's "One Child" policy in the early 21st century had led to millions of abortions and eventually to a population predominantly of men. That in turn led to China's excessively aggressive stances in the mid-21st century despite their collectivistic culture of thoughtful restraint.

Cultural and religious issues were discussed next, though Haarkonan thought it sounded more like a verbal brawl than a discussion. Everyone wanted their religion or heritage to be accepted, and everyone blamed other religions or heritages for encroaching on their rights. Plexar again listened well and affirmed his intent to continue to reconcile the issues as long as people went about making complaints in a proper manner and did not take things into their own hands.

One small swarthy-looking representative Haarkonan didn't recognize broke into Plexar's calm tones by waving his hands and yelling, "Wait just one minute!" Plexar clearly didn't appreciate the interruption but stopped in mid-sentence anyway and nodded at the individual.

"You keep saying everyone is equal and all that, but we all know you and those from the future favor The Way as a religion. Most of us here who are complaining are doing so because we feel your majority religion is encroaching on our beliefs. You need to set a policy of toleration and reign in The Way's influence."

Plexar looked at the man with understanding and hesitated a minute before answering him. "I know you're Muslim, and what you're referring to is our habit of treating Sunday special with fewer duties rather than Friday, and how we do not officially celebrate Ramadan and other holidays but do celebrate The Way's holy days. I know this must be frustrating to you because on Earth your official religion was enforced by law, and now it seems we only tolerate your religion.

"While I understand your plight, let me be clear in this: The Way is the only religion that led to true democracy, individual rights, and the ability to have a pluralistic society without disintegration. In Earth's past, most other religions and even atheistic communism tried the extermination route, simply killing those who didn't conform to their views. Back then, even though The Way was fractured into Protestants, Catholics, and Orthodox believers, it still formed the foundation for a stable diverse society because it required believers to respect all others as God's creations and as equals. The Way recognizes that we cannot make a person become a certain religion but instead insists that faith is a personal choice. True followers of The Way never coerce but instead seek to win over hearts and minds by reason and acts of service.

"You must understand this. *Horizon* is not tolerant of other religions in spite of following The Way; we are tolerant *because* we follow The Way. We honestly think our religion will prevail in the marketplace of ideas, so we're not intimidated by allowing other views and beliefs to be held and proclaimed. Just before the Great Nuclear War on Earth the United States had begun to erase its religious heritage, accepting tolerance and hedonism as their new gods. They did away with their religious cultural glue in order to create a more pluralistic society, but it quickly resulted in disintegration. The forces of community tying their society together couldn't cope with the forces of individualism pulling it apart, and the belief in every god led to no sincere belief in any god, which in turn led to people using their liberty as a license to do wrong."

Plexar scanned the whole room as he continued, looking deep into everyone's eyes. "On *Horizon*, we will not simply tolerate your religious and cultural heritages, we will respect them. We will even work around every specific area you feel is being encroached and attempt solutions. But what we will not do, what we cannot do, is compromise our own heritage in the process, for I see our culture as the Petri dish that allows all the other cultures on *Horizon* to thrive. I hope you can live in harmony here with that understanding."

After a few more minor discussions people realized the main issues had been clarified, and so the meeting was adjourned.

Delegates exited the room still in a mild uproar, but Plexar affably stood by the door shaking their hands and exchanging final pleasantries or ripostes. Dr. Entwater simply stormed out of the room on his own, skipping Plexar's handshake. He obviously was still upset he didn't get his way in cancelling all further colonization efforts.

When everyone else had left, Haarkonan approached Plexar and patted him on the back. "Well done there, Ian. You ran that one like a pro. I don't know what you're going to do about all those complaints, though."

"I just did what can be done about them. I listened to them. Most of our leaders know the problems are unsolvable—they just had an obligation to represent their people and they wanted to make sure I understand their plight. I do. I really do get the fact that we are too multifarious for harmonious occupation of this small living space. I also understand we cannot stop being who we are."

"You did great," said Haarkonan.

"Thanks. I must say, though, that I'll be glad when Winston gets out of orientation and can start taking over some of the administrative duties. He'd probably have handled that meeting better. I'm chuffed just to have survived it without inciting a riot."

The two men chuckled as they exited the room and walked a little way in silence. It was a comfortable silence, born from mutual understanding and respect. Haarkonan knew the difficulty of managing so many people and was willing to offer a listening ear should Plexar need to vent his frustrations.

When Plexar did not say anything, Haarkonan decided to prompt him. "Rowdy bunch, aren't they?"

"Yes, but I don't blame them for being upset. I can't imagine being ripped out of my reality, pulled into a completely foreign context, and tasked with saving the human race."

"If we're all like that lot, it rather begs the question of whether humanity's worth saving."

Plexar stopped abruptly, forcing Haarkonan to do likewise. Haarkonan felt a little uneasy as Plexar scowled at him, and then softened before replying.

"We can't think that way. All life, and especially human life, is precious to the Creator. I don't know why He's allowing the Narcoid to ravage Earth, but I do know humanity is worth saving."

"What gives us any more right to live than the Narcoid have?" Haarkonan asked. "If you value all life, why should it be right to kill one kind of life to save another?"

"I don't know, exactly. I think the answer must lie in why we have value. What do you think—where does your value come from?"

"I guess it comes from the United Earth Constitution. It says I have rights, so I guess I also have value," Haarkonan replied, a bit uncomfortable that the conversation had taken a philosophical bend rather than being the venting session he'd expected.

"Even the UE Constitution, patterned off the old United States Constitution, declares that we have been endowed with rights *by the Creator*. It's from the Creator that we gain our value. If I build two robots, I can decide their relative values. I can destroy the one and love the other, because I created them. So it's our Creator who gives us value, and we become more valuable when we strive to please Him and behave as He'd have us behave. I believe He created all life and made us in His image. That's why humanity has value."

"So who made the Narcoid? In what image are they created?" Haarkonan asked, genuinely interested now.

"I would guess God made them too, just like He made men who can choose to be either good or evil. I don't know how God values them relative to us, but I do know He really loves us. In fact, I believe He loves us so much that He became incarnated to show us how to live and to initiate a better relationship with Himself. He died to save us. Maybe this is our chance to die to save the Narcoid. In any case, because the Creator values human life, I value it too, and I feel we have the right, maybe even the obligation, to defend ourselves from extinction."

"You sound like you want to save the Narcoid too."

"I do. We're to love our enemies. If we can find a way to save ourselves without killing the Narcoid, that'd be best. That's why I'm pouring all my research time into trying to develop a way to skip through present 3D space. It's so frustrating that we can transit through the fourth dimension but we're stuck using slow fire-based methods to travel in our own time."

"So you'd just run away?"

"We have enough people now, and we certainly have enough variation in the gene pool, so we could do it." Plexar looked briefly contemplative and then continued in a rush.

"No, you're right, we can't just leave now. We've an obligation to rescue the people of Earth, and maybe Earth itself. But if that were not the case then yes, I'd try to put as much space and time between us and the Narcoid as possible, and we could start over."

"So you were as worried as I was about that vote on colonization."

"Absolutely. I'm relieved that the back-up colonization plan passed—it's essential, though without faster propulsion it's probably futile. Space is too vast, and I can't tell you how frustrated I am that I can't figure out how to modify temporal technology to unlock space-time-skipping. If I just had a dedicated team and five more years, there's a real possibility we could get it. But we don't have five years, and the human race must fight if we are to enjoy any more years."

The men continued down the corridor again in comfortable silence. Haarkonan marveled at a faith that could love the enemy even while striving to kill it. He had no such faith. The Narcoid had killed his wife. He hated them and believed the only good alien was a dead alien.

The two men paused near the StarShot pub.

"There's something else I want to confide in you, just to get it off my chest," said Plexar in a softer voice. "I haven't told anyone this before, and I trust you will keep it in confidence. I'm worried about overuse of the temporal transition machine. I don't see any evidence that it's having deleterious effects on the space-time continuum, but I simply can't be positive. There's a chance that every temporal interference, even despite our precautions, is in effect bunching up space-time and contracting the Universe's duration. I can't help but think how selfish that is, if we are doing it."

Haarkonan just nodded his head to acknowledge that he had heard the good doctor's concern. He didn't fully understand and was not sure how to reply.

Eventually he decided to offer what comfort he could. "I'm sure you'll let us know if you find any evidence that we're doing something like that. For now, we need time travel. Need it. Must have it if humanity is to continue. Like you said, let's keep this concern private for now."

"Of course," said Plexar, looking a bit relieved to have finally told someone about his fears.

Haarkonan wanted to further unburden the scientist. "Tell you what; I'll guarantee that should you discover that we're doing something terrible, I'll back you up on whatever decision you make to stop the atrocity. But for now, we go on doing what must be done."

"Yes, of course. Thank you, Admiral. Seeing as how we're here, would you like to stop in for a drink?"

"Sorry Ian, maybe another time. I have a lot of work to catch up on."

The two then said their brief farewells and parted ways. Haarkonan strode down the white hallway toward his office, his mind already wandering ahead and not looking forward to the stacks of paperwork that were piling up on his desk. As he approached he saw SSgt. Eada reading her tabcomp outside his door. She looked rather upset, and didn't have the same jaunty energy she usually possessed. SSgt. Eada looked up as he approached, so he gestured for her to precede him into his office.

"Take a seat," he said, waving her to a chair. He walked around his carbon-gray metal desk and sunk into his own chair with a sigh. The day had already been long, and from the signals Eada was sending, what she had to say would only make the day longer.

"What've you found?" he asked without sounding too expectant.

"Sir, I have some troubling information, first about Dr. Entwater and then about Dr. Plexar."

"Plexar?" Haarkonan couldn't help blurting. He caught himself and reminded himself that this wasn't about defending a friend, but about following the evidence wherever it led. "Tell me about Entwater first," he said, keeping his face impassive in an attempt to not show how much he'd like to arrest the pestilent doctor.

"Sir, I have reason to believe Dr. Entwater knew about the *Ark of Time* explosion in advance and that he timed his return to his room to provide himself with an alibi." She then went on to explain the time stamp evidence.

Haarkonan listened intently before responding. "You may have reason, but you have no proof," said Haarkonan with disappointment. "No judge is going to rule he is guilty based off a meticulous personality and what may be coincidental round-number time stamps."

"Yes sir, I know, and I'll keep digging into it. I just feel it's too much of a coincidence to ignore."

"Sure, keep looking into it. Now, what have you discovered about Plexar that may be related to the *Ark of Time?*"

"I'm not sure it's related sir, but a few hours ago I went out to the landing pad where *Ark of Time* exploded, wearing a pressure suit, of course. I didn't think I'd find anything, but I didn't have any leads. We investigators are taught that if we have no leads we should return to the scene of the crime, and I realized I hadn't even inspected the scene of the crime. Anyway, while I was out on the spacewalk I noticed a satellite of sorts, and I was curious if maybe it was a communications satellite and had some footage of the *Ark of Time* from another angle."

"Fascinating," Haarkonan said, truly intrigued. "I didn't even know we had a satellite in *Horizon* orbit. I wonder if that is a security concern too—it may make us more visible to the Narcoid."

"My thoughts exactly," said Eada. "That's why I looked into it…and got nothing. No one knew about it, and no database I found had information on it. In fact, our own observation software has protocol written into it to ensure the satellite is never reported. The only reason I spotted it was because I was looking around carefully in person and not using augmenting technology."

"That just can't be right," said Haarkonan puzzled. "Who has access to rewrite observation software—and who would want to do that? Whoever put it there, it must have been done after my crew and I landed on *Horizon*, or else we would have seen it back then. You can't just launch a satellite and then hide all evidence of the launch."

"I was worried about that too, so I spent some time commandeering telescopes from our observation center. Here are the pictures I took." Eada passed Haarkonan her tabcomp. He promptly punched through the photos, staring in astonishment.

"That's a killer satellite!" he declared, looking carefully at the small defensive lasers and single, large offensive laser. "That thing's pointing straight down the access tube from the landing pad! If it were fired it would probably fry all the labs and research areas, and very likely destroy this whole station!"

"Yes sir, that was also my assessment. It obviously is not Narcoid but of our own manufacture. Understanding the gravity of the situation, and since you were in a protracted meeting, I used the access codes you secured for me and did a trace of all personal records, to include diary entries and personal communications. I know that would normally be a breach of privacy, but it seemed to me that a search was justified since we're talking about the very existence of *Horizon*. I also didn't think that reading what people say about satellites would constitute undue privacy interference."

"What'd you find?" Haarkonan asked, feeling a small tingle of apprehension at the back of his neck knowing a killer satellite was poised to strike his location at any moment.

"Sir, the only person who seems to know about the satellite is Dr. Plexar. He makes no notes about it in his professional log, but he made a private entry saying he had launched the 'doomsday satellite.' I can only assume he means the one pointing at us from point blank range. I then came straight here to tell you and see what to do next. If he is our saboteur, I don't know how to confront him. It seems to me that we can't let him know we're onto him. We don't know how he intends to fire that laser, so if we don't catch him unawares we could tip him off, and he'll fire it before we get a chance to arrest him."

"Arrest Plexar?" Haarkonan said aloud. He couldn't think of a more dangerous thing to do. Plexar was a friend and was the primary leader of *Horizon*. Without him at the helm everything would unravel. People would talk of a military coup, and the general dissention would decay into anarchy. Everything would be lost as surely as if *Horizon* had exploded. How could Plexar be planning to destroy *Horizon*? There had to be some kind of mistake.

"Are you sure that satellite isn't defensive?" he asked, already knowing the answer as he stared again at the photos in front of him.

"Yes, sir. As you can see, it's definitely pointed at us, and it's in geosynchronous orbit with no thrusters that I can see. Why you would send a satellite like that up there with heavy shielding but no thrusters is beyond me, but it ensures not only that it is pointed at us, but that it can't be pointed in any other direction. That doomsday satellite is meant to destroy *Horizon* in one great burst of energy. And Dr. Plexar put it there."

CHAPTER 8

Death Dare

Valerius' body shuttered as he died. It was as if his spirit were fighting to remain in control of his body, while being irrevocably called away from it. At last his spirit pulled away, somewhat boosted by its repulsion from the pain his body was experiencing. As his spirit came lose, he drifted up toward a gentle warmth. He had shrugged off his mortal coil and was now floating above himself. How strange to be looking at yourself without the aid of a mirror. As he considered his body below he experienced two diametrically opposed thoughts simultaneously.

He felt gratitude as he looked at his body lying motionless in the machine below. That mass of blood, flesh, and bones had served him well, and he had done his best to take care of it. He also despised his body. It was so limited, only able to access five senses, and those imperfectly. He wondered why he hadn't overcome his body earlier.

That line of thought led him to realize he was experiencing death. It was so peaceful it felt more like a sublime sleep with full awareness. He looked around and discovered that while the room around him was still there, it looked more like a shadow than tangible reality. All the physical objects were present, but they had become background, unimportant compared to the things of the spirit. The spiritual things seemed much more real, though visibly they were more like lights and glows and pathways rather than objects. He was stunned by the vibrant colors that didn't exist when he was in the body. He felt a strong desire to explore, to see what was in the tunnels, and to get far away from here. He was somehow certain the farther he went from his physical body the better he would be able to experience this new life. He started to float toward what seemed to be a light tunnel and was intrigued to see the outline of someone just inside it.

Suddenly he was grabbed from behind as if by the arms of a powerful warrior. He struggled against the pull, but it had him firmly in its grasp. He was being tugged inexorably back down toward his body. Every particle of his spirit screamed negation and wrestled trying to break free. Then his spirit started to reintegrate with his body. The shock was like jumping into an arctic lake. It was like being instantly frozen, where the cold is so cold that it burned. His body felt thick and slow and stupid. He was blind, and he felt nauseating claustrophobia as he finished reintegrating back into his flesh and bones.

Then he opened his eyes. Disorientation and nausea remained. A soft whirring noise made by small motors opened the console and he looked up to see Otho still standing by the DeathDare machine with a look of sheer condemnation on his face.

"Are you a goddess?" Valerius croaked out with a sly grin.

"Yeah, and you're a carrot," Otho said in his characteristically disgusted tone. "What you really are is an idiot. How can you play games with death? We can't afford to lose you like this."

"I'm the idiot?" Valerius retorted with mock surprise. "Which one of us was caught dipping his drinking cup in a toilet?"

"It was perfectly good water! Sure looked like a mini well to me! And drinking a little potty water isn't endangering my life."

"The DeathDare machine is very safe," interjected a female voice to Otho's left. Valerius blinked and looked that way to see Rachel standing there with an unabashed smile. Now that's closer to a goddess, Valerius mused to himself. His strength was quickly returning, and he decided to stagger up to his feet.

"Easy now," Rachel said, offering him a hand and then letting him wrap an arm around her shoulder when his legs went wobbly. "You just died remember? It takes a few minutes to fully recuperate."

"I can't believe it! I was dead. This is no joke, right? It's not like the moving picture machines just telling a false story? I really died in there, right?"

"You sure did!" bellowed Otho, tremors of fear evident under his tone of wrath. "I saw you shake and then stop breathing. I almost ripped the machine apart, but I was afraid that might be even worse for you."

"You're right there," said Rachel with a smile. She glanced over at the machine's settings. "You were dead for about 20 seconds and revived with no difficulties. The machine can sustain your death for up to two minutes, so you really just experienced a very mild death sensation. Oh and look there," she said pointing at a purple light on the side of the control panel. "That means you may have the psycho-determination to control temporal insertions. You'll probably get a notice to test for that. It's a rare gift."

Valerius wasn't interested in gifts, as he was still in mild shock from the DeathDare experience. "It was so real. Light and colors there were so much more vivid, and I felt…alive! I was somehow more myself, unencumbered by this body. It was amazing!"

Otho just scowled. He was clearly interested in what happened after death, but he also still distrusted the DeathDare machine.

"Did you see anyone there?" asked Rachel while steadying Valerius on his own two feet.

He steadied himself and reluctantly removed his arm from her shoulder. That contact had been pleasant while it lasted. "You know, I think I started to see someone just before I got pulled back."

"Yah. It really is hit or miss on seeing much using the 20 second setting. You should try a bit longer sometime."

"Try longer!" exclaimed Otho. "Doesn't the risk of permanent death increase?"

"Sure it does, but this machine is safe for up to two minutes. Over one minute and the DeathDare machine takes over brain functions for your body while you're gone. Much over two minutes, however, and your spirit can't find its way back to your body. The chance of something like that happening on this machine is less than one in a million billion, and even then it may have simply been your time to die rather than the machine's fault."

"I felt like I was there forever, and yet when it ended I thought it had gone by far too quickly."

"Yes, that's how many people feel about it," said Rachel. "Without the body's natural rhythms of pulse and breath the brain seems to measure time very differently. What did the person you saw look like?"

"I have no idea. It was more an outline or a shadow really. Whoever it was they seemed to be concerned for me, almost watching over me."

"That was probably what we call your 'guardian angel.' Almost all of us see a similar form and somehow feel as you do that the person has our best interests in mind."

"You believe in angels?" Valerius asked with incredulity. "What pantheon of gods do you believe in?" While he was always critical of the idea of gods, his recent experiment with death was already making him question former beliefs.

"I don't worship a pantheon," said Rachel. "I used to just call myself a Christian, but I guess they call it 'The Way' now. I'm still getting used to that, but in general we believe there's only one God who manifests Himself in three persons."

"How does one god have three personalities?" asked Valerius.

"It's not personalities, but persons. He's both one and three at the same time. You remember how we were learning that space and time are both dimensions? And that String Theory posits that we have ten dimensions plus time?"

Valerius nodded, a little confused about how talking about god had put him back in physics class.

"Well, for you and me 'sameness' means sharing dimensions. If we stood in the same place and shared length, width, height, and time we'd be one being. However, if we just shared length, width and height and not time, we'd be completely separate. With 10 dimensions, God could share five dimensions with Himself, making Him more one than we can even fathom, and still be separate in five dimensions, making him more three individual beings than we can imagine."

"Sounds like a religion only the moderns could have invented," Valerius scoffed.

"Actually, the concept of the Trinity was there from the beginning of Christianity and far before anyone thought up String Theory."

"OK, but I don't think it should take a physics lesson to understand god. And I can't believe Christianity became a major religion! It was just a minor cult in my time, hardly worth noticing! Its adherents were devoted, but so were the Jews. You're saying this belief in a Jewish carpenter outlasted the noble worship of Zeus or Mithras? What about Zoroastrianism? I can't believe it."

"Yep," replied Rachel with a big smile. "Let's go to one of the booths and get some drinks and I'd be glad to catch you up on religious history."

"No thanks," Otho grunted. He had been standing protectively close to Valerius, making certain his commander was okay. "I'm going to go get some workout time in. You two enjoy."

Rachel led Valerius over to a booth and slid in beside him. She ended up close enough for their arms to slightly touch. Did she intend that?

After ordering drinks, Rachel returned to their discussion about religion. "I can see how you'd find it unbelievable that Christianity became a world religion. It's one of the most unlikely events in history. A man with little religious training, who was persecuted by his own religious sect, and never wrote down a word that we know about, somehow founded our current majority religion. What's even more remarkable is that Jesus was killed at the age of 33. Some say the rise of Christianity is a miracle and is itself proof that it's the one true religion."

"One true religion?" asked Valerius. "Aren't there other religions still?"

"Of course there are still other religions, but even in my day in the 21st century the major religions were all Jesus-centric or at least Judaic-centric. Christianity had split into various groups called Catholics, Protestants and Orthodox, and Islam also had two sects called Sunni and Shiite. Judaism had become more of a tradition than a religion, but that was inevitable since your people destroyed their temple and with it their ability to be forgiven of sins. Once they gave up the sacrificial system all they had left was the law, so they made that the cornerstone of their beliefs. Laws just don't work very well as a religion."

"But what about the pantheon of gods, or the Eastern mysticisms?"

"The pantheon of gods was already being disbelieved in your time, I think. And the Eastern religions were more philosophies than actual religions. The Bible-centric beliefs were the only ones that claimed to have actual validity, historic accuracy, and dealt with the big questions of religion such as where we come from and what we should do in life."

Valerius had been so intrigued by the conversation he hadn't noticed Dr. Plexar had entered the room and drifted over to their table. "I hope I'm not intruding," he said with a mischievous glint in his eye. "You two looked pretty engrossed in something."

"Not at all," replied Rachel. "Please join us. We were just discussing religion and could use your insights on the subject."

No matter how much he liked Plexar, Valerius couldn't help feeling a little regret at losing Rachel's full attention. That thought quickly vanished when Rachel scooted further into the booth to allow room for Plexar. Valerius rather enjoyed the coziness. Their drinks arrived just then, and Plexar order his Dr. Pepper with a twist of pomegranate before Rachel resumed the conversation.

"From what I've learned on *Horizon*, it seems many vestiges of other religions persisted until the 22nd century. I know there was a slow evolution from the pluralists who think all religions worship the same god to the true monotheists who said only their God was the right one. Really, in the monotheist camp only the aggressively evangelistic beliefs of The Way and Islam had staying power. When time travel was invented, followers of The Way lobbied to make a trip back to see if there really was an historic Jesus. Whereas most religions didn't want their religion declared true or false, followers of The Way insisted theirs was a logical and even provable religion. The Pope, the acknowledged leader of The Way after unification, even decreed that if the resurrection didn't really happen, he'd renounce the faith and call it all a hoax. That was too big of a challenge for scientists, many of whom wished to terminate all religions."

Valerius was even further confused. "Why would anyone want no religion? That's like condemning hope and tearing away any reason to be moral when others aren't looking. We Romans put people to death for such an affront to common sense."

"Yes, I know. In fact, you put Christians to death for the crime of "atheism," claiming Christians were "godless" since they believed in only one God Who couldn't be seen nor represented with images and statues."

"So did this resurrection of Jesus occur? Surely either He came back to life or He didn't, and that would solve the matter."

Dr. Plexar cleared his throat and Rachel nodded at him to let him into the conversation.

"As you know, time travel on Earth was banned soon after it was proven possible. That's why we built all this," he gestured around to indicate *Horizon* as a whole.

"Do you follow The Way too?" Valerius asked bluntly. He then realized how the question sounded and added, "If it's alright for me to ask?"

"Of course you may ask. I think The Way is the closest religion we have to the truth, and I'm a worshipper of the truth."

"If you think that, then surely you must have sent a time ship back to see if Jesus existed."

"You're right there. We did indeed authorize that mission, and I went on it myself."

"Then you must have found proof that Jesus existed and ended the religious debate for all time."

"Not quite. No one ever doubted whether or not Jesus existed. What people doubted was his identity and by extension the miracles that He is said to have performed. But you must know this: people have to have faith to believe anything. We believe the moon is not made of cheese because we have faith in books and astronauts who have been there. Even the staunchest atheist basically says, 'Give me the one miracle of the Big Bang when everything was created from nothing, and I'll explain the rest.' We seem to accept the need for faith in every realm except religion. In this case, when we could show that Jesus existed and performed miracles, many people simply invented a higher standard of belief."

"So you did prove Jesus is God?" Rachel asked transfixed.

"Jesus' identity is still up for debate. His resurrection is still believed by the faithful and disbelieved by his critics. When the *timearcs*, that is, time archeologists, traveled back, they found that a man named Jesus existed and that the Bible gives an accurate record of the last three years of his life. They even visually recorded Jesus' death and the scene at his tomb during the resurrection. They were absolutely incredulous when they saw Jesus living again, and ministering for 40 days past his death. I can certainly see why His disciples were so convinced that he was divine."

"So that settles it. God actually visited mankind in human form, and we Romans put him to death. Unbelievable," said Valerius. "That must be why God turned on us and destroyed our empire."

"Unbelievable is exactly what people who reject The Way say. Many of them began suggesting that Jesus was actually a man from the distant future, who went back in time to create a religion so as to make the world a better place. Some think he had a twin, and it was he who reappeared after the crucifixion. Others think the future may have ways to revive the dead, or clone the dead and include a soul. Basically, those who do not want to believe can still come up with all kinds of reasons for their disbelief. Even with the evidence of history, only those who choose to believe must believe."

"But surely you could go back in time and install equipment to detect what happened in the tomb, or interrogate Jesus to discover the truth."

"We can't interfere with time without unleashing unknown consequences. Messing with Jesus would be a highly risky endeavor, as he was a key figure whose life has ramifications all the way to today. Any minor disruption in his thinking or being could prove catastrophic and so will never be authorized. In a way, the equilibrium has been reestablished: faith is a choice, just as it always has been. Faith doesn't come from seeing, but stems from hearing the words of God, whether spoken by the Holy Spirit to the heart of man or through the Bible."

"If what you say is true, then I'm not sophisticated enough to argue against the evidence of Jesus' acts. To me, things either are as my eyes see them or else they are deception. Still, I have *seen* things in the last few months that I would never have dreamed possible: miracles of flight and time travel and even heating food by pressing buttons. The more I know the more I realize there is a huge amount I don't know."

"But you just experienced death," interjected Rachel. "You just saw there is an afterlife and an angel waiting for your soul."

"I don't know what I saw. It could be as you say, but if I have a choice, then for now I choose not to believe in this Jesus-God. He was just a Jew. Jews were just some small religious sect in a backwater of our empire. If there is a god, he should just appear. Like I've always said, if Zeus appears and gives me a command, I'll obey. If a god can't appear to me then I don't want to serve that god. Begging your pardon, and no hard feelings meant, of course."

"Of course. It's your choice," said Plexar with an agreeable smile. "One of the greatest truths we believe here at *Horizon* is that we each must choose our religion. I just had a similar conversation with various leaders on this installation. No one can force you to believe anything, and on my station no one had better try. Since it entails your eternal destiny, it should be your individual choice. Just realize that what you're saying is that god must meet you on your terms, rather than being the maker of the terms Himself."

"That's true," said Valerius with even more respect for the lead scientist for not being offended or too forceful with his religion. "I'm not saying I won't believe someday, just that it's all too much for now. But if this Jesus-God is true, I also wish to make peace with Him and respect Him. Is there some offering I can give that will placate Him from anger at my unbelief?"

"No," Plexar shook his head slowly. "He accepts your words, but the only sacrifice that He deems acceptable is your total surrender. The Way claims that God is the 'one and only true God' and so requires His supplicants to either give all or not be a follower at all. It's a total commitment or no commitment, a complete faith or an absence of faith."

"But there are plenty who say they believe in Jesus yet who do not follow His teachings," said Rachel. "Are they not partial believers?"

"The book of James says faith without works is dead. It never says faith is simply sick. People may claim faith, but if their actions speak otherwise they will be among the many who on the final day will wake up to the harsh reality that they loved their own conceptions of God rather than the character of the true God. In the end, a 'partial faith' as you call it is not faith."

"This is too hard for me," said Valerius. "I have much to contemplate. I'd always thought Christianity was for weaklings and the poor. I want a God of strength and perfection."

"But The Way is exactly that," said Plexar with an amused smile. "It's your misconception of perfection that's blinding you. God is perfectly sovereign—so much so that He can give up some of His sovereignty to allow free will. God's so powerful that He can forgive—and one who can forgive is truly frightful. The one who only has vengeance is weaker than the one who can forgive. Peace is more powerful than war, love trumps hate, and light must first be defined to even consider what darkness is."

"Now you sound much more like a priest than a natural philosopher," said Valerius with a smile.

Plexar laughed. "Why not? Religion and science are very much alike."

"How do you figure?" asked Rachel. "In my time we saw them as competing truths."

"The prime question of physics is very similar to the important question of determinism in religion. Both the discipline of physics and the field of religion attempt to understand causality. In physics we're trying to determine what force and matter do when they interact. Religion often attempts to understand how to interact with God and how He interacts with the Universe. Both are asking the big 'why' questions, but whereas science is inductive, religion is deductive."

"I never thought of it that way," Rachel shrugged.

"Even here in my own time most people missed the obvious fact that science involves understanding the laws of God. Perhaps the greatest scientist ever was a man named Einstein who lived not long before Rachel's time. Though he once spoke of trying to know the mind of God, he believed everything was predetermined. His famous quote is that 'God does not play dice with the Universe.' While he was right about many things, including the concept of a universal constant which he called his greatest mistake but that later proved to actually have some truth behind it, he was wrong about causality. There is room for free will in the Universe—indeed, it looks like the Universe was created intentionally to allow free will."

"What do you mean?" asked Valerius. Rachel also looked interested as she sipped from her exotic-looking red beverage with green swirls. Plexar took a drink of his Dr. Pepper brew before continuing. Valerius briefly wondered why a drink was named after an advanced degree, or if only doctors could drink the stuff. And who would want to drink a liquid pepper?

Having placated his thirst, Plexar leaned back and continued his musings. "Science has advanced so far that it's merging with religion, and much of the intersection involves the notion of free will. Somehow the human will helps create its own reality, and the physics of the Universe is designed to offer true free will."

"There you go again," said Valerius with some exasperation. "Confusing us ancients. Exactly how does religion and science intersect at the issue of free will?"

Plexar collected his thoughts before beginning again. "Either all things are predetermined, or we actually have free will to create our own futures. I think science has conclusively sided with free will. After all, what we now know is that there is no way to determine the future given the past. Quantum theory suggests that multiple possibilities exist simultaneously, and observation makes one more permanent than another. "

"Is that something like how we understand electrons revolving around an atom?" Rachel asked. "They somehow exist in multiple shells at once until we pin them down and make them chose a location?"

"Yes," said Plexar with a smile, as if pleased with a star student.

Valerius was not a star here. "I'm sorry, but you both just lost me again. I never understood those concepts very well. Can you make it a bit simpler?"

"Sure…how about this," replied Plexar. "A scientist named Heisenberg proved that we cannot know both the position and direction of particles smaller than a certain mass. Our very observation would move the particles, since our least intrusive method of observation still requires us to use light to bounce off an object. When we strike these particles with light, we change them, and hence our observation changes the particles' orientations. From this we realize that we can never know everything, but instead we can only create probabilities for where particles are and what they are doing. In short, we have proven that we cannot determine the future based on the present, because the present is not fully observable. If the future cannot be known from the present or past, it cannot be solely determined from the past. This means determinism fails—the Universe is created to allow free will."

"I think I'll just accept your word on that," Valerius said. He glanced over at Rachel and saw that she was deep in thought. Maybe all this made sense to a modern mind.

Valerius was shaken from his brief reverie by Haarkonan's firm voice behind him. "Dr. Plexar, will you please come with me?" Valerius craned around to see Haarkonan towering over the seated group. He knew the question was actually a command. He looked

125

past Haarkonan and saw two security officers by the room's doorway, trying unsuccessfully to look casual.

Valerius looked over at Plexar. He looked pale and visibly shaken. Plexar stood up hesitantly. "Sure, admiral, if you need me for something all you need to do is ask."

Valerius knew of the coups in ancient Rome, and this certainly looked like a coup. Still, Haarkonan was known to be best friends with Plexar, and didn't seem like the kind of man who needed more power or authority. Indeed, if he had to guess, Haarkonan would have been happier retiring than being second in command of *Horizon*. This was all out of character, but he wasn't about to let a military coup cut down Plexar. Valerius stood up and stepped away from Haarkonan, putting a little distance between them and leaning forward into a ready fighting stance. If this turned into a fight Haarkonan's huge frame had the advantage close in, but Valerius was younger and better trained for hand to hand or martial arts fighting.

"What do you want with Dr. Plexar?" Valerius demanded.

"Stay out of this, Valerius," Haarkonan growled. "This doesn't concern you."

"It does if I say it does," Valerius replied. "I don't like the look of your security detachment, and I don't like your ordering the good doctor around either. If you came to start something, you'll have to go through me first."

"Please, gentlemen, let's not make a scene," Plexar broke in. "I'm sure Haarkonan knows what he's doing, and that he has the best interests of *Horizon* in mind. Let's retire to my quarters to gain some privacy and discuss this further."

"Sorry, Ian, but we can't let you go there either. I really hate to do this, but we need to take you somewhere else. How about my quarters?"

"I'm coming too," said Valerius. "This obviously is big…and so concerns me too."

"OK Valerius…I'm okay with that, as long as you vow not to interfere until you hear us all out."

"I can stand that, but with one condition of my own. Since I don't know what you're up to, I'd like your word that Rachel here is free to go. Deal?"

"Sure, that's no problem," replied Haarkonan nervously.

Valerius turned to Rachel who looked very scared. The room had quieted a bit and people had begun to stare at the tense command staff. He reached down and helped Rachel stand up from the booth while quickly whispering in her ear. "Tell Otho we're in Haarkonan's room. Tell him Caesar may be meeting with Brutus, and if I don't contact him in two hours he is to assume the worst." Rachel nodded slightly, clearly understanding the reference to one of the greatest coups of all time.

As she started walking out of the room, Haarkonan gave Valerius a quixotic look but seemed to be OK with him whispering to Rachel. "Let's go then," said Haarkonan with a tight insincere smile. "I'll buy the drinks," he said loudly enough for all to hear. He proceeded to scan an excessive amount of credits into the *tablecomp* before turning and following Plexar and Valerius out of the room.

Once in the relative privacy of the hallway the security men each grabbed one of Plexar's arms. Valerius started to react only to be brought up short by an arm bar from Haarkonan. "Wait for it Valerius. This is the way it has to be. I hope to God I'm wrong, but you promised you'd hear out our case first. We won't hurt Dr. Plexar, we're just ensuring he can't reach into his pockets."

Valerius gave Haarkonan a menacing look, but backed down. He then followed after the two security men and Plexar, with Haarkonan taking up the rear. Valerius noticed out of the corner of his eye that one of Haarkonan's hands was now in his pocket, probably handling a small firearm of some sort. He used his stoic training to tell himself that he was now locked into this course of action and had no choice but to see it to conclusion. He chuckled internally as he thought about how such a predetermined outlook went entirely against Plexar's earlier form of reasoning. Sometimes life looked like you had many choices, but sometimes there seemed to be no good choices at all.

The group went to Haarkonan's office rather than his quarters, but that didn't bother Valerius too much. The two security officers drew their weapons once inside the room. As he glanced around he noticed a young lady in the far corner. Valerius knew her as the *Ark of Time* explosion investigator and was glad she was present. More people made for poor coups.

"Sir," one of the security officers said addressing Plexar, "We need you to stand with your arms out while we remove your lab coat and search your personage."

"This has gone far enough," Plexar said, turning around to face Haarkonan, but keeping his arms straight out as he was instructed. "I trust you, but I don't understand what you're doing here. These men work for me, not for you, and you don't have the right to abduct me and take me wherever you wish. I need an explanation, and I need it right now."

The security officers gave the coat to the lady in the corner who started going through the pockets while the guards patted Dr. Plexar down. "Sir," Haarkonan said, "I really don't want to do this either, and I guarantee that I'm not trying to take over as head honcho of this operation. I'm close enough to the job to know I don't want it. But we've found disturbing information about your past actions and we need some answers."

"Found it!" said the young lady in the corner. Valerius looked over to see what she had found. She was inspecting a small remote control device like the ones used to control tabcomps from a distance when voice control was off, only this one had fewer buttons and they were all encircled around a large red button.

The young lady continued. "This looks like a remote firing device, with encoding buttons. " She looked up at Dr. Plexar. "I bet this is linked to the killer satellite you put in orbit that has a laser trained at *Horizon?*"

Plexar seemed momentarily stunned. "How did you know about that?" he stammered.

Valerius looked even more shocked, and glanced at Haarkonan to see what he was thinking. Haarkonan looked exhausted and disappointed.

"Never mind that," said Haarkonan. "Just tell us why you did it. Why were you planning to destroy *Horizon*, and why did you destroy the *Ark of Time*?"

"You don't understand," pleaded Plexar, regaining some composure. "I had nothing to do with the *Ark of Time* exploding."

"And I suppose this just appeared in your pocket by magic?" inserted the young lady, in full interrogation mode.

"No, of course not," said Plexar. "I understand how this looks, but I can explain. I had nothing to do with the *Ark of Time's* tragedy, but I did launch that satellite and I do carry the remote around on my person 24/7. No one was to know about it, but I consider it a failsafe. If the Narcoid discover this facility, we'll do everything in our power to defend her, but in the end I don't believe we can prevail against their superior technology and numbers. I had that doomsday satellite put in place so that we can destroy *Horizon* as a last resort. Whatever happens, we must never allow the Narcoid possession of time dilation technology. We owe that much to any other sentient life God has created in the cosmos."

Valerius heard Haarkonan sigh in relief and could see the strain drain from his face. The young lady was still skeptical. "So why not put thrusters on it so you could use that laser to defend *Horizon* if it came to that?" she demanded.

"Because I'm weak," responded Plexar, a sad expression spreading over his face. "I knew that when my friends started dying I'd be tempted to use it against the Narcoid, compromising my ability to destroy our time dilation technology. I just could not have that, so I made sure that laser only has one purpose."

"Thank God," boomed Haarkonan, an infectious smile beaming on his face. "I thought for an hour there that you were the saboteur, and I just couldn't understand how that could be the case. This makes much more sense. I'm so sorry I ever doubted you."

Plexar relaxed. "I understand how it happened, but I hope in the future you'll trust me a bit more and ask me about things instead of using these heavy-handed tactics."

"That's my fault," said the young lady in the corner, clearly wanting to defend her boss. "I wanted you to be shot outright, and it was Admiral Haarkonan who decided to have you arrested instead. I was worried you'd just fire the laser the moment you knew you were caught. I'm glad the admiral had a more level head and knew you well enough to give you a chance. Here, you can have this back." She handed Plexar his remote device and lab coat. "I'm sorry too."

"All is forgiven," said Plexar tenuously, then continued with more gusto. "Now we need to be seen throughout the ship having a good time together to dispel any rumors this little incident may have created. We can't have people wondering about their leadership. Bill—you're buying the drinks for the party."

"Yes, sir—it's the least I can do."

"I'll be with you all in a moment," said Valerius. "I need to call Otho first and tell his strike team to stand down. If I don't miss my guess, by now he'll have half the Romans ready to storm this room."

"That's what the whispering to Rachel was all about?" asked Haarkonan. "I sure hope we don't need to ever suspect you of anything."

"You won't," said Valerius smiling. "Not only am I not guilty of anything, but I'm a Roman. I could do intrigue around you moderns with half my brain lobotomized."

CHAPTER 9

Chinese Resurrection

It was the greatest force humanity had ever assembled, or indeed would ever assemble. Wei-Phung remembered how over a million Chinese soldiers gathered in Beijing, assisted by the newly constructed system of canals that had brought north and south China together. A strident Emperor Yangdi had decided to unify all of Asia at the start of the seventh century and declared war against the pesky Koreans who refused to stop raiding China's southern border region.

Wei-Phung was proud when he left Beijing as part of that force. It was so large that it took 40 days just to leave Beijing, and the line of marching men stretched over 400 km. They had such high aspirations, until things started going wrong. The main force was quickly bogged down with logistics issues, raiders, and the need to bridge the Liao river.

Even then he had been proud of his work. Wei-Phung had helped construct one of the three massive bridges that eventually were long enough to span the mighty Liao. It was hard work, and since he could swim he'd been selected to be part of the crew that worked on boats to build the base in the middle of the river. He was filled with a sense of pride and wonder as he considered how his bridge would be a testament to the glory of united China for centuries to come. He had even enjoyed working on the boats in the river and was glad to be chosen as a part of Admiral Lai Huni's naval force of more than 200,000 men who had quickly sailed to the enemy capital of Pyongyang.

Arriving at the Bay of Daedong well ahead of the more than 300,000 invading ground forces, the Chinese naval contingent fought a small skirmish before the Korean naval forces retreated and holed up in their great citadel. Admiral Lai Huni was emboldened by the quick naval victory and decided he had enough men to take the fortress even without the army. After all, he should use the surprise he had earned by his swift sailing, and if he could take the enemy capital before the army even arrived he would earn honor for both himself and his emperor. Nearly the full naval force quickly disembarked and began the march uphill to assault the enemy stronghold.

It was not Wei-Phung's place to question his admiral, but he had been a soldier much of his adult life and had learned from the writings of Sun-Tzu that one major principle of war was not to divide ones forces but to instead use overwhelming numeric superiority to crush the enemy. Still, surely this large of a force could destroy whatever defensive army the Koreans had managed to amass.

Wei-Phung adjusted his armor of boiled leather and wiped the sweat from his brow with his dusty hand, smearing reddish brown mud across his forehead. The hike to the Korean capital's fortress was only a few miles, but even that short of a hike was hot and difficult when in full battle armor walking uphill and carrying a pack both for provisions and to haul off potential loot. He also felt like he was suffocating from being crammed so close to so many other warriors. And he was lucky, as he marched toward the front and near the right edge of the formation. He couldn't imagine what those in the middle and back felt like, since they had to contend with the dust churned up by the warriors in front of them.

Wei-Phung looked again at the houses and taverns that lined the way from the docks to the citadel. It was a ghost town, as few people had stuck around to see the invaders enter their city. Wei-

Phung spotted one lady down an alley, but she quickly disappeared into a building.

He marveled at how strange the Koreans looked, with their pale-looking skin and high cheekbones. And they were tall! All the Koreans he had seen in the previous skirmish seemed at least a hand's height taller than the average Chinese warrior.

He stumbled into the man in front of him as he hadn't realized the formation had halted, his face colliding into the man's backpack and slung leather shield. Before he could apologize he was pushed from behind too, as the man behind him had also not realized the line had halted. Wei-Phung looked back and saw the entire mass of men crashing into each other and then quickly untangling themselves before craning their necks upward to try to see why they had halted. Wei-Phung looked up and forward too, and saw the light-grey walls of the citadel looming above him. It seemed strange that they had arrived so close to the walls without being fired upon.

It was oddly quiet on those walls. Squinting up against the sun's bright rays that were further magnified by the light grey color of the citadel's walls, Wei-Phung scanned the enemy's fortress. Try as hard as he could, he could not locate a single enemy soldier on the walls. When he looked toward the center of the wall he saw something stranger still. The massive doors built to withstand sieges were flung wide open, as if inviting the invading army to enter.

His first thought was that it was a trap. But what kind of trap allowed an enemy access to a fortress? Surely the Koreans would have had a better chance of victory if they made the mighty Chinese invaders pay in blood for every footstep of advance. Battle drums sounded out, calling the men to raid the fortress. Commanders shouted, passing down orders from their admiral.

"Watch for a trap!" Wei-Phung heard his commander yell, relaying the order he himself had just heard. "No one is authorized to loot! We must first destroy the Korean defenders; then we'll have time to take all we want!"

Wei-Phung smiled at the orders. Of course Admiral Lai Huni was clever enough to look for a trap! He should have confidence in his commander, who was appointed by the great emperor himself.

The men at the center of the column were already shuffling into the citadel opening as fast as they could go, and it was not long before Wei-Phung was also pushed with the flow of men storming the open gateway. He barely had time and space enough to pull out his shield and sword before he was squeezed through the massive front gateway.

As he emerged from under the dark archway, his sight blurred as his eyes struggled to adjust back to daylight. He paused to let his eyes adjust but in the process almost got run over by the men behind him. He looked around and noticed that Korean weapons and valuables lay strewn about the large courtyard, as if the enemy had thrown down their weapons and gear and fled the scene. The goods pulled on him like gravity. He wanted to break ranks and grab all he could, but he resisted the urge and continued to shuffle forward. Then he spotted a grisly scene. Two Chinese bodies lay dead near the center of the courtyard, decapitated by their own leaders for disobedience. His overwhelming desire to plunder quickly abated.

Chinese officers inside the citadel continued repeating the order not to loot, and soon the army was once again marching as an orderly mass of men toward the center of the huge fortress. They passed a few walls and interior battlements and still caught no sight of the enemy. Either it was all a trap, or some calamity had overtaken the Korean defenders.

The way narrowed somewhat as the army entered a fancier gateway that then expanded into the courtyard of a Buddhist monastery. Wei-Phung was not fully through the pink and gold arches when he heard Korean battle cries just ahead. So this was where the ambush was set! The narrower pathway would restrict the Chinese superior numbers from being able to concentrate, but the smaller space also meant the enemy would have a hard time bringing their full force to bear.

Wei-Phung charged into the courtyard and ran straight at the nearest enemy he could find. He heard swords clashing and was jostled to his left as more of his own men rushed beside him to assist with the fight. His entire world narrowed to a single Korean warrior directly in front of him who had already begun a strong downswing with his slightly curved sword. Wei-Phung was too crowded to maneuver, and his shield was in the wrong place, so all he could do was raise his own sword to try to deflect the powerful arcing enemy weapon.

Iron screamed against iron as the impact jarred him to the bone. A tingling sensation shot through this forearm all the way up to his shoulder. Paying no attention to the pain, Wei-Phung decided to use his momentum and rushed forward to slam his shield into the other warrior's body. The taller Korean was also thinner and when rammed spun backward onto the paving stones.

Wei-Phung followed up with his sword, skillfully seeking the joining space between the defender's belt and breast armor. He lunged with his sword point, putting his full weight behind the blow.

His sword sunk deep into the enemy's stomach, and the Korean cried out in pain as Wei-Phung's body also landed on the man's chest. He twisted his sword for maximum effect, then pushed against it to stand back up. With one foot on the now-dead enemy's shoulder, he pried his sword out before glancing around for another fight.

The battle was already turning into a route, as the Koreans were again pulling back, receding through the many exit points like water down a drain. Admiral Huni's own body guard of elite warriors had entered the temple and were quickly killing the few Koreans who were buying time for their comrades to escape at the cost of their lives.

The Chinese army let out a cry of victory that echoed off the walls and was raised again by the men who had not yet entered the temple. Indeed, Wei-Phung smiled proudly as that cry reverberated all the way back to the original gatehouse, with men all along the way taking up the chant of "Admiral Huni the victor!"

Stunned by the ease of the battle, Wei-Phung was slow to notice that his fellow warriors had begun to plunder the enemy capital. The admiral was allowing his own guard to take fallen enemy weapons, so it must have been authorized. Men everywhere began to disperse and look for valuables throughout the city.

Wei-Phung slung his shield on his back and climbed the stairs leading up to the ramparts to get a better view and decide where would be the most lucrative place to gather goods. He was one of the few Chinese who had not immediately grabbed plunder, and that fact alone may have been what saved his life.

At the top of the stairs to the left was a doorway and entrance to the temple building, while to his right was the wall battlements. He hesitated by the door, wanting to enter the temple and plunder whatever riches he could find there, but it felt wrong to take from a temple, even if it was Korean. His pious instincts won the struggle, and he went to the right and leaned over the wall to look around. Not far below him he could see a thatched roof of a house that had conserved stone by using the temple's wall as its backing. He looked back in the direction he had just traveled. From this height he could easily see the entry gate and initial courtyard area. Chinese warriors there were in a state of chaos, grabbing not only plunder off the ground but even fighting each other for the more valuable pieces. Everywhere he looked he saw Chinese men cheering and raiding.

Behind him he heard a soft creaking and then some grating of metal on stone. Wei-Phung whipped around just in time to see the door behind him start to open, and then a huge explosion ripped through the courtyard area below. The wall he stood on shook as fire and metal fragments wreaked havoc on the Chinese who were still in the courtyard. Smoke filled the air, but through it Wei-Phung saw the temple door open all the way and a mass of Korean warriors stormed out, streaming down the stairs to kill the shaken Chinese warriors below.

As the smoke dissipated some of the Koreans spotted him on the wall and ran his way. With his shield hanging on his back and his sword sheathed he had no chance of stopping the Koreans, who now let out a blood-curdling battle cry of their own. These were not dispirited and defeated troops: these were men who believed they had a plan to win the day. They had intentionally allowed the Chinese into their fortress so they could detonate barrels of powder and create a massive killing ground.

Thinking fast, Wei-Phung tried to leap over the thick wall, but was weighed down so much that his feet failed to clear the battlement, causing him to clumsily topple over the side. His legs careened forward, and he scraped the back of his helmet on the wall as he did a half flip during the downward journey. As he plunged, his arms flailed about trying to get a view of something other than the pale-blue sky above. His shielded back crashed into the thatch roofing, absorbing much of the impact.

That roof saved his life! It also created enough whiplash to hurt his back and neck. Slightly disoriented at first and coughing from the dirt that had been released by his fall, he tried to focus on the top of the wall from which he had fallen. The Koreans up there weren't about to follow his leap and instead just shook their fists at him before leaving the wall to join their comrades. Not having any projectile weapons, they must have decided to join the fray in the courtyard rather than chase a single enemy.

As Wei-Phung tried to gather his wits on the roof top, a Korean *cho-ko-nu* crossbow archer reached the battlements and took aim at him. Wei-Phung grunted in fear, rolled over, and tried to scramble away, but couldn't seem to gain any traction on the thatched roof. He didn't even realize he had lost his backpack in the roll until he stood up and tripped over it in his haste. He once again found himself falling. A crossbow bolt plunged into the roof with a heavy *thunk* right where he would have been had he not tripped. This time his flailing in mid-air oriented him enough to land on his feet with a jolt, but his legs quickly collapsed under his weight augmented by his leather armor and shield. Sprawling beside the house, he reached out to slow himself and instead jammed his already hurt shoulder into the ground. Looking up, he realized the good news was that he had fallen on the far side of the structure, away from the crossbowman. The bad news, however, was that he was now effectively separated from all his comrades, who were probably battling for their lives against a serious ambush, and he didn't have his backpack anymore. Indeed, looking around at the maze of foreign buildings, he knew any one of them could house more enemy ambushers, and he didn't stand a chance fighting on his own.

Stripping off his armor, Wei-Phung decided speed was more important than protection. With some effort of will, he forced his aching joints and bruised body to start running toward what he hoped was the front of the citadel. Weaving in and out of structures, he saw very few enemies in that part of town, and when he did see them he didn't stick around even long enough to know if they saw him too.

He desperately weaved his way between houses, hoping he was still moving in the correct direction. Occasionally he heard more barrels exploding in the palace area and knew it would be chaos in those narrow spaces with the Korean army flooding in to kill those who survived the blasts. He skidded around a corner so fast that he ran into the back of a Korean pike man. The man shouted something, but Wei-Phung ignored him and instead leapt back up and continued running. The pike man didn't bother following, knowing he was far too laden down with armor to offer effective pursuit.

By the time he reached the citadel's entrance, the few Chinese who survived were running in a full rout. Bodies lay everywhere, and Wei-Phung joined the tidal wave of retreating Chinese as they rushed down the hill and back toward their ships. He saw blood everywhere and smelled its thick sour scent. Fear and pain were in everyone's eyes as the enemy's cheers and crossbow bolts followed close on their heels. Gone was Wei-Phung's sense of pride and patriotism. If he could just get home, just get to safety, he would not need any plunder to make him happy. Why had he joined this army? It was one thing to feel good about being strong, but in the heat of battle all one felt was terror and the desire to stay alive.

Some men ran up the ramps on the docks to the few ships that were still moored there. Others ran to the left and down into the white sandy beach to board paddleboats and try to get back to their ships further out at sea. Wei-Phung went with the latter, knowing the large boats moored to the docks would never launch in time.

He joined eight other men pushing a paddleboat out and then scrambled into it as the water reached shoulder height. He looked back at the city and saw the first fire arrows pelt down on the moored ships. The majority of the Chinese army would burn on the docks or burn fleeing the docks. One way or another they would burn.

Fire arrows then started raining down on the paddleboats. A sickening, hollow sucking noise heralded a warrior to his right being skewered in his neck by a fire arrow. The sticky tar on the arrow burned even while being drenched with the man's blood. Soon nearly all the paddleboats were ablaze. His own boat was hit by one of the burning tar arrows, and men scrambled to push water on the blaze to no avail. Wei-Phung, unencumbered by armor, was one of the few who had the ability to abandon ship. He dove into the warm waters, welcoming the wet after feeling the searing blaze of fire that had erupted on his paddleboat. No one from his paddleboat followed him into the watery haven.

***

To Valerius, the Chinese Sui forces' withdrawal looked more like a sprint to the safety of the ships than a military retreat. Men scared for their lives flung down spears and slightly curved swords and ran for the landing paddleboats that remained on the white sandy beach. Hundreds of Chinese were cut down from behind as they tried to escape, and many more were stapled to the ground and docks by a hail of spears and *cho-ko-nu* bolts. The Korean warriors under Gohuryeo were fighting to defend their homeland and were not about to give the invaders quarter. In fact, they were intent on making the retreat turn into a bloody rout.

Those fleeing men who did access small landing craft were still far from safety. Already dozens of the barely sea-worthy craft had capsized on their way toward the larger sail ships, being driven under the violent waves by the weight of too many armored men. Then a hail storm of fire arrows spewed after the small craft, as volley after volley sought to thwart all escape.

Valerius knew the history. The Chinese Navy had foolishly mounted a land war rather than waiting for their army comrades who were mired in muddy marshes. While torrential weather was common during Korea's rainy season, the resulting swampy land had caught the Chinese invading land force by surprise and broken their invasion strategy into a series of losing coastal engagements. It had also delayed their assault on Pyongyang.

Peering into the tri-screen, Valerius watched the brutal combat below from the comfort of a padded, white chair in the command room aboard the *Time Raider*. Since the explosion of the *Ark of Time*, the *Time Raider* was one of the two largest ships in the human fleet. It had been specially fitted for time insertion missions, while the *Valkyrie* would be repaired as a last-resort colony ship.

Though the people fighting below were Asians from the beginning of the seventh century, Valerius easily recognized the courage of individual men and the hopelessness of the Chinese position. This type of fighting was much easier for him to understand than the three dimensional space battles using beam and projectile weapons he had been studying back on *Horizon*.

"I'm glad I'm not down there," exclaimed Lt. Col. Staci Minker, formerly the defensive measures operator for the *Valkyrie*, but serving as *Time Raider*'s Captain until the *Valkyrie* was repaired. Valerius was in command of the ground operations, but it was her show until boots hit the muck. He grunted agreement with her statement, even while knowing he would soon be down there in the middle of it all once again.

Their mission had already been a success, as they had picked up hundreds of men from the Chinese army that was strung out for hundreds of miles to the North. The huge Chinese land force had quickly given up large-scale operations that were made near impossible by the marshy terrain and ponderous logistics. The Chinese had therefore broken their army into many groups that were acting independently and facing fierce fighting everywhere they went on the Korean peninsula.

While the Chinese had suffered many losses from disease and desertion, they had been especially astonished at the Korean use of a large dam. The Korean leader had craftily waited for a large Chinese force to enter the lowlands and then torn down a dam to flood the area. Tens of thousands of Chinese were drowned in minutes, and the survivors were maimed and disoriented. Though Valerius had tried, the time travelers had not been able to take many men from that massacre because the Korean forces had stuck around to finish the killing and take plunder.

The news just got worse for the Chinese. If history were allowed to run its course, the bulk of the Chinese navy would be sunk in less than two hours, and tens of thousands of people would go under with it. History recorded that less than 10% of this half-million-man army and navy would make it home.

Valerius watched as one Chinese warrior refused to run but instead stood his ground against the advancing Koreans pouring out from the citadel. The waves of enemy crashed against him, and though he killed a few he quickly succumbed to the Korean bloodlust. That was a man Valerius wished he could have gotten to before he died. It was that kind of heart they most needed to combat the Narcoid. War had a way of killing the best and most noble while sparing the timid and cowardly.

Was all this death worth it? Valerius chastised himself for thinking like a Greek. Here he was witnessing an incredible battle, and instead of feeling the exhilaration and glory all he could do was ask philosophical questions. Still, he wondered if anyone really won when tens of thousands of fathers and sons lost their lives in combat over a simple matter like which leader would have the higher title. Maybe the Narcoid would never have been able to invade Earth had mankind refused to kill one another over petty issues in the past and instead devoted its energies to building culture and roads and science. These were not the proper thoughts of a Roman Centurion. Maybe the *Horizon* instructors were succeeding in making him more acclimated to their ways of thinking.

As he continued watching the battle below, Valerius marveled at the clarity of tri-screen "sight" that penetrated the thick gray clouds below. The *Time Raider* was hovering just a few dozen feet above the storm clouds but was surrounded by bright sunlight and apparent tranquility. He allowed himself a wry smile as he thought of what the men below would give to trade places with him. "How long until insertion?" he asked, never taking his eyes off the tri-screen.

"Insertion in 30 minutes. Better get the team assembled," Minker replied. Valerius still found taking orders or even suggestions from a woman uncomfortable, but he couldn't argue with Minker's professionalism or competency. He sprang out of the chair and trotted toward the egression room.

Dr. Entwater was already there fiddling with his Jensen Four Replicator when Valerius arrived, and beside him was Vinny Walscott, a fairly recent acquisition from the 17th century. Valerius had hand-picked Vinny for the mission, given his extensive knowledge of the sea and ships. Walscott was a British officer turned pirate, and while you never wanted to play cards with him, you could trust him to have your back and fight like a lion.

Dr. Entwater nodded to him as Valerius entered.

"Are you ready with that thing?" Valerius asked, giving the large J4 Replicator a slight scowl.

"Everything is operating within normal parameters," replied Dr. Entwater in his most official tone before breaking into a smile. "You always act like the Jensen Four is some kind of monster. I assure you, there is no magic to it—just simple DNA replication, protein hyper-accelerated growth, and micro temporal jumps to create aging when necessary."

"I know," replied Valerius as he regained a neutral face. "But it seems to me that replicating a person's body is…creepy."

"There's nothing 'creepy' about it. It's necessary for us to replicate bodies so that this history records the dead and has the evidence of death. As you know, the Jensen Four only replicates dead DNA—we cannot create life itself. If we could do that, this whole mission would be unnecessary—we could simply replicate or clone ourselves and create an army that way. That's actually what the original designers of the Jensen Replicator intended. As it is, this bit of failed technology is now allowing us to harvest from time and give back the required dead bodies. "

"I know that too. What I don't understand is how it works. I gather that you receive instructions on how to create a person by getting a DNA sample, but then it seems rather complicated."

"It's not that complicated. The Jensen Four stores all the atoms needed. You may find it interesting to know that 99% of a human body is just oxygen, carbon, hydrogen, nitrogen, calcium, and phosphorus. We also store the other trace elements and even contaminants like mercury in case our snatch happens in a time period where they would be appropriate. We then constitute a body from the DNA code, insert any necessary scars or identifying marks if it is an important person who will be inspected before burial, and then use micro jumps to further age the body and scars."

"So you also use temporal transit?"

"Yes, when necessary. I have a temporal transit rating, and it isn't that hard to focus my will with the machine to push the bodies through a quick series of micro jumps. I can even do it close to large populations since my jumps are so small and I'm only taking one body through. It's really a much less taxing job than a temporal pilot faces."

"It's just strange to think that you're duplicating people."

"We are *not* duplicating people," Dr. Entwater insisted, a bit perturbed. "We *cannot* create a soul or even an animated being. All we're doing is copying a body. The cloned body is not a person, just a body."

"I know," Valerius muttered. "It still seems eerie to me, but thanks for the clarification."

Valerius marched past the doctor toward his egression plank. He still got a chill when he considered that he had been replaced with a dead body that exactly resembled himself. He knew they only cloned a few people at each take so that at least some evidence remained behind, but he figured he was probably one of the people chosen since they usually tried to leave bodies of commanders and leaders who would have the highest chance of being recognized. His dead clone body seemed to seal his fate, for he could never return to his own time if a dead replica were already there taking his place.

As he walked up to his egression station, he looked around at the mulling multitude and was satisfied that most of his egression team had already arrived. Valerius rubbed his well-oiled brown leather cuirass as he watched the gaggle assemble. He'd insisted on having his old Roman armor recreated for insertion missions, explaining that he knew it best and wanted its protection should it be needed. While some of his temporal insertion team had adopted modern clothing and armor, most seemed to prefer their own period's attire, making their gathering now look like a kaleidoscope of colors and time periods.

Instead of launching smaller craft to shuttle people down and then back up from the sail ships, the *Time Raider* would simply hover near a target location and send out long ramps. The egression teams would then strip unconscious bodies, bring them up the ramps, and allow some of them to be replicated by Dr. Entwater's machine. Later they would haul the replicated dead bodies back to be redressed. Water "takes" were preferred because it was easier to believe the missing bodies had become fish food or simply decomposed in the tumultuous waves.

Walscott came up beside Valerius. "We're all present and accounted for, mate. Egression team one is green for current ops."

"Thank you, Vinny," Valerius replied. "I expected nothing less." He mentally activated his DataPort com unit to call the bridge. "Captain, we're green for insertion."

Lt. Col. Minker didn't waste time responding with words. Valerius felt the *Time Raider* rumble into action, beginning its smooth descent through the clouds toward the sailing ships below. After a minute or two a red light flicked on, and the room quieted naturally. Everyone watched the monitor that showed the naval armada below, some ships already keening over. The picture then went bright white as the *Time Raider* fired a broad beam of charged ions into the storm clouds and pulsed the sea with sonic beams to counteract waves and calm its surface.

The artificial tranquility beams worked well, quickly quelling the storm in the immediate vicinity. Valerius heard a few chuckles as the team watched the Chinese below stare up with incredulity. Many of them started making superstitious signs with their hands, or even fell prostrate in worship, clearly thinking a god had arrived. Valerius remembered that feeling and smiled in sympathy. The *Time Raider* continued its smooth slide down toward the ships, and about 100 yards away ripped the air with its powerful subsonic sleep inducer. The men below grabbed their heads as their skulls were blasted into unconsciousness, then fell limply onto their ship decks.

The *Time Raider* stopped just a few feet from its targeted destination ship and then hovered. Valerius felt the floor under him vibrate as the combat ramps smoothly slid out like serpent tongues toward the awaiting ships. The *Time Raider* was built like a large ugly swan, with the "head" being the command deck and the wings and back housing six large thrusters. On the "neck" just below the command deck was a large bulbous projection that housed the tranquility beams, sonic beams, and the huge ramp that was now quickly extending.

Valerius hit the door button as soon as the indicator light turned green and then calmly marched out to lead his temporal insertion corps specialists down to the waiting ships.

Valerius found his visceral reaction to stepping aboard an ancient Chinese vessel to be confusing. On one hand, Earth's fresh air cleansed by the storm that revolved around them was invigorating, and he felt a pang of homesickness as he considered that just a few thousand miles west would be the Roman forum and coliseum and a semblance of home. On the other hand, he was once again aboard a sea-going vessel, complete with slimy, water-soaked deck and the pungent smell of sweaty and wounded men. His feeling of nostalgia quickly abated as he remembered that the last ship he was aboard should have been his coffin.

"Let's go!" he shouted, waving his arm forward in the age-old tradition of a commander on a battlefield. He knew his verbal admonition was not necessary, but it felt good to be in command once again. Thinking of all the other ships he wanted to harvest, and the extreme conditions that would conceal their activity, Valerius decided to slightly alter the standard protocol.

"Change of procedure!" he bawled to his team. "We'll haul 'em up, *then* strip 'em down and send a few through the replicator. We can dress up the replicated bodies while still on the *Time Raider* and just throw the bodies overboard. There's no need to carry 'em back to this sinking ship."

Valerius' crew of about 50 people went about their tasks efficiently. The Chinese soldiers who looked wounded were simply ignored, while the able-bodied ones were quickly stripped and put on a cart that then made a series of trips up and down the ramp. Valerius could have simply supervised, but instead he joined the process and helped the loading and hauling. As he lowered a soldier onto the transport cart, he saw Walscott doing the same thing at the other end. Walscott was moving quickly and simply let the unconscious Chinese soldier's head drop the last ten centimeters.

"Be careful there!" Valerius instructed. "That's a new recruit."

"He'll be just fine, sir" retorted Walscott, his cockney English accent coloring his Anglisk. "Look, the man didn't ev'n wake up. 'e's still sleeping like a baby!" Walscott smiled at his own jest and turned to fetch another soldier. Valerius was glad Walscott hadn't been around to handle his own temporal transition, or he'd probably have had an even worse headache when he woke up.

Within fifteen minutes the entire ship had been stripped of all its healthy people, and Valerius ordered his crew back up the ramp. He walked the full length of the deck, making one last sweep to ensure nothing anachronistic would be left behind. As he neared the far end of the ship he noticed Walscott slipping something into his pocket.

"Vinny, what did you just take?"

Vinny hesitated as if debating whether he could get away with a lie, then reached into his pocket and showed off a golden coin. "Just a little momento, capt'n. A keepsake, that's all."

"You know you need to put it back."

"Right ya'r capt'n. Right ya'r. I jus' don' see how a little souvenir makes a difference."

Valerius was prepared for the complaint. "The problem is, we don't know what here gets found and what's not important. We must get approval from Research and Scouting to harvest resources. Imagine if someone down the time stream is supposed to find that gold, and uses it to save their brother, who eventually will have a distant ancestor named Napoleon."

"Then I wouldn't mind settin' that 'poleon fellow right by takin' this here coin," Vinny said with a grin. "From what I learned, he wasn't an upstandin' character."

"OK, but what if it were Lord Wellington, or some other character you do think is upstanding? With every rock we move, and certainly any gold coins we lift, we're endangering the time stream. History can't record everything, but the laws of physics can be affected by anything. That's why this business is so crazy. If humanity weren't about to be exterminated anyway, I'd never be a part of this."

"So we can't take their stuff," Vinny said, dismay clear in his voice.

"Right. If you want a coin, we'll make it for you on *Horizon.* While bones in the ocean will quickly decay and shouldn't be missed, gold could stay here for hundreds of years. It's rather ironic; we can't take any mere material object because it could affect the time stream eventually, but the thing that has the most value, human life, won't be missed once it is consumed by death, so we can take people. Kind of suggests the soul's not really meant to be on Earth anyway, doesn't it?"

"Ahh. I know yous 'ave it rights, but I'd still like that bit o' gold."

Valerius shook his head in amused disgust. You can take the man out of 17th century piracy, but you can't take the piracy out of the man. "You don't get it. Just trust me—taking that coin could cause far more harm than it will bring you happiness. And we can give you an exact replica on *Horizon* if you need one."

"Aye, but where'd be the fun in that?" Vinney flipped the coin over his shoulder as he proceeded up the ramp. One his way he paused a second to offer one last objection over his shoulder. "You're afeared about alterin' the future? Seems to me that that is exactly what both the past and the present were meant ta do." He then shook his head bemusedly and continued up the ramp.

Valerius grinned and gave one last look around before also starting up the ramp. About a quarter of the way up he heard a flopping noise over the ship's side and spun around as something sloshed toward him. He was just in time to meet Wei-Phung's knife attack. He caught the small Chinaman's wrist and tumbled over backward, hitting the deck hard. While grappling, Wei-Phung's knee jerked up and smashed into Valerius' side, but his Roman leather body armor protected him, and it was Wei-Phung who let out a gasp of pain. Valerius rammed the man's knife hand against the deck, failing to dislodge it but at least distracting his assailant enough to then slam his right elbow into the man's face. Wei-Phung screamed and rolled away, clutching his face in one hand and still clinging to the knife with the other.

Both men recovered and stood to face each other in crouched attack stances. Valerius wasn't sure he'd be able to stop the knife this time, since the man had space to slash with it. Suddenly a net spiraled through the air enveloping the Chinaman. Fully ensnared, the man fell to the ship's deck.

"Leave him—let's go!" shouted Walscott who was now standing half way down the ramp and holding a snare gun.

Valerius started to turn to go, then checked himself. "No, he's seen too much. And we can't leave the netting. This man's spirit is exactly what we most need to fight the Narcoid. Come down here and help me carry him up."

The Chinaman clearly didn't understand modern nets that tightened with movement and by now his thrashing around had resulted in almost complete immobility. Walscott stomped on the Chinaman's knife hand, then kicked the knife aside. Valerius and Walscott then knelt down, grabbed Wei-Phung, and easily hoisted him to their broad shoulders to transport him up the ramp.

"How di' 'ee resist the knock-out blast?" asked Walscott as they carried him up the ramp.

"Don't know," grunted Valerius. "He came at me from the side of the ship. Maybe he was swimming and had water in his ears."

Even before they reached the top of the ramp Valerius noticed that his team had returned to work and were starting to toss more replicated and clothed bodies back into the sea. He was proud his team had resumed their efforts without needing his orders. Valerius wanted to get to many more Chinese ships over the next few hours, and the longer they took the more ships would capsize before they could be harvested. Since time travel on a large scale was only possible away from Earth, and it was expensive to travel back and forth, their policy was to never leave Earth to skip back in time and return to harvest from the same event. That practice also prevented them from unintentionally meeting themselves.

Dumping the net-entangled body beside the pile of unconscious Chinese who had already been stripped, he then strode over to Dr. Entwater who was sitting beside his machine reading his tabcomp.

"Have you already completed your duties replicating bodies?" Valerius asked.

"We don't need many this time," Dr. Entwater said, looking up. "There're many wounded down there who we left behind. Some of those should wash ashore. The ones we took will be written off as missing in action. Especially since there was also a lot of burning."

Valerius raised his eyebrows in understanding and nodded his acknowledgment of the point, then returned to one of his former disputes with the doctor. "I still don't think it's right for us to knock people unconscious and then leave them to their fates. At least when they were awake they had a fighting chance."

"Like I've told you before, Valerius, their fate is death. History doesn't record a single name who survived this retreat into the sea. From the entire force, fewer than 3,000 men will make it back to China. Had the Sui been successful it's possible all of Asia would have been dominated, Korea would have ceased to exist, and much of the future would unfold very differently from what history records."

Valerius wondered if Wei-Phung would have been one of the surviving 3,000. He certainly had the spirit for it. His thoughts were interrupted as Walscott yelled to him.

"All present and accounted for, sir."

Valerius left Entwater and strode toward his insertion team. Raising his voice for everyone in the hangar bay to hear, he said, "Good work people! Now strap in—we've got a lot more people to save!"

The *Time Raider* rescued Chinese warriors from five more ships before the hold was full and they decided to head back home to *Horizon*. Valerius dropped into his own acceleration chair, secured his straps, and after a few minutes felt the *Time Raider* shudder slightly as it began its acceleration to break the earth's gravity. *Horizon* was home for now, he thought, but it would never truly be a permanent cradle for humanity. He glanced at the viz-screen and saw the earth rushing away before being blotted out by the gray clouds, then reappearing again as they hurled through the exosphere and finally into space. The earth was more beautiful every time he visited it. The blue skies were stunning, and the grassy fields seemed somehow a luminescent green after weeks of only seeing dull white and gray walls.

More important than missing the earth's beauty, Valerius wondered if he really could overcome his deep-seated heartache and get on with life. He missed his olive groves and the glorious marble forum, but most of all he missed his sweet daughter Lilah. He had justified leaving her for duty in Egypt by telling himself it was too dangerous to take her along, and that after his command position he would be able to return to Rome and spend the rest of his days as a senator and work on enjoying her company and securing her a good marriage. How could he go on living without his only child? Protecting and raising her was all that got him emotionally through his wife's death during childbirth. He didn't need beauty, and he could live without the comforts of Roman civilization, but could he ever call *Horizon* home without his daughter? People are what really makes a place home, he decided. And he had Otho and many of his fellow legionaries. And there was Rachel.

A shrill shrieking sound burst into his ears, tearing his thoughts back to the present. He almost panicked as he heard what must be the hull being torn apart. But how had the Narcoid discovered them in the past? They had yet to transit into the future. He looked around frantically and noticed no one else was even excited. The craft was also not being jolted around but kept a steady course as if nothing were amiss. Still the shrieking noise continued in his mind, undulating and digging into his eardrums as if it were boring into his brain. Could this be Narcoid language, or possibly a new sonic weapon, trained only at him?

He fought down panic as his eyes wildly swept the room, trying to understand what was happening. To Valerius' immediate right, strapped into his seat, was Walscott, who was now looking straight at him with a toothy, mischievous grin. The ex-pirate then let out a bawl that served him as laughter.

"Are you responsible for this noise?" Valerius demanded, not seeing anything to smile about as he wondered how much more his brain could take before it started melting. All of a sudden the insane noise ceased, and he let the blessed silence wash over him.

"'ats not noise, sir." Walscott replied, clearly amused at Valerius' dismay. "'At der was bona fide music. The moderns call it 'rock and roll.' Jus thought I'd share it wit cha, I did. Didn't mean no harm."

"If we weren't heading for temporal transit, I'd get out of these bonds and teach you something about rocks and rolls! I thought I was under attack!"

Walscott just laughed some more and turned away.

Valerius slowly recovered and smiled as he realized he may have overreacted, but he had nothing with which to compare such a blaring, squealing noise. How could people listen to that on purpose? He decided to soothe his disturbed eardrums by listening to the greatest composer of all time, according to Dr. Rachel Rais and quite a few moderns who would know. The old movie scores of John Williams began to massage his mind and his thoughts drifted back to ancient Rome as the *Time Raider* passed Mars' orbit.

Mars' orbit. Mars was the Roman god of war, and Valerius had been told that the Narcoid vanguard force that first attacked Lunar One were spotted erupting from the red planet. He wondered if the Narcoid were there now, in this seventh century. Most scientists believed the Narcoid had arrived millennia earlier, possibly when Mars had liquid water on its surface and a much thicker atmosphere. If that were true, then humanity's mortal enemy was even now somewhere beneath the surface of the red planet. Could they detect the *Time Raider* flying by? Were they already creating plans for their conquest of Earth, possibly calling in the much larger force that would arrive a millennia and a half from now? Valerius decided he wanted to take a trip to Mars someday. Maybe it would have to be Mars in the future so as to protect the time stream, but he wanted to see the Narcoid lair and try to discover something about their plans and motivations.

The temporal transition warning indicator lit up on the command deck, and a verbal warning sounded in his head as his DataPort was connected wirelessly to the command channels. He knew exactly what was about to happen because he had received some training in temporal transitions, but he didn't think he'd ever get used to it.

While he didn't know it at the time, the DeathDare machine had tested him for psycho-determination, and his positive scores had been sent straight to a lab. *Horizon* scientists had subsequently discovered that he was one of the rare individuals who could push through time with his will power enhanced by Plexar's temporal transition device. In fact, he had the second highest potential yet discovered, right behind Dr. Entwater, who supposedly had laughed at the notion and refused to get trained as a pilot. Valerius had received some preliminary training, but full training to become a temporal transition pilot was postponed since he had too many other command duties.

Valerius felt queasy and a sense of wrongness in his gut. He knew that the *Time Raider* pilot, linked directly into the craft through a hardwire that attached to the DataPort embedded at the base of his skull, had begun easing them all toward the future. The key was to visualize the destination time while never forgetting the vessel you were in. You mentally pulled the spaceship forward, slogging through a thick haze, much like a man might attempt to walk upstream through a torrential tide while pulling a boat. Time swirled around and eddies buffeted the ship, but the pilot kept his mind on the goal and refused to be distracted. He also had to have complete confidence that he could indeed move through time, and never lose faith in the final destination.

One of the techniques Valerius had been taught was to repeat over and over that he was already at his desired destination time. Toward the end of the time transition it started to feel like falling into a hole rather than pushing against a tide. The pilot felt like he was being sucked in and downward, but he had to hold the whole spaceship in his mental awareness so that it came along too. It actually hurt, and felt a lot like dying in the DeathDare game. It was terribly exhausting, and the temporal transition instructors had told him that the pushing and pulling was actually fighting against mentally-enhanced gravity wells, which was why it was so much harder to do near human populations.

Toward the end of the transition the pilot reached a place of despair where he had to give one final mental push before everything eventually emerged and synchronized, resuming the standard flow of time relative to the desired three-dimensional speed.

All of a sudden Valerius knew the transition was over. It felt like his body had flipped inside out and back again a few times, and he battled down a wave of nausea. After a few minutes the queasiness gripping the pit of his stomach eased, and he heard Walscott throwing up beside him. He grinned as he heard the ex-sailor curse and spit stomach bile. Maybe it was beneath him to gloat, but Valerius was proud that his stomach somehow weathered temporal transition better than the sailor who felt so at ease on a boat in the roughest of waters. The *Time Raider's* sensors rebooted, as they always went blind during a time transit, and the passengers were slowly pushed back into their chairs as the ship began accelerating.

He decided that the past was fascinating, and the future held many marvels, but he would probably always prefer the sights and sounds of his own time period. Soon he would need to unstrap and begin indoctrinating the new recruits, but for now Valerius felt content. His mission was a success, time traveling had once again not resulted in disaster, and Walscott was still getting what he deserved. That rock and roll noise should be outlawed for all time, he thought. Period.

CHAPTER 10

A Split *Horizon*

Haarkonan slammed his fist into his desk. Though he was typically a fairly emotionally-reserved man, remnants of his Scandinavian ancestors' fiery temper flared as he considered the sheer audacity of the present crisis. "Don't they realize we saved them from certain death?" he roared into the tri screen. "Haven't you told them that we're trying to keep the human race alive?"

In the tri screen SSgt. Eada blinked at the admiral's vehemence before quickly gaining her composure and answering calmly. "Yes, sir. They say life is overrated and that they'd rather have died and gone to Valhalla or some such Viking afterlife. Nothing I can say will persuade them. In fact, they read about Ghandi in their assimilation studies and have decided to gather at in-processing room three for a nonviolent sit-in protest. They demand a physical fight with enemies or to be returned to their time period."

"Vikings read Ghandi? And learned from him? I wouldn't have thought that possible. Is it just me, or does a non-violent protest to be given the opportunity to do physical violence seem strange to you too?"

Haarkonan grinned at his own jest, but SSgt. Eada seemed unamused. "How many are we talking about?"

"At least a few thousand...most but not all the Vikings snatched in the ninth century. I think only the ring leaders have a philosophical purpose—the others are here out of clan loyalty or just to see what mischief they can accomplish. What do you want me to do?"

"Let 'em sit there and rot. They may think they can do non-violent protests, but I'd bet a month's pay, if we ever start getting monthly pay, that the Vikings won't be able to actually stomach the patience that's involved. Speaking of stomachs, make sure you flood the bay with smells of steak at dinner time. We'll let nature take its course on this one."

"Yes sir. I'll contain the situation and attempt to dispel the protest with fumes of good food."

"Thanks, sergeant. I'm late for the morning command meeting, but since they'll ask, do you have anything new on the murder investigation?"

"Not really, sir. The recent kills have all been covered up and seem equally impossible to trace. The only new finding I haven't gotten around to telling you is that I confirmed your hunch; no murders have occurred while Entwater was away with temporal insertion teams. That could be coincidence, of course. We've very little else that points in his direction."

"We have very little that points in *any* direction. Alright, thanks, sergeant. Haarkonan out."

He quickly tidied up his desk and briskly strode toward the command meeting room, his soft soles making a soft thumping sound on the metal flooring. Haarkonan hated being late, and he dreaded giving his usual report of no progress with regards to the murders. He couldn't even tell them about his suspicion of Entwater, seeing as how the man was on the command team and in the meetings. As the door swished open he saw the meeting had started without him, so he tried to quietly slide into his chair beside Ian Plexar who sat at the head of the table.

His arrival caused Plexar to pause and look at him. Haarkonan heard the circulation fans revving into high gear, pumping warm air into the room. The faint floral smell of oxygen mixed with sterilizing chemicals to prevent diseases quickly permeated the room.

Plexar acknowledged his arrival with a small nod before getting right to business. "So how many murders does that make?"

Haarkonan felt uncomfortable and angry. These morning meetings were getting harder to attend when he consistently had to give out the bad news and still had no leads on the murderer. "We've lost four scientists since the *Ark of Time's* explosion. All of them were specialists with critical expertise for our upcoming war with the Narcoid. The latest was a Dr. Sorenson, who was working on miniaturization of the *vlaser*." He looked around the room and saw a few faces that looked confused, and so he continued.

"For those of you who didn't know, the vlaser is a nuclear-vapor charged laser. It's what we consider to be the most promising space weapon, so that we can go on the offensive and not just hide behind our new repulsar shields."

"Any leads on any of the murders?" Plexar looked calm and merely interested, but Haarkonan felt inadequate. Even if Plexar didn't seem to be judging him, he was judging himself and felt lacking. He wondered if Plexar held a grudge from being arrested, but decided his strong sense of condemnation stemmed from internal rather than external causes.

"No sir. Nothing substantial. All of the bodies are cold and completely wiped clean of prints by the time we find them, and the trail to the killer has gone cold with them. Whoever it is, they know our systems better than we do. They're entering the computers and deleting camera footage and other details with impunity. Eada—SSgt. Eada—who is our chief investigator, believes they have a back door encryption that operates at a deeper level than we can. No amount of encryption on our part is effective. What's driving me crazy is that only a handful of people could have this level of knowledge of our systems, and they all perished with the *Ark of Time*."

"I understand. Could someone we thought was killed on the *Ark of Time* have escaped that explosion and now be hiding somewhere on *Horizon*?"

"I doubt it sir. I've personally reviewed the footage of people entering the *Ark of Time* and confirmed all who were reported on board. Of course, that footage could also have been altered, for all we know. Still, I think our regimented environment with scarce and guarded resources would make hiding out on *Horizon* almost impossible for any length of time. Even if they had a secure location in one of the uninhabited levels, they still have to get power, food, air, and other necessities. The only way something like that could happen is if they have collaborators feeding them resources, and that seems a bit far-fetched."

Now Plexar did look a little disappointed. "Do you have any leads? Anything positive to report? I admit I'm just as baffled by all this as you are. Where do we go from here?"

"I do have a plan of sorts, sir, but given that we're clearly dealing with someone who has authority in the computer system I'd prefer not to discuss my plan in this forum, or even at all unless you think it's necessary."

"Does that mean you suspect one of us?" interrupted Dr. Entwater with a suspicious sneer. "Surely you can relay your plan to this command committee."

Haarkonan was tempted to reply in anger, but checked himself and sighed instead. "Dr. Entwater, I suspect everyone I'd even suspect myself if I didn't live with me 24/7. But it's not just that. Since whoever is doing this has a superior command of our own systems, I can't rule out the possibility that what we're saying here is being recorded somehow. I figure the safest thing I can do is keep quiet and spring my plan without notice." Haarkonan didn't add that Entwater was the only person in the room who was on his short list of potential perpetrators. He rocked slightly back in his chair and nodded at Plexar to confirm he was done talking.

Plexar looked at Entwater to ensure he was satisfied with Haarkonan's answer before continuing. Entwater looked unhappy but remained silent. "Alright. I like your logic there and I hope your plan succeeds. Don't tell anyone about it. Up until now fratricide has been hurting *Horizon* more than the Narcoid, but unfortunately that may soon change. I regret to have to inform you all that the Narcoid have been systematically searching the solar system and have discovered and eliminated every other satellite or human outpost that we know about. Titan Three, Foray, and the Uranus Observatory are all gone. The Narcoid have even discovered our lunar relay and took it out with a few spacecraft that hit with the force of a small nuclear device. That's a bit of an overkill for a mirror, but it certainly did the job. Recently we've seen a lot of unusual activity, and analysts believe the Narcoid may be scourging the solar system in our direction. I think it's a foregone conclusion that *Horizon* will be discovered sooner or later. We must step up operations and get this war back on Earth where it belongs."

There were general murmurs of agreement as Plexar looked nervously around the room, as if deciding if he should say more. Haarkonan had seldom seen Plexar be nervous, but clearly the scientist didn't like what he was about to say. Plexar cleared his throat, waited for silence, then continued.

"There's one more reason we must try to accelerate our efforts. Earth is suffering. At current rates we expect the ecosystem will largely be destroyed in under one year, meaning that life as we know it will be unable to live on the planet's surface without augmentation. Furthermore, before the relay was destroyed we learned that Earth Resistance actually saved a human who had been cocooned for two days in a Narcoid body. It took the individual a few weeks to recover sufficiently to communicate, and she'll probably never fully recuperate, but while partially cocooned in a Narcoid body she started to get impressions about their intentions. From what we can gather, the Narcoid are actually many alien species all cocooned into a host shell, and hence they call themselves "The Many" or "The Swarm." We still don't know why they chose to come to Earth, but we do know they are after resources such as salt and heavy metals. They're also using humans as a food source and a recruiting pool for their swarm. The longer we wait the more our planet will suffer, our people will be consumed, and the Narcoid will grow stronger."

Many people in the room had disgusted looks on their faces, and a few of the scientists looked like they might even be feeling ill. Plexar drove on. "There is some good news. We now believe that the cocooning process can be resisted, as humans with strong wills and intense feelings of pain or hatred seem to irritate the Narcoid hosts, resulting in either a longer and less complete cocooning process or in human death. I know I'd rather die than be turned into part of The Swarm. In any case, now that our primary source of information has been severed, we simply must create an invasion force with all due haste."

The rest of the meeting involved more mundane issues, most of which stemmed from being such a diverse bunch of people locked in close proximity with scarce resources. There were also some minor inventory discrepancies, and it seemed theft was up and a black market developing. Probably the strangest theft to date had been in the small Museum of Time *Horizon* staff had created. While only a few tangible items were on display, it did boast a nice holo-video of how temporal mechanics had developed, and it was a common stop when introducing newcomers to the reality of time travel. The main purpose of the museum, and why it was started in the first place, was to store old equipment that had made history and that may one day be of value to a museum on Earth. It seemed a few crates were missing, and while the curator swore they had been taken, most people believed there was a far better chance the crates had simply been mislabeled or misplaced. Haarkonan doubted there was any value on the black market for old machines that were mostly failed attempts to build a temporal transition device. Survival in the present far trumped any concerns for posterity.

Haarkonan left the meeting still upset at his lack of success finding the murderer, but he was pretty sure the new subroutine he had created would do the trick. The small program was geared to act like a virus, duplicating itself throughout the web and searching for official data that was being replaced. It probably would also capture an incredible amount of inconsequential data, and it was a flagrant violation of individual rights, but Haarkonan decided the ends justified the means this time. While he hoped the subroutine's data would lead him directly to the guilty party, at the very least it should be able to detect the access computer and backdoor codes that were being used to change data recordings and hide the murderer's trail.

He would never have thought it could be so hard to trace down crime in such a sterile, highly recorded environment. Then again, he would never have considered having to go against an opponent who had more control of the central computer system than he did. Not for the first time he grumbled that he'd rather be on a warship with guns blazing than have to do all this clandestine sleuthing, but he would of course serve where he was needed most.

After sifting through various reports on his tabcomp all morning, he decided to go to the John Glenn Cafeteria. He wasn't really hungry but wanted a distraction and figured he had to slurp down some globs of nutrition sooner or later anyway. After filing through the short line he took a corner seat and started eating automatically. His thoughts wandered, and in less than ten minutes he noticed that he was consuming the last bite of gray mash. While the color and texture were bland, it actually tasted like a mix of bread, corn, beans, and steak. Steak really lost something when it became the texture of drippy mash potatoes. He grunted with disappointment that he had eaten so quickly, as he dreaded returning to the paperwork. Since he had not been out of his office long he decided to prolong his hiatus by walking around a bit.

He heaved himself up, disposed of his tray and utensils on the conveyer belt to the kitchen, and then headed toward the weapons development lab. He had clearances to go anywhere he wanted, and while he hadn't formulated exactly what he wanted to do at the lab, he had a vague notion that he should inspect it and ask around to ascertain exactly how much chaos the various murders had caused to the vital weapons development program.

As he passed through security he saw Rachel Rais in the break room having a heated discussion with one of *Horizon's* temporal physicists. She was a friendly face, so he decided to start his inspection by asking her a few questions. He regretted the decision the instant he entered the small break room, as he overheard they were discussing some deep philosophical questions. He started to turn around, but Rachel caught his eye, flashed him a smile, and waved him to a seat.

Haarkonan obediently slid in beside her, thinking that being near her beauty would somewhat compensate for having to listen to the discussion. If he were a decade or two younger she would most certainly be at the top of his interest list, but as it was he felt almost a paternal affection for her. He looked at Rachel with her big smile and gleaming white teeth and wondered if she and Valerius were getting closer. Love and the tempest of new relationships was for the young.

Was his lack of interest really due to age or was he still healing from his wife's death? Maybe even just recognizing that Rachel was pretty was an indication that the pain in his heart was slowly healing. And what if it did mend, then who would he be interested in? Certainly none of the ancients attracted him. He needed a first class mind from his own time period. Strangely, the first person he thought of was Lt. Col. Staci Minker. He decided to leave that train of thought, but was somewhat comforted to know that an option did exist for a potential intimate relationship.

As the two scientists continued their discussion, Haarkonan watched an experiment in progress through the break room's transparent Plexiglas. The break room was suspended over the lab room proper and could double as an observation lounge when important experiments were taking place. It looked like they were creating a contained nuclear cloud, which Haarkonan knew was important to power *Horizon's* latest offensive weapon. He had read the specks on the new vlaser but had never seen it in action, and he was amazed at the colorful array that formed. Its resplendent beauty was only matched by its lethal violence, and the cloud which had started with every color of the rainbow began to turn a florescent violet color, laced with brown and tan streaks as the lasers agitated the atomic nuclei.

"I'm surprised to see you here, admiral," Rachel said, pulling his attention away from the forming vlaser cloud. "This is Dr. Stevenson, a psychokinetic researcher who's one of the leads working with Dr. Plexar to modify temporal transition technology to skip through 3D space." The pale scientist across the table with a shock of red hair gave him a small nod of acknowledgement, but was clearly more interested in Rachel or his argument's point, or possibly both, as he quickly resumed his eye contact with her and lunged back into his discussion.

"So as I was saying, it was the quantum effects of observation collapsing the fields into reality that most convinced scientists of The Way. Our reality is not created until it is observed. As the Schrodinger's cat experiment suggests, the cat is neither dead nor alive, or maybe it is both dead and alive, but neither state can be confirmed until it is observed. Reality doesn't happen without observation. The tree that falls unobserved in the woods doesn't really fall until it's observed, and by observation pulled into the matrix of the rest of reality."

Rachel interrupted with a smile. "If that's true, then Descarte was not far astray when he postulated 'I think therefore I am.' Somehow thinking makes things real. Until I think I am not. When I think I observe, and so become. Of course, in order to justify the rest of the objective Universe, Descarte resorted to pulling in a God as the ultimate observer."

"Exactly!" Dr. Stevenson said enthusiastically. "The only way to have an objective reality for us is if it is being observed by someone else. God is the force that observes all reality, who knows not only the reality itself but every contingency and probability that reality will unfold."

Haarkonan noticed the vlaser was now pulsing with energy and saw that the scientists in the lab were chatting excitedly and jotting down notes on their tabcomps. He glanced back at Rachel and Stevenson and noticed Stevenson had his lunch in front of him, completely untouched. Clearly food for the mind took precedence to food for the body for this wiry genius, who pressed ahead in a high-pitched excited voice.

"Dr. Gookenker thought up the 'Ubiquitous Observer Hypothesis' in the mid-21st century in an attempt to understand how reality coalesces without resorting to the multiple worlds explanation.

While he never labeled a being 'god,' he argued that if there were a being who could watch all quantum-level interactions, such a being would be able to determine the outcomes of those interactions. Because that being would have some sort of agenda, it would make sense that a fairly stable statistical matrix could be developed for when each interaction would produce each kind of result, creating natural laws. However, since this being would act with purpose and presumably must be adaptable and able to be persuaded by circumstances, there would exist a random element to natural laws, which constitutes the spiritual or realm of luck. Thus the ubiquitous observer would be the key behind the Universe, and the Universe's laws are based on that being's will rather than on consistent physical reality that exist separate of intelligent observation."

"That makes such good sense!" Rachel yelped, her shiny white teeth evident as she smiled excitedly. "So miracles are possible, not as aberrations in the natural laws, but as a consequence of them. A miracle is simply a minor intervention at the quantum level created by the Ultimate Being changing its mind. Prayer is asking this Being to observe a new reality at the subatomic level which creates unusual outcomes from our macro perspective. At its core, it is all science."

"Yep. Every good scientist would have to admit that all we really do is trace back causality. Scientists discover what matter or energy led to the present matter or energy so that we can make the same kind of conversion in the future. However, at some point in the past the causality line must have originated. You can name that "Ultimate Cause," "Mother Nature," or "Singularity," or anything else, but I prefer to think it is a Creator who has a purpose and plan and gives all the rest life and meaning."

As the two scientists reached a contented pause in their discussion, Haarkonan decided to interject his questions. "I see the vlaser cloud is functioning well. If you don't mind my asking, how's the whole project coming along? Are the murders setting you all back very far, or were they more peripheral to the central production task?"

Dr. Stevenson seemed a bit annoyed to be interrupted while he was connecting with a pretty woman in the only way he knew how, but he quickly overcame his irritation. "I'm afraid Dr. Sorenson was vital. Absolutely vital! We're still raiding his files to try to discover his thought processes. Let me put it this way. If your job were to slow down our research, he was exactly the right man to take out. In fact, each scientist who has been murdered was in a break-through area. It's as if the murderer knows exactly who to kill. I admit I've even had misgivings, thinking that if I develop a great idea it might be better to work on it silently rather than make myself a target. I wouldn't do that, you understand, but the thought sure has occurred to many of us."

"So the murders are perfectly targeted. That suggests the murderer is a scientist who knows exactly what is being developed." Haarkonan paused to consider the new angle for investigation.

"Not necessarily," said Rachel thoughtfully. "He needs some scientific knowledge, but really all the murderer would need is access to all the scientific chatter on the web. It wouldn't be difficult to see who is being lauded or talked about the most and just pick that person as a target."

"That may be true for some of them, but Sorenson had just formulated his ideas on how to condense the size of the vlaser, and most of his thoughts weren't published yet. Unless someone could tap into his personal files, I don't think the general web had time to get excited about his breakthroughs. I'd say your murderer is vatic, or awfully lucky. Look at how Sorenson was killed!"

"What was unusual about that?" asked Rachel.

"I don't like discussing ongoing investigations, but I admit it was strange," said Haarkonan. "Dr. Sorenson got off work and soon thereafter cleared his schedule, wrote a will, and then went to a remote wing of *Horizon* on the third basement that is being prepared for the next batch of people from temporal insertions. The place was deserted. It was almost as if he knew he were a target, and stranger still, that he knowingly went to a place where he could be quietly killed."

That revelation served as a conversation stopper. All three watched the vlaser in bemused silence before Rachel slowly pushed herself up and said something about getting back to work. Haarkonan also stood up and excused himself. Dr. Stevenson waved them away, giving Rachel a warm smile and Haarkonan a cordial nod. He then looked down at the food in front of him and seemed surprised that it was still there.

As Haarkonan strode back toward his office he contemplated the murders. There was something to this murder mystery that he just wasn't getting! Why would humans kill each other when they were locked in a fight with the Narcoid to prevent their own extinction? Why would key scientists be targeted, and how did the killer know exactly which one to attack? How could the scientists know they were about to die and even cooperate with the murderer?

He reached his office and saw a warning light on his computer was blinking. It was his subroutine to track unofficial tampering with the net. In his excitement, he punched the button to see what had been discovered without even bothering to sit down. After a few minutes of scanning the data, a small smile crept across his face. That kind of power usage in an unauthorized area was indicative of only one kind of technology. And that kind of technology was exactly what his prime suspect was trained to handle. It was an excellent lead, and it aligned well with his suspicions. With this program running he knew he would succeed in discovering the killer, and he suspected he would enjoy making the arrest.

***

Valerius was a bit depressed. He was overworked, and while he tried to put a good face on everything, at his core he didn't think humanity really had a chance against the Narcoid. The morning briefing made it clear that the aliens were scouring the Milky Way looking for outposts like *Horizon*, and there was just not enough time to develop and build spaceships capable of repelling the strange creatures.

His attitude perked up a bit as he strode toward the Earth Recovery planning room. On top of his insertion team duties, he had been put in charge of developing the planning team to retake Earth, and so far he was rather proud of the team he had assembled. They were some of the greatest military minds of all time, though they also could be some of the most demanding personalities.

The automatic doors swished open as he reached the room and entered. It was still an amazing sight to behold. Gathered in front of him, carefully peering down at the holo-table map of Earth, stood generals who were legendary in their own times. As he entered he heard the world's two greatest conquerors arguing.

"We must free the most humans first so they can join our army," said Cyrus the Great. "That means invading China and Arabia first. Then, with sufficient human resources, we can proceed to retake the rest of the earth."

"That's madness!" exploded Alexander the Great, his petulant young nature rising to the fore. "Maybe in your day the number of people you commanded was most important, but history suggests power today stems from manufacturing. We attack Europe first, secure the most advanced industrial base, and then we can generate the weapons needed to push the Narcoid off Earth."

"You realize, of course, that your argument is premature," interjected General Antonio Scalerio, hero of the Great Nuclear War and head planner for the invasion. "What we need to consider first is how to gain space superiority. Whoever has the high ground also has the ground. The only way a land invasion can succeed is if we first have defeated the Narcoid air and space assets."

Alexander turned his fury on General Scalerio. "So you keep saying! You and your space power advocates can work on that aspect. Cyrus and I will continue to discuss the ground war. We have no interest in flying things, except where they impinge upon our ground maneuvers."

Scalerio took Alexander's anger in stride. Famous for his unflappable countenance, Scalerio was the perfect person to lead the team of temperamental and impetuous leaders. Valerius didn't know what he'd do without him.

Valerius halted beside Scalerio, who moved aside slightly to let Valerius peer at the holo-globe. "Do you have any more intel on what kind of space craft and weapons we'll be working with?" he asked Valerius. "I can't plan an invasion without knowing our own capabilities, and the information on the Narcoid is almost a week stale since we lost contact with Earth."

"I have good news for you on that front," smiled Valerius. "I've loaded into your tabcomp the latest capabilities projected for the repulsar web, which we expect is only weeks away from its final testing phase. While these are still projections, by now we have a pretty good idea of how much pounding it can take. I can also confirm that we'll have a new offensive weapon in the next month or so. We're calling it a vlaser."

"And what is a vlaser?" asked Scalerio.

"It was explained to me to be a nuclear-vapor modified laser and should be capable of much more power focused on a much smaller spot. You'll probably understand it all much better than I do."

Scalerio glanced down at his tabcomp to verify he had received the document. "Excellent. Since we'll clearly be vastly outnumbered, our only chance is to create a weapon that they can't counter. I'd hoped the repulsar web would do it, but I don't think it'll be capable of handling their brute melee assaults forever. Having a superior offensive weapon might just tip the balance back in our favor."

Valerius smiled, glad to have made Scalerio happy. Even though Scalerio's Italian heritage was filtered through his American citizenship and two thousand years of history, Scalerio still reminded Valerius of generals from his own time. Or possibly even senators of his time. Valerius briefly wondered if Scalerio had aristocratic ancestors but decided not to ask. Not only would Scalerio probably not know, he probably would be even happier if he were only of plebian blood. Such was this strange future age that gloried in things the past disdained.

Valerius looked over at the holo-globe and saw an actual general of his time, or more precisely, a legend from a few centuries before his time. Publius Cornelius Scipio Africanus, famous for fighting Carthage and having never lost a single battle, had intervened between Cyrus and Alexander.

"You both make valid points," Scipio said in his oratory-trained voice of command. "But there is one other possibility. Instead of focusing our initial attack on liberating either of your homelands, maybe we should address the problem by first destroying their strongholds. It seems to me that the Dead Sea has particular importance for them, and that we should strike them where it most hurts them rather than where it offers us more resources."

Valerius smiled as both Alexander and Cyrus reacted well to the praise and mild rebuke, and began looking at the problem from the perspective of what would most hurt the enemy. Scipio led the discussion, pointing out the locations of Narcoid concentrations.

Scipio had insisted on keeping his Roman traditions alive, and while most of the other leaders including Valerius had adapted in various ways to modern attire while on *Horizon*, Scipio had insisted on clothing that simulated his Roman armor even on the outpost. His current attire was made of modern plasti-ceramics, making it lighter and tougher than his original armor, but it was molded to perfectly match his old armor. He wore a dark red *paludementum* similar to the capes worn only by emperors during the Republic, a synth-leather baldric, a scabbard, and a *sporran* pouch on his belt. He even had a sheathed *gladius* sword. Of course, his *caligae* sandals were not shod with hobnails but instead enjoyed a layer of serrated rubber, but to appearances he looked like he just walked out of the history books.

Valerius felt a stab of nostalgia. He missed Rome. He missed home. Most of all, he missed his daughter. What would become of Lilah now that he was thought dead? While Valerius had a small estate, it wouldn't make a large enough dowry to tempt anyone of real prominence. And though Valerius loved his daughter, he knew she was rather plain in appearance, unfortunately inheriting some of his stony features rather than being graced with features from her beautiful mother. A day didn't go by without him thinking of going back to her, if not to stay with her then to at least see what had become of her life and possibly nudge fate in her favor.

The war room continued with its arguments as Valerius' thoughts turned toward his deceased wife. Sweet Felicia. He had lost her four years ago in child birth, and the child also perished from the ordeal. What would have been one of the greatest days of his life, the birth of his firstborn son, ended in tragedy as both mother and child died. It was a breech birth, and the child had suffocated with the umbilical cord around his neck while Felicia had bled too much to recover.

It all seemed so unfair! The technology that surrounded him now could have been employed, and he was certain it would have saved both his wife and son. Why did the gods grace one generation with the power to preserve life while another age languished in ignorance and death? Were these people of more value in the gods' eyes? It was so strange to think that people had so many blessings in their lives simply from where and when they were born, and most people never appreciated their fortunate circumstances.

But what if Valerius went back to save his wife? He could rescue her and his son...no, it should not be done. It should not even be contemplated. If what little he understood about time were true, he'd do real damage to others, and all for a selfish cause. But what if he just returned to his own time to watch over his daughter? Surely it was possible that in the actual timeline he had survived the shipwreck and then spent some time finding his way back to Rome? History reported Julius Caesar had endured a similar experience. And what about Wei-Phung? He'd been snatched and there was at least the possibility that it was an error...that Wei-Phung still had a future in his own time. Yet there had been no negative repercussions for that. Maybe Valerius should never have been time-snatched, and he would actually be repairing the timeline by returning. There was so much that history failed to record! His insertion missions had convinced him of that.

Valerius was jerked back to reality as Scipio laid a hand on his shoulder. "I was wondering if I may make a request of you," asked Scipio with some formality.

"Of course," replied Valerius.

"I've been reading history, and I can't help but to notice that I'm regarded as the second greatest general of Rome. It seems to me that we need the very best. Would you be able to suggest to the leadership that we time-snatch Julius Caesar? I would very much like to meet the man and have his opinion about how we intend to execute the upcoming invasion of Earth."

Valerius smiled. "I'd like to meet him too. Actually, he's always been on our list of potential recruits, but his death was rather public and very significant to history. We haven't given up on the idea, but for now we're only snatching people who are easy to get."

"That makes sense," said Scipio thoughtfully. "That messy business with Brutus and the senate would make it difficult. I was thinking you could perhaps warn Caesar and use some modern technology to simulate blood from the senators' knives. Do you think that'd work?"

Valerius didn't reply immediately, as his mind had started wandering. Caesar was less than two centuries prior to his own time, and if he went back in a disguise to snatch Caesar he might be able to also make a small time-jump forward and check in on his daughter. He had begun training to become a time transition pilot, and in the process he had learned that an individual could actually time-jump even on Earth if they had the talent and right equipment. The mental inertia of all those people prevented items with large masses from jumping because larger masses had their own gravity wells, but a single person could do it. If he could just get the mission to retrieve Caesar approved…

"You look exhausted, Valerius," Scipio said, interrupting his thoughts. "Why don't you go get some rest and we'll keep working these issues and let you know how it's going when you return?"

Valerius blinked and felt ashamed to have displayed weakness before such a legend of Rome. "Yes, I do need some rest. I'll reconsider how we might retrieve Caesar, but for now I'll be in my quarters if anything comes up that needs my immediate attention."

Retreating through the door, he heard Alexander expositing how real war was like chess, and that they needed plans to pin the enemy in place, fork their most precious assets, and only when all was in place let them discover the real threat.

As he walked through the white halls glowing with recessed sterile light, his thoughts wandered to Rachel. He wanted to take the relationship to the next level, but had no idea how courting was accomplished in this new era, or in her home era, or even which era's rules he should follow. Maybe it would be better to put off courting until after the war? But what if there would be no end to the war? It was all so frustrating.

Just before the stairs to his level he passed the pub where the DeathDare game rested. He wanted to have another go at that machine, but not until he had rested and cleared his head of the gloomy thoughts. To be honest with himself, what he really needed was more time to build up his courage in order to submit to death again. The first time he had been facing an unknown, and his pride had fueled his courage. Back then death was a nebulous concept that honor demanded be faced without fear and be doled out to all enemies of Rome. But now he knew more about death. And he knew the game really did mean facing death. He was unsure if that was a good idea. Maybe it was best to wait and experience death when it was his natural time? If the Narcoid had their way, that time would arrive soon enough.

CHAPTER 11

Battle for *Horizon*

The Narcoid had discovered *Horizon*. You could feel the tension in the air, like electricity crackling and jolting the senses to a heightened awareness. Such had it always been when war loomed, mused Haarkonan as he glanced at the faces of the leaders who had been assembled for this emergency command meeting. Everyone looked tense, with furrowed brows and strained expressions. A few people quietly chattered and occasionally let out loud bouts of nervous laughter, but most sat solemnly battling their inner demons. No one wanted to admit to the intense fear that seized the pit of the stomach and if let loose would drag a man into panic.

Haarkonan had felt this primal sense of rage mixed with despair before, and he knew it was fatal to give in to the surging raw emotions. Humanity, unlike the animal kingdom, didn't wage warfare from emotions but was at its most deadly when cold and calculating. Haarkonan greeted his fear and channeled it into hatred for the Narcoid and a drive to survive. Every generation of mankind since the dawn of civilization had faced external threats that they had to protect against or lose their livelihoods. Now it was not just a nation, but humanity as a whole that had to fight to survive. Haarkonan was not confident they would win, but he was confident that all the strife of the past had made humanity strong enough to at least make a good showing for itself in this final fight for species survival.

The room smelled of sweat and fear as Dr. Plexar entered, trailed by bustling aides who were trying to hound him about various issues. Those lesser things may all have constituted emergencies in their own right, but they were dwarfed by the present crisis, and Plexar waved at them to leave the room as he hurriedly seated himself. Haarkonan noted that a few people on the command team had not yet arrived, but Plexar nodded to Lt. LeMoray to begin the briefing anyway.

The lights dimmed and LeMoray pointed at the screen that covered the wall on the far side of the table from Plexar. "These two points of light are in fact Narcoid craft. A careful search of past records conclusively tells us that they've been circling around and observing *Horizon* for at least a fortnight. These craft have an extremely low heat signature, and are almost impossible to detect. In fact, they were first spotted by human eyes on the observation deck, and then only a concentrated search through our databases revealed they have been circling around us in intelligent paths that initially seemed to be random but in fact gave them a 360 degree look at us. Our conclusion is that these are Narcoid craft that have been reconnoitering *Horizon*.

"Two weeks!" Haarkonan couldn't contain his outburst. "What are they waiting for? They've known about us for two weeks! Do we know if they ever waited to destroy human outposts before?"

"No sir, to the best of our knowledge they usually just attack. But we're the biggest target since they took out the earth and moon, and it's possible they did reconnaissance on other targets but were never detected. These things are small and very hard to detect."

Plexar looked confused too. "So does anyone have a guess as to why they would just observe us?"

"Maybe they want to be friendly this time," Entwater sneered with derision, drawing a small chuckle of nervous laughter from the commanders who needed to release some of their stress.

"If I were them," Haarkonan said thoughtfully, "the only reasons not to destroy this station immediately would be one: they changed their objective with regards to destroying humanity, which I doubt. Two: they see some advantage in treating us differently rather than destroying us outright, which would suggest that they know about temporal mechanics or our weapons research. Or three: they're distracted by something else right now and cannot get overwhelming force in place. Lieutenant, where has their main space fleet been? Maybe more importantly, where is it now?"

LeMoray raised his eyebrows in a brief look of surprise at the accuracy of the analysis. "I think it's option three, sir. The Narcoid have certainly been acting distracted. While they left two thirds of their forces on Earth, doing some pretty devastating things to its environment I might add, about two weeks ago they sent a third of their fleet back into space. We initially thought it was an all-out search for our location, but since then we noticed that most of them massed together and headed straight toward the Kuiper Belt. What's interesting is that it was quadrant 4-E, exactly the place from which the original Narcoid fleet emerged. You'll remember last week that I told you we thought they might be sending those craft back home, but we don't believe that now, as they have reemerged from the belt and are headed our way."

Behind the lieutenant quadrant 4-E dutifully lit up and then expanded, and some sketchy details of the Narcoid fleet's craft were noted. Haarkonan grunted as he saw how huge that fleet was. He also noticed that quadrant 4-E was fairly close to *Horizon's* future orbital path, but it was nevertheless far enough away that it would not be a natural place to gather forces for a raid on *Horizon*.

"Something in there not only had their attention, but created losses," continued LeMoray. "Look at this. What you're seeing is the force entering and then emerging from the Kuiper Belt. You'll notice that there are 15% fewer craft when they emerge."

"Do you have any idea what they're doing in there?" asked Plexar while staring at the screen.

"Could be resupplying before battle," interjected Haarkonan thoughtfully. "But it seems unlikely since they don't expend projectile weapons."

"They could be resupplying," said LeMoray, sounding impressed once again at Haarkonan's quick analysis. "That's what we thought at first. However, we now believe that they either sent some ships back to a Narcoid home world, or that they've split their forces while hidden from our radar, most likely in a strategic move to flank us."

"What do you mean our light-radar can't track them?" asked Haarkonan. "Is it just the density of the Kuiper Belt in that area?"

"No, sir," said LeMoray. "We're actively being jammed and can't see a large section of quadrant 4-E."

"How do you know it's jamming?" asked Haarkonan. "They never evidenced that capability before."

"When we analyzed the data, we noticed that before the Narcoid fleet entered that area we could easily discern their various masses. Every Narcoid ship has a distinctive mass, which indicates that they probably don't use mass production techniques. As the fleet continued into the quadrant, we first lost mass data then we lost the ability to detect them at all. That suggests a graduated field of some sort that is cloaking their light signatures."

"That bit about not having mass production is fascinating," said Plexar. "An advanced race that still creates everything uniquely. Be sure to pass that observation on to the xenologists."

"Yes, sir." LeMoray agreed, then waited a second to see if there were any more orders before continuing. "Having different masses has also made classification of enemy vessels difficult. We've just settled with dividing them into small, medium, large, and mother classes. We could also just call them Frigates, Destroyers, Battleships, and Motherships, but those terms suggest actual classes of similar ships.

"Having unique masses does give us one advantage, as our computers can estimate each ship's mass and identify each vessel precisely. The ships that left their formation were almost all small and medium-sized craft, as well as one Mothership.

"Unfortunately, we don't know where the smaller force is now. It seems reasonable that 4-E contains a base or a gateway of some sort that leads to the Narcoid home world, or at least one of their worlds. It would be worth investigating to see if they have some sort of transportation device in there, like a warp gate or a controlled wormhole. Wouldn't it be amazing if—"

"Lieutenant," Haarkonan broke in without apologizing, "This is not the time for theorizing. Where is that large fleet *now*, assuming it's not jamming our light-radar."

"Yes, sir. Sorry, sir. We know exactly where it is." The map switched from a close-up on 4-E to a strategic overview of the Milky Way.

Haarkonan heard what sounded like the entire room collectively draw a breath as they saw the size of the force that was arrayed against them. There was no doubt that the alien armada was headed for *Horizon*.

"As you see, they are on a direct intercept course with *Horizon's* orbit," LeMoray continued. "We estimate that they have a couple hundred smaller craft, dozens of medium-sized ones, and maybe 10 large battleship craft. Surprisingly, there are no Motherships in the main force."

"What's the ETA?" asked Plexar nervously.

"I expect we'll have to host these visitors within the week, sir. Their speed is erratic, but I'd guess we have at least two and a half Earth days, and probably three, until their fleet engages at our location."

The room erupted into gasps and comments about not being ready. While the vlaser had proven effective and a few large defensive batteries had been constructed on the surface of *Horizon*, it had not gone into its full production phase. Worse, fewer than half of the human spacecraft had smaller versions of the vlasers installed. The repulsar technology was also untested in battle, though its predecessor technologies were now well-established, as they formed the basis for the dampening ray that was being used to calm storms during temporal abductions.

Haarkonan saw the fear on every face. Almost every face. Entwater's face was inscrutable. Haarkonan never thought the man would be brave, but in the face of this danger he seemed unflappable. Haarkonan's respect for the man edged up a notch. His suspicions also increased.

"OK people," Plexar said, trying to regain control of the meeting. "We knew this day was coming, and we've been preparing for it. I want as many vlasers as possible produced and installed on our spacecraft. We also must have repulsars on every ship in our fleet."

More emergency directives were given, and workers reallocated from research and other areas so that everyone would be working to bolster the defensive capabilities of *Horizon*. The meeting was swift and efficient, and in the end Haarkonan left with a huge to-do list to prepare the small human fleet of under 80 spacecraft for action. He was glad that the waiting was over, though he knew that part of his happiness was irrational, stemming solely from the joy of pushing aside his administrative duties and concentrating on military matters once again. He was also relieved that he didn't have to oversee *Horizon's* few defensive batteries and lead the small ground defense force. Those tasks had been assigned to Valerius, as all temporal operations were suspended in preparation for the imminent Narcoid attack.

The highest priority was launching the *Valkyrie* which had been repaired sufficiently to once again serve as a colonizer. Plexar was taking on that task. The second priority was to install repulsars on as many spacecraft as possible. Surprisingly, Dr. Entwater had volunteered to head-up that endeavor, so Haarkonan would concentrate on getting the vlasers built and installed.

The last time he met the Narcoid in space his pitiful Earth Defense Fleet had made do with mining lasers and no shields. He smiled at the thought of using real military-grade beam weapons this time around. Sure, this defense would probably prove just as futile as the last one, but he was resolved to exact as high a price as possible from the enemy. Even if humanity would have no future, he hoped to at least etch this final fight into the Narcoid collective memory.

***

Haarkonan punched the button on the *Time Raider's* command chair to pull up *Horizon* command on the viz-screen. The joy he had felt for the past 12 hours of finally being back in command of a warship and small fleet was muted by the similarity this experience had with his failed attempt to protect Earth. While the *Time Raider* was a bit smaller than the *Valkyrie* he had then commanded, this ship was equipped with much more powerful defensive and offensive weapons, and he hoped it would be enough to hold off the Narcoid while the *Valkyrie* escaped with the few humans who would be tasked with keeping the human race alive.

Haarkonan was surprised to see Dr. Plexar's calm face in the viz-screen. "Sir, what're you doing on *Horizon*? I thought you were in the *Valkyrie*?" Then he remembered the killer satellite Plexar had in orbit, and realized the scientist had probably stayed behind to burn *Horizon* before the aliens could obtain the time technology.

Plexar looked haggard and tired, but managed a kind smile anyway. "I know. I changed my mind. I decided to stay here with the people I've known these past few decades and share their fate. That was a tough decision, and I didn't want you to worry about it, but now it doesn't matter anyway. The *Valkyrie* is returning to *Horizon* and will equip itself to join your armada as soon as possible."

"But why?" Haarkonan asked. He felt his spirit drop as the full weight of the news hit him. If there were no *Valkyrie* escaping the solar system, then there really would be no human race. He had planned on fighting to delay the enemy, but what was the point in delaying an enemy if the destruction of humanity were inevitable?

"Admiral, we all knew the *Valkyrie* was a long shot anyway. But now we have new data that made it no shot at all. Please view the new long range scanner data that we're uploading into your system."

Haarkonan nodded at Lt. LeMoray to split the viz-screen so that Plexar and the new data were side by side. The bridge crew stared at the screen in disbelief. Lights of various sizes showed the main Narcoid force decelerating to combat speed with an ETA of less than an hour from the *Time Raider*'s position. The human fleet had traveled about 10 hours away from *Horizon* to meet the aggressive aliens, hoping to be able to delay the attack and use the space to wage a fighting retreat as needed. But other lights now lit up as new data streamed in from *Horizon*. It appeared that the Narcoid had split their fleet, with a much smaller second wave of invaders closing in on *Horizon* from another trajectory. Telemetry data showed that the second wave was coming from the Kuiper Belt on a heading that placed it directly between *Horizon* and Alpha Centauri, and thus directly in the path that the *Valkyrie* had been using to escape. Lt. Colonel Minker, now Captain Minker and in charge of the *Valkyrie* expedition, had turned the colonizing ship around and was about nine hours from landing back at *Horizon*. It seemed that the Narcoid had known where the humans were planning to flee and had taken measures to ensure their victory would be complete.

"As you see, the *Valkyrie* had to be turned around since that second fleet was detected. I can only assume from this that the Narcoid know about Alpha Centauri, and probably already destroyed it. They then correctly surmised that we would flee in that direction and so sent this smaller fleet to trap us on *Horizon*. The small fleet is also using some kind of jamming device that is making them hard to see on our scanners. At first we thought they had a very sizable force, but the closer they come the fewer of them seem to be showing up on lidar. We can't get any determinative size data this far out, so we've sent a scout to check it out."

"There's another possibility," Haarkonan growled with disgust.

"Yes, I thought of that too." Plexar paused, clearly considering his next words to be distasteful. "Maybe there *is* a human traitor among us who gave our plans away. At this point it doesn't really matter. What matters is that you realize we're no longer fighting to delay. We must now fight to survive. We're fighting this battle to win it. There's no back-up plan."

"Got it." Haarkonan paused to consider the tactical situation, then continued. "We'll need to fight the main Narcoid armada and hopefully have something left to deter that smaller fleet when it arrives at *Horizon*. Since we're fighting to win, I'm pulling back the fleet so we can be supported by *Horizon's* vlaser batteries. It makes more sense to fight with massed firepower than to allow them to chew us up piecemeal."

"Whatever you think's best," Plexar said with a wan smile. "War is your area of expertise, not mine."

Both men simply nodded a farewell to each other, effectively saying without words that they wished each other luck. Admiral Haarkonan then began messaging the fleet, explaining the situation, and ordering the *Time Raider* to come around and accelerate toward *Horizon*. Most of the human fleet were smaller ships that didn't have to turn around but could instead just flip and rotate to a new trajectory. Soon the whole human fleet had reversed direction and was accelerating behind the *Time Raider* on a return course to *Horizon*.

The retreat was going to be close. Luckily, the Narcoid were nearly fully decelerated to combat speed in order to engage Haarkonan's fleet, and they seemed to be continuing their deceleration rather than realizing that their prey was withdrawing. Haarkonan brought up an intercept probability program to see exactly how close the race back to *Horizon* would be. Even while he was running through his second scenario a green acceleration arrow lit on the Narcoid fleet, indicating that the Narcoid had resumed acceleration. That was the most important variable the program needed, and so it quickly recalculated using the known capabilities of the human and Narcoid craft.

Haarkonan grimaced at the results. It was possible for the Narcoid to overtake the human fleet before they even reached the defensive protection of *Horizon*. That would be devastating. If both fleets were traveling at speeds that were too fast for human ships to maneuver, the Narcoid would be able to strike the human fleet from behind. However, if the Narcoid chose that option, they would also overshoot their objective, and *Horizon* would be able to pour fire into them as they finished decelerating and turned back to engage.

The alternative was for the Narcoid fleet to start decelerating earlier so that it would arrive at maneuver speeds near *Horizon*, in which case the human fleet should be able to arrive first and get some good shots off as the Narcoid finished decelerating. Haarkonan wouldn't know which alternative the Narcoid would choose until the aliens started decelerating, which needed to be about four hours from *Horizon* if they did not want to overshoot it. If the Narcoid did not start decelerating at that point, Haarkonan would need to scatter his fleet so that the Narcoid would not have a concentrated target. That would also mean a very messy engagement at *Horizon*, as his defensive fleet would arrive piecemeal.

He smoothed out his black Space Command uniform and sat back in his command chair. This was his least favorite part of battle. The waiting game. This was when he would run a million scenarios through his mind so that he was prepared for any contingency. As he started to consider the possibilities, he glanced around the command deck and smiled. He had never seen a crew that was so diverse. People came from every part of the earth, and even from various time periods, though most were moderns. Many of the people on board wore civilian clothes, as the textile industry had been somewhat negligent in preparing uniforms for this war. Most of his crew wore some kind of jumpsuit, though he saw one guy wearing shorts. Those who had served in space command wore their black uniforms trimmed with silver piping and decorated with rank and merit badges. Haarkonan's own uniform included a cluster of high-level merit medals constituting his "salad bowl" of decorations on his left breast pocket. While those were nice conversation starters at cocktail parties, they meant very little when battle loomed.

Hours passed and everyone suffered the intense acceleration. At five hours from *Horizon* Haarkonan barked the order and the human fleet flipped around and began decelerating. It felt the same as acceleration since the *Time Raider* had simply rotated 180 degrees and then resumed firing its thrusters. The brief minutes of rotation felt like nirvana, quickly banished by the resumption of the relentless thrusters and six Gs of pressure. Haarkonan thought he could feel his entire skeleton squeezing up against his softer membranes and organs. The thrusts were also not completely smooth, meaning that passengers felt a constant shaking that was quite unnerving over long periods of time. Humans could not take much more than six times

Earth gravity, even in acceleration chairs, and even six G's was a frightful amount to endure for any sustained length of time.

Haarkonan hated waiting. It seemed that as human warfare advanced, so had the time spent waiting lengthened. War in space was basically extreme boredom punctuated by moments of sheer terror. Even on Earth, as weapon systems and strategies evolved from killing the guys on the other side of the field to destroying civilizations on the other side of the planet, generals had to increasingly give the "hurry up and wait" command. Militaries often deployed then sat and waited as diplomatic solutions sputtered toward failure. The extreme distances in space compounded the problem, with communication lags and seemingly interminable waiting.

Haarkonan was grateful that Plexar had allowed him to plan the defense, and that no politics had interfered with this war since the invasion of Earth. So far there had not been any diplomatic contact with the Narcoid whatsoever. Humanity had not been treated as a fellow sentient race but instead was being exterminated just as humans would hunt out an animal infestation. There was no dialogue, no understanding of where the conflict originated or where each races' goals came into opposition. There was just war and death.

It was easy to hate the Narcoid. While Haarkonan had killed humans before, it was never with relish but always with a sense of duty and even a kind of respect that the other side was just doing their duty. Haarkonan was startled to realize that he *wanted* to kill the Narcoid; all he felt for them was hatred. While his armada raced back to make a stand at *Horizon*, Haarkonan reflected on the fact that his hatred indicated a heart that thought of the Narcoid as animals rather than sentient beings as well. He knew that the best way to defeat an enemy was to understand that enemy, maybe even to empathize with them. If you could see through their eyes you could predict their moves…he had to learn to respect his enemy.

As another hour passed Haarkonan continued to worry about the upcoming battle. The Narcoid spacecraft were easily more nimble than the human fleet, and they had about a dozen large vessels that were so thickly armored that they were probably best avoided. He'd leave those to the *Horizon* vlaser batteries, which were far more powerful weapons that anything that had been installed on space craft. His own fleet was mostly medium and small ships that had formerly been used for scouting or mining, and he intended to deploy them like a net to push the Narcoid within range of *Horizon's* large defensive vlasers. The advantage he had was that the Narcoid seemed to always fight melee battles rather than using distance weapons, and there was a good chance that the new repulsar shields fitted to every human ship could deter a melee attack for some time. But not forever, he reflected wryly. Nothing could hold off the Narcoid forever.

"Sir, do you think they'll slow down?" asked Lt. LeMoray, clearly starting to ponder the same issues Haarkonan was contemplating.

"If I were them, I'd strafe the fleet and shoot past *Horizon*. But I don't think they'll do that. From what I can tell, they're very straightforward and like to attack whatever is first in their path. Still, if they don't start to decelerate soon, we'll need to assume a strafing and try to scatter as best we can."

The human fleet was now three hours from *Horizon*, and the Narcoid weren't far behind them, but still the alien armada had not reversed thrust. Haarkonan knew that the aliens could sustain more Gs than humans, but the computer indicated that in another ten minutes even the aliens' extreme deceleration abilities would fail to slow them down to combat speeds before reaching *Horizon*. Maybe his guess was wrong, and the Narcoid would indeed make a devastating pass on the human fleet? If they did that, they would devastate the human fleet, and then they could take their time attacking *Horizon*. He punched in another quick simulation and grunted as he saw that at current velocities the Narcoid would overrun his fleet just under an hour before they reached *Horizon*. The enemy might even have enough time to destroy *Horizon* before Haarkonan's small fleet could arrive at the battle.

He was about to give the order to scatter the fleet when the tracking screen abruptly updated and showed that the Narcoid were flipping around and going into full deceleration. The computer projected that most of the Narcoid would be at an optimal attack speed just as it arrived at *Horizon*. However, all of the medium craft were decelerating just a tad too slowly, and it looked like they wouldn't have enough time to slow down. They were on a collision course to slam into the dark asteroid!

Haarkonan started to feel elation at their navigation mistake, but then he realized what this really meant. The medium ships were probably assault craft, and they would ram into the planet and release ground troops. He had to take some of those out before they reached *Horizon*!

He quickly drafted orders and sent them to the rest of the fleet. The medium Narcoid ships would be the primary targets, as a ground assault on *Horizon* would probably result in the end of humanity no matter what happened during the space battle. *Horizon* had to hold on to its atmosphere and was simply too fragile to take much of a beating. Even a single enemy troop carrier could spell doom for *Horizon's* inhabitants.

The human fleet finished decelerating, and only had a few minutes before the leading edge of Narcoid craft began to appear on near-range sensors. The first wave was all smaller craft, most likely sent ahead as a screening force that would give cover to the larger craft behind them.

Haarkonan flicked on his fleet-wide transmitter. "OK people, this is it. You have your orders. This is a day that the human race will never forget. This is a day that calls for courage. This is the day when humanity scores its first victory against the lobsters!"

Haarkonan paused as cheers swept through the human ships, then resumed. "I know you're afraid. Everyone's afraid. You don't want to die. But there's more at stake here than our living or dying. The entire future of humanity rests in your hands, in your minds, in your brave hearts. We will not allow humanity to die. Channel your fear into resolve. Let's show the Narcoid that humans don't quit without a fight."

More cheers echoed down the halls of humanity's defenders, but the cheers subsided quickly this time. "One last thing. I know your orders explain it, but I want to reiterate it here. Those medium-sized ships are probably troop carriers, and they'll smash into *Horizon* and tunnel in to kill the people you love. We can't let that happen. Target them first, even at the cost of your own safety. Do *not* let them reach *Horizon*. After that, your job is to stay alive and skirmish. Our ship-board weapons will not be decisive in this conflict, but if we can herd the larger Narcoid ships toward *Horizon's* vlaser batteries, we have a chance. No matter what happens today, I want you to know I'm proud of you. It has been a pleasure serving with you."

"And also with you," came the traditional reply from dozens of ship commanders.

"God bless and protect you. Haarkonan out."

With *Horizon* looming darkly behind them, the human fleet formed up and began a slow acceleration toward the incoming Narcoid. Their battle formation was a pattern of tight-knit 3D triangles, designed by Haarkonan to maximize defensive fire that would flay Narcoid borders from sister ships.

The first Narcoid ships plunged forward straight at the leading human ships. Human vlaser beams streaked out, striking the small Narcoid vessels to great effect. The alien craft were sliced and holed, flung spinning to the side, or simply continued forward as dead husks. Haarkonan smiled as he saw one small Narcoid ship hit by four vlasers simultaneously. There was a brief pause and then the primordial heat disintegrated the alien into pieces so small that it looked like a large puff of dust more than an explosion.

Then the overwhelming numbers of the Narcoid armada arrived, and the alien craft began slamming into human ships. Bright blue and white fields flashed around the human ships as the repulsars heated from the impacts. The *Time Raider* shook as small Narcoid craft evaded the vlasers and rammed into shields, attempting to cling and eat through the hull. Warning claxons sounded as the repulsars labored to dissipate the intense energies formed by the striking Narcoid.

"Give sympathetic fire!" Haarkonan shouted as he saw the shields on one of the ships near him start to wink out. The *Time Raider* retrained its fire to scorch Narcoid craft off the human ships in its vicinity. As they were designed to do, the repulsars were not only slowing invaders from reaching ship hulls but were also keeping the alien craft at a small distance from those hulls. Even just that small of a distance greatly improved the ability of friendly ships to wipe away the aggressive Narcoid without also doing fratricidal damage. Human tactics had improved and sympathetic fire was greatly extending the survivability of the human fleet.

Even so, the first human ships began to explode, making brief incandescent balls of flame before their onboard oxygen reserves were depleted and they faded into the dull black of empty space. Life and love and complexity was turned instantly into death and darkness and oblivion.

Haarkonan didn't have much time to reflect on losses as the medium-sized Narcoid craft approached his position. "All fire stations, retrain on incoming medium vessels!" Haarkonan directed. Other human craft were also redirecting their fire, at the cost of allowing the attached Narcoid to keep burrowing through repulsar shields on fellow human ships.

Vlaser beams thrust forward from the majority of the human fleet, but this time it took more than a minor hit to dissolve the alien ships. Clearly the medium-sized craft were better armored, and only multiple vlasers or a sustained beam resulted in destruction. The medium-sized Narcoid craft were also all traveling faster, making targeting much more difficult.

Haarkonan swore as the computer reported multiple over-heating failures on his vlasers. Nothing *Horizon* scientists could invent had yet been able to properly cool the nuclear-charged laser beams. The recently miniaturized hand-held versions of the vlaser were worse, often overheating and burning users. Despite the danger of overheating, the vlaser was still the most effective instrument of death against the Narcoid, and Haarkonan was glad he at least had an effective weapon, even if it often burned itself out.

He heard a cheer and looked up to the general viz-screen. Explosions were everywhere, but a larger one was already dying out in front of him. Then he saw a flash of light and another explosion and realized why people had cheered. *Horizon* ground batteries had entered the fray, firing the largest and most powerful version of the vlaser. Lighting-like streams streaked out and crushed into Narcoid craft, disintegrating them with impunity. It was strange that such intense explosions made no sound, as they were swallowed up by the silence of space. Haarkonan was glad that even the heavily-armored medium alien craft could not withstand the force of a full-sized vlaser battery hit.

Destruction tore at space for many cubic kilometers as the human force tried desperately to arrest the Narcoid advance. Haarkonan felt pride in his fleet and their new weapons, but he had a nagging feeling that it would not be enough. There was a continuous tide of smaller Narcoid, and now the largest concentration of medium craft were assaulting his fleet. Behind them were the larger craft with an even denser swarm of the small alien ships. This was the critical moment. They had to prevent the medium craft from impacting *Horizon*.

The battle swirled around the *Time Raider*. Each ship was locked in its own struggle for survival, yet commanders knew the only chance of the fleet's survival was to free resources up to assist each other. The best officers died first, as they selflessly directed sympathetic fire rather than concentrating on their own defense. Narcoid swarmed in and attached themselves to human vessels, with sometimes as many as a half dozen striking the same target. Shields failed, hulls creaked and cracked, air was tainted by smoke, and human ships dissolved into charred remains that reflected bits of light as explosions continuously flared on the viz-screen.

The *Time Raider* continued to target medium-sized craft, but its vlasers were beginning to fail, and Haarkonan saw one medium alien craft scream past on a direct path toward the surface of *Horizon* near where the *Valkyrie* was being refitted for war on the landing pad. He was filled with an intense sense of shame as he realized it would be his fault that one got through. Just before impact a vlaser battery near the landing pad swatted the Narcoid craft into oblivion and Haarkonan let out a deep sigh of relief.

He quickly punched up *Horizon* command. Instead of Plexar he was greeted by a cool Roman face.

"Scipio—you saw that one?"

"We saw it, Admiral Haarkonan."

"I don't think we can hold them all. I don't know what you can do to protect yourself, but if I were you I'd assemble a team and have them head toward the landing pad area. That seems to be where they're concentrating."

"We're already on it. Valerius put me in charge here while he assembles an emergency defense team. We'll send them toward the landing pad. But I have to tell you, I don't think our ground forces will be effective. From the recordings I've seen, the Narcoid ate through Earth's ground defenses with impunity. We have to stop them in space."

"I know. I just wanted to warn you about where they seem to be aiming. It's certainly our weakest point, if they can evade the defensive vlasers."

Scipio was nodding agreement as he cut off the transmission with a curt "Haarkonan out." He then quickly returned his attention to the battle and saw *Horizon's* sure demise. A tightly packed bundle of about a dozen medium-sized craft were streaking toward *Horizon's* landing pad, surrounded by a swarm of smaller escorts. The human fleet couldn't get a good shot at the troop carriers because the smaller craft would intercept beams, paying with their own lives. The two leading medium-sized craft accelerated and peeled away from the main cluster, darting toward the nearest vlaser battery. The battery fired desperately, taking out the first troop carrier before the second one plowed into it and churned the whole area into black dust. Nothing could survive an impact at that speed, the force of which rivaled the meteor that had once struck the earth millions of years earlier and caused an ice age. Black rock and dust erupted from the surface, and when it settled nothing was left of the alien or the vlaser battery except a large crater.

Other troop carriers began accelerating and peeling off to wreck similar havoc on the rest of *Horizon's* massive vlaser batteries. This was not war but suicide. The Narcoid had no fear for their own survival, but fought with everything they had, to include giving their lives in order to eliminate the human race. Seven alien troop carriers remained in formation and were decelerating as they angled toward the first large crater, probably believing that a crater was as good a place as anywhere to begin burrowing into the rock toward the human settlements.

Haarkonan tried desperately to find a way to stop them. The *Time Raider* had too much speed and inertia to flip around, and he didn't have time to circle around so that his main weapons could be brought to bear. Even if he could get around, he didn't have enough firepower to knock out all of those troop carriers.

Other potential defenses also looked futile. While a few smaller human craft had flipped around and were directing fire at the cluster, they would take out one alien ship at the most. All of *Horizon's* defensive vlaser batteries in that area were now either obliterated or temporarily out as their crews tried to repair damage from near-hits and over-heating.

Haarkonan admired Valerius, but he knew that there was no way the few soldiers who remained on *Horizon* would be able to repel the full complements of seven troop carriers. Only a handful of mini-vlaser rifles had been developed, and other weapons would either be too weak to hurt the invaders or so strong that they risked cracking the rock and letting out the artificial atmosphere.

Haarkonan stared in horror as he saw the medium ships hurtling toward *Horizon's* black surface. They were fast approaching the crater near the landing pad area where the human habitation was closest to the surface. He felt intense despair and knew he had once again failed to stop the Narcoid threat.

Then Haarkonan saw a bright flash and a blur as something streaked up from the surface of *Horizon's* landing pad. The *Valkyrie* lunged forward and managed to get in front of the Narcoid cluster. Since the Narcoid ships were traveling too fast, they could not maneuver around the huge vessel and so started slamming into it, one after the other. The *Valkyrie* must have made an emergency take off and did not have time to turn on its repulsar, as Haarkonan didn't see the now-familiar glow of blue and white light. Instead, the *Valkyrie* was rocked back and forth and then erupted with explosions that tore it into four chunks that spun away from each other. Those chunks then quickly burst into incandescent flames, and the *Valkyrie* was no more.

Haarkonan wilted inside at the devastation. It wasn't just his beloved former ship. It was his friend. Lt. Col. Staci Minker had been given command of the *Valkyrie*, and most likely it was her sacrifice that had saved *Horizon* from certain destruction.

Pieces of the *Valkyrie* and the destroyed Narcoid craft slammed into the surface of *Horizon*, as did the last two enemy shuttles that had only suffered minor damage as they burst through the remains of the *Valkyrie* and struck the surface. Haarkonan lost sight of them as they burrowed deep into the rock and coughed out their invasion force, swarming toward the heart of the human settlement.

Haarkonan felt a lump in his throat and swallowed hard. Despite Minker's sacrifice, that was probably the end of *Horizon*. He couldn't fire accurately enough to hit the burrowing Narcoid, and even if he could he would risk damaging the human tunnels and habitations. The death and destruction those creatures would wreck on the civilian families deep inside *Horizon's* womb was unimaginable. His brief reverie was then harshly interrupted as more warning lights signaled the arrival of the large Narcoid ships.

The huge Narcoid battleships were even more powerful and better armored than Haarkonan had feared. He saw one of them take multiple vlaser beams and easily shrug them aside while closing in on a small human scout ship. The Narcoid craft slammed into the human ship in a collision that instantly smashed through the human ship's repulsar shield and hull, pounding it into dust and debris.

Haarkonan wished he had a few nuclear weapons, but the scant nuclear materials mined from asteroids had been invested in the vlasers which took far less fissile material for greater effect. He had pushed Plexar to allow teams to bring large quantities of Uranium and Plutonium in from Earth's past, but the scientist had rejected the idea outright. Plexar insisted that there never be nuclear material in temporal transition, since it could constitute deleterious temporal interference. The radioactive decay of nuclear material constituted a type of internal clock, thus any temporal transition could prove to be a paradox for the time stream.

Haarkonan knew his small fleet was doomed. His only hope had been to try to push the larger Narcoid craft into range of *Horizon's* large vlaser batteries, but most of those were now destroyed. *Time Raider's* main vlaser might prove of some effect, but it looked like most of the rest of the human fleet's weapons could hardly scratch the surface of the large Narcoid craft. He quickly ordered the fleet to try to evade the larger craft and concentrate on the smaller swarming Narcoid spaceships.

"Sir, the second smaller wave of Narcoid are now approaching *Horizon*," reported Lt. LeMoray with anxiety. "And sir, while they're still jamming us, we have some new data. We know the first ship in their formation is a Mothership. After that things get hazy. On their way in we kept seeing blips of medium-sized craft at the fringes of the jamming zone and what looked like a trail of destroyed ships. It's confusing, but I think there is a real possibility that they have assault shuttles following that Mothership."

Haarkonan grunted acknowledgment and tried desperately to discover how to wage a war against such superior forces. Soon he'd be surrounded and destroyed.

"So we're finished?" asked LeMoray.

"We might be, but that doesn't mean we're giving up," said Haarkonan gruffly. "I almost gave up once before, and then we discovered *Horizon*. It's true that we're pretty useless against these battleships, so let's disengage here and try to intercept that new group of invaders. Those medium-sized craft may be shuttles, and they're still our first priority. Please pass those orders on to the fleet."

"Yes, sir," said Lt. LeMoray, clearly glad to be doing something useful.

It wasn't a great plan, but at least it was a plan. Haarkonan reflected on one of his favorite historic quotes from a guy named General Patton. "In battle, a good plan now beats a great plan later," or something like that. As far as he could tell, no plan would save *Horizon,* and the fight for survival of the human race was as good as lost.

CHAPTER 12

Invasion on the *Horizon*

Explosions rocked the hallways, shaking dust from the ceiling and slowing down the emergency defense strike team. Valerius felt sweat trickle down his back as he shuffled on despite the lurching floors. Moving ground felt just like being on a ship, he thought with disdain. He could not imagine the magnitude of explosive force that must be impacting the surface of *Horizon* to create such turmoil this far from the surface.

The vlaser batteries had fought bravely, but most of them were now in ruins as the Narcoid ships had hurtled themselves en masse into the external guns. Valerius' defensive strike team of twelve men was now hurrying toward one such destroyed battery located near the landing pad that Scipio and Haarkonan thought was the epicenter of the Narcoid ground invasion. Warning lights lit in his visor informing him that Narcoid ground troops had landed and were penetrating the tunnels that led from the external vlaser battery toward the inhabited lower regions of *Horizon*.

Valerius worried about the possibility that his strike force would be simply sucked into the vacuum of space without getting a chance to engage the Narcoid. Surely the Narcoid also needed protection from space and would seal off their aggression point. Valerius tried to toss his fear aside, and swore at himself in his native Latin for dwelling on what could not be known or changed. He feared an ignoble death rather than the death of battle, and nothing could be worse than being swallowed by the silence of cold space. Well, maybe being swallowed by the silence of cold water, which was exactly what fate had originally intended for him, he thought with a wry smile. He simply had to trust the designers of *Horizon* who had installed multiple airlocks in order to prevent vital atmosphere from bleeding into space, and multiple indicators to ensure he didn't enter an area that was open to space.

Just as the thought crossed his mind the small group of defenders turned a corner and piled to a halt at a closed airlock door. This was where the well-lit and wide tunnels of the inhabited area transitioned to the thinner outer tunnels that spindled out to various locations on the surface. Valerius slipped through the few members of his strike team who had gotten ahead of him and looked at the instrument panel. He didn't know what all the atmospheric data meant, but the most important indicator light shone steady green, suggesting that the door was safe to open because behind it was a viable atmosphere. Valerius punched in his code and took a short breath before striking the enter button, as if one last breath would help should the door open into vacuum.

The door slid aside and warm air rushed by, seeking the narrower and less pressurized outer tunnels. One of his defenders pushed ahead and led the way through the airlock. Valerius recognized him as Wei-Phung, the feisty Chinaman he had brought back from ancient Korea. Wei-Phung was also their scout, as he had the most experience exploring these outer tunnels. Other members of the defensive strike team scrambled after the Chinaman, and Valerius followed his trusted primus pilus Otho through the doorway, leaving the rest of the twelve to squeeze through behind him.

The tunnels here were not just narrower, but were also more rough as the natural black rock was not lined with plastic like it had been in the inhabitable area. It still looked fairly smooth as it had been bored out with excellent robo-mining equipment. Valerius thought he detected a musty wet smell as he would have expected on Earth in dark tunnels, but then he realized it was just a combination of the colder temperature and his expectations. *Horizon* was far too cold this far from its molten core to have any significant degree of precipitation.

Otho, running in front of him, almost looked like a steam ship as his massive body churned out a cloud of cold breath. His body then plunged through the cloud, leaving behind a plume of disturbed mist. Even though they had been running for nearly 20 minutes, their pace never slackened. These were well-trained men in their prime, and Valerius felt honored to lead them. He had personally selected this team originally to be a kind of special forces for the retaking of Earth, and it just made sense for them to be the primary response force for a Narcoid breach.

The dark rock of the tunnel seemed to soak up the meager light emanating from the intermittent overhead light panels. It seemed like he was running from twilight into almost pitch black before he spotted the dawn ahead once again and repeated the process. Valerius slowed down and reached out as he saw Otho stumble in the darkness in front of him, but Otho quickly caught his own balance, and both men lumbered on into the darkness.

A screaming high-pitched metal-scraping noise slammed into the group like a wall, and the tunnel shook and filled with reverberations. The team jostled to a confused halt, and Valerius pushed his way to the front to assess the situation. Otho, with a bit more pushing, managed to follow Valerius to the front of the group.

The squealing was nearly unbearable, grating and whining as if steel were being shredded into confetti. Valerius turned to Wei-Phung, who had been leading the group. "Any ideas what that is?"

"None, sir," replied the Chinaman with a slight bow.

"How far are we from the surface?"

"At least a mile or two, sir."

"Probably the Narcoid widening the tunnel," shouted Sergeant Johnson from behind Valerius. Johnson was the only modern in the strike team. He was originally a technician on *Horizon* who had retrained to be a combatant. "I'd say that's the sound of grinding through this rock. Maybe our tunnels are too narrow for the bugs."

Valerius nodded his head to acknowledge the opinion from behind, and decided they really had no choice but to push on and see what was happening. "I'll take point," he said as he swung his weapon up to a more prepared two-handed position and started forward at a cautious pace.

Each squad member carried a prototype *mini-vlaser* rifle, which was thought to be up to the challenge of searing through even the Narcoid shell-armor. The weapons were known to have overheating issues, and no one liked to take an experimental weapon into battle, but they really didn't have a choice. Explosives strong enough to be effective against Narcoid shell-armor also risked cracking a hole to the surface and letting out the atmosphere. On the other hand, conventional bullets were ineffective against Narcoid armor.

After just a few minutes Valerius spotted in the distance the cause of the noise and tightened his grip on the mini-vlaser. The entire tunnel was now visibly shaking, and the men had put in ear plugs to try to dampen the screeching noise that chilled the blood and seemed to dig into the very soul of a man. Somehow the earplugs made everything surreal, and Valerius felt isolated and alone whereas just a few minutes earlier he had felt part of a team.

Warm air brushed by Valerius' face. Ahead was indeed a drill of sorts, grinding into the tunnel and probably doubling the tunnel's size. The drill point looked white-hot as it spiraled through the dark rock and gave off its own eerie alien light. It would be a difficult shot from this distance, but that drill had to be stopped.

"Otho, Wei-Phung, aim at the center of that drill and on my order we'll fire simultaneously!" Both men just gave him a confused look, clearly not being able to hear him over the scream from the tortured rock.

Valerius wondered if they even could concentrate their fire with all the shaking, but he still went forth with his plan, making gestures until he felt they knew what he wanted. He knelt and opened fire as the other two men shot over his shoulders. Lethal streams of iridescent violet, red and blue streamed out of the weapons toward the distant alien machine. At first nothing happened, and Valerius marveled at the strength of the drill material. Then the mini-vlaser streams all met at the center of the drill head and the screeching sound was replaced by a great *woosh* noise followed by a burst of light and a blast of heat. The huge drill imploded into itself as its center was seared into individual nuclei, and then a great roar erupted as the spinning outside of the drill fragmented and blew apart like a grenade. Pieces of the explosion bit into the walls creating a small cavern, while other parts blew down the tunnel toward the humans. Luckily the pieces fell short of their position and just littered the tunnel in front of them with white-hot debris.

The sound of the explosion echoed down the tunnel, being eventually replaced only by a soft sizzling sound from the charred remains of the drill. Valerius' ears were ringing as he removed his ear plugs, but he kept the presence of mind to hold his men back from rushing forward. That debris had to be cooled before they approached it, and he had no idea what lurked behind the drill. Brown smoke curled through the tunnel, oddly reminding Valerius of the peaceful morning mists that rolled through the valleys of Tuscany.

After a few minutes the sizzling subsided and the white fragments cooled to dull red embers. He could not be certain, but he thought he saw some motion through the smoke. He waved his men forward, exaggerating his efforts to avoid the charred drill's remains so that his men would get the idea and do likewise.

The drill had indeed been massive, and the hole left behind was roughly cone-shaped and the size of a parade ground. The widest mouth of the cone was where the drill head used to be and where Valerius was now entering the cavern. The cone then tapered down to the far side where the freshly-drilled tunnel was still at least twice as wide as the human tunnel had been. The alien tunnel was also perfectly circular, not enjoying the flat floor that lined finished human tunnels. Even though the overhead light panels had been burned into oblivion, the cavern flickered with ominous light from the debris that was strewn not just across its surface but clung to the walls and ceiling as well.

The human strike force instinctively fanned out into the cavern in fire team pairs, avoiding random flaming chunks of former drill and making evasive maneuvers around odd-shaped rock that somehow escaped the blast. Then Valerius spotted the Narcoid pouring in from the far side of the cavern.

At first it looked like the floor was moving where the tunnel met the cavern, and there seemed to be a brownish sheen on the ground almost like running muddy water. Then Valerius realized it was actually huge creatures propelling themselves on their bellies using multiple legs like insects, and the sheen was their armor reflecting the flickering, fading light. At first it was a trickle, then the far side of the tunnel erupted with a flood of Narcoid, swarming on top of each other as they rushed to destroy the small force of human defenders.

"Take cover and fire!" yelled Valerius, leaping behind a large chunk of debris and taking aim. Otho hustled to join him and started firing around the other side of their makeshift barrier. The rest of the team also scattered into positions and began pouring lethal mini-vlaser fire into the massing Narcoid menace.

It was difficult to get a good aim as the flickering, smoldering light seemed to refract in strange directions from the Narcoid mottled brown shell-armor. Human eyes were not used to tracking the brown on black, and Valerius had to fight against a primitive fear that attempted to make him go berserk with battle-lust or fear. While his body pumped him full of adrenaline to flee or fight with insane rage, his self-discipline and training held him in check. The best killer was not heated rage but cold precision—that was the Roman way. He swallowed, symbolically downing his liquid fear, and unleashed the hellacious heat of his vlaser.

Narcoid armor was good, but the mini-vlaser fire chewed into it and eventually blew huge holes into the invaders. The humans cheered as they blasted the first wave of Narcoid and saw that their new weapons were effective in actual combat. However, even with holes in them, the Narcoid advanced a dozen or more paces, in effect shielding the healthy Narcoid behind them.

Dozens of Narcoid were now motionless, but many more swarmed into the cave. A putrid smell like burnt lobster mixed with dung filled the cavern. Huge chunks of the invader splashed against the back wall that was now also being pocked from the mini-vlaser fire. Many more Narcoid were seared with holes, but the tide didn't seem to be ebbing.

Valerius forced himself to think like a leader and not just a warrior filled with blood-lust. He looked around at his men and approved of their locations. Most had done as he had and sheltered themselves behind rocks, often using the barriers to stabilize their rifles. Vlaser fire was pouring into the enemy, but then Valerius noticed two of his men had tossed their weapons onto the ground.

Valerius felt extreme anger at their cowardice and then realized that the two men had burned hands and their weapons were glowing slightly. The mini-vlasers were already overheating. One of the two was Johnson, who was slightly ahead of Valerius' position, and who now was pulling out a large-caliber pistol. Surely the man knew that would be ineffective?

Without the power of a mini-vlaser there was nothing those men could do to hurt the Narcoid. Valerius called out to try to tell them to fall back if their weapons malfunctioned, but even his battle-trained voice could not be understood over the din of battle. Looking back at the Narcoid mass, Valerius knew the humans were exacting a great price, but at this rate the enemy would soon overrun their positions. There was no reason to die if they could escape instead, and since they had destroyed the enemy's drill they could probably collapse this tunnel and be reasonably certain that the Narcoid could not advance any further toward the habitable regions of *Horizon* from this vector.

Valerius waved at his men, signaling them to fall back. Johnson and Wei-Phung were further ahead than his position, and therefore could not see his signal. The rest of his defensive force got the message and had begun a firing retreat, carefully backing toward where they had emerged into the cavern while still spewing primordial fire toward the advancing Narcoid.

Valerius planned to act as the rear guard to cover his men's retreat, but it was now obvious that Johnson and Wei-Phung still had not noticed the order. He had to get their attention! Valerius slipped from behind his barrier and raced forward. The advancing tide of Narcoid was getting close, and one slightly larger creature in front made an impossibly quick rush forward, leaping with the strength of all its legs.

Otho, who had been following Valerius forward, saw the danger and stopped to pour his fire into the creature, but it continued forward and crashed into Johnson's rock barrier, throwing Johnson and Wei-Phung violently to the ground. Johnson hit hard, but then quickly rolled and got up with his pistol trained at the enemy. He emptied his clip into the Narcoid's head region at point blank range, spraying thick globs of green puss on himself and the surrounding area. The creature nevertheless whipped forward an appendage like an arm that ended in two blades that were longer than *spatha* cavalry swords. Before Valerius could react the blades reached for Johnson's waist then snickered together like giant scissors, neatly slicing Johnson's torso from his hips.

Valerius now had his vlaser up and firing, as another appendage shot out toward Wei-Phung who was still struggling to get up. Wei-Phung had lost his weapon, but he saw the Narcoid arm coming for him and instead of diving away from the blades he instead leaped forward, doing a flying somersault through the blades. His back foot cleared the sharp edges just before they sliced together. Wei-Phung rolled and tried to run, but another arm came forward and caught his ankle while yet another arm whipped out a scythe-shaped claw aimed at Wei-Phung's neck.

Valerius stepped forward yelling a blood-curdling war cry and shooting his vlaser at the holding appendage. The fire ripped through the Narcoid arm, severing it, but the claw still didn't loosen its grip from Wei-Phung's ankle. Valerius then saw the razor-sharp edged arm whipping toward Wei-Phung and was helpless to stop it as his vlaser coughed and jammed from overheating.

Otho rushed forward, using his overheated vlaser like a club, barely parrying the Narcoid's death blow. The scythe-like arm struck the rifle with a resounding clanging noise, pounding Otho to the ground but deflecting the sharp edge enough that it didn't sink into Wei-Phung's back. Wei-Phung pulled himself forward, scrambling on all fours behind Valerius, with the Narcoid claw still clinging to his ankle. It was clear by the way the Chinaman shuffled on all fours that the ankle was broken, and possibly completely shattered.

The other Narcoid were now closing in, but the closest one was still the real threat. Valerius tried once again to shoot his vlaser but it just let out a slight coughing noise as if it were trying to fire but could not. Otho was in real trouble now, as the nearest Narcoid changed targets from Wei-Phung to the much larger man. The scythe-like arm didn't bother to raise itself much, but simply shot out at full speed from its position on the ground, skimming about 30 cm above the tunnel floor.

Otho saw it coming and tried to thrust himself over the blade, but was not quick enough. He pushed hard against the ground, trying to elevate his body above the blade, but didn't get his left arm off the ground in time. While his torso and most of his body leapt over the blade, his left arm was still retracting when the blade sliced completely through it. It was a clean cut, straight thorough Otho's left bicep, and his body seemed to pause for a moment in the air before coming crashing down on top of his freshly-severed arm.

Valerius rushed mindlessly forward, not knowing how he could help but refusing to leave his long-time friend. He held down the vlaser's trigger in a vice-like grip, but nothing happened. Then he spotted Wei-Phung's rifle that had been thrown back in his direction. In a single motion he sprang forward, dropping his weapon and scooping up the Chinaman's vlaser. As he rolled forward and rose to his knee beside his friend he let out a silent prayer that the weapon would still work before squeezing the trigger, firing into the embattled Narcoid's center of mass at point blank range. Surprisingly, a streak of lightning violence erupted from the rifle's muzzle, obliterating the creature, and spraying a wash of black and green fluids everywhere.

Otho was staggering up now, his right hand clutching at the stump-remains of his left arm. Even Otho's huge hand could not adequately staunch the spurting life blood. Clearly the big man was fighting shock and pain and seemed disoriented. Valerius pushed him back toward the tunnel and screamed for someone to come help. The next full wave of Narcoid were now about 50 meters away, and Valerius tried to spray them with fire as he quickly retreated toward the mouth of the tunnel and pushed Otho ahead of him.

Luckily, his men had not simply fled, but were waiting for him at the entrance to the tunnel. Three men were still firing their vlasers while the others clearly had held on to their weapons a bit longer than they should have and so suffered burnt hands and forearms.

Despite the wounded ankle, Wei-Phung had not abandoned his commander either and had heard Valerius' call. He came scrambling forward again, grabbed Otho and pulled him out of the cavernous area and a little way into the tunnel. There the men with burnt hands started applying a spray-on battle-triage plastic bandage to Otho's arm stump. The spray quickly expanded and hardened, completely covering the wound. Otho was then injected with a stimulant that provided nutrients and helped clear his mind from the shock.

Valerius sprayed fire as he stumbled backwards, retreating into the tunnel mouth. "Run!" he cried over his shoulder as he kept firing from the tunnel mouth. His firing was not without effect, as another Narcoid crashed to the floor, crumpled, then was swarmed over by its fellow creatures.

Valerius felt his weapon starting to get hot. The leading Narcoid had just passed the place where Johnson's divided body lay, and Valerius realized that they would all be dead and *Horizon* lost if he didn't figure out a way to blow down the tunnel. He decided this was where he had to take a stand to at least buy his men some time as they began scrambling away from the carnage.

As the other men fled, Otho actually stumbled forward and yelled, "Come on sir!"

"Go!" Valerius shouted over his shoulder. "That's an order!" He vaguely was aware of Otho turning back down the tunnels before he turned his full attention back to the flood of Narcoid and silently prayed to whatever god could hear him. He would not run—his men needed time to get ahead of these demonic creatures. He was going to face death, only this time it wasn't a game. He raised his vlaser and kept spraying the pursuing enemy with nuclear-charged fire. The creature that had been in closest pursuit must have already been wounded, as it quickly collapsed and slid forward to a screeching halt only five meters from Valerius.

He wanted to scream a final challenge of rage and defiance as his rifle spewed forth death, but defiance wasn't really what he felt. What he felt was fear. His soul seemed to be gasping for life, trying to think of anything that could stop his inevitable demise. His own squeamish emotions humbled him. He had expected to be beyond fear, to be caught up in the moment of battle and not have a care for his own personal wellbeing. He had faced death on a battlefield before and had not experienced this sense of loss and guilt. As he felt the vlaser start to burn his hands, time seemed to stand still while his mind raced through all that he had left undone. He would never see his daughter again. Never give her away in marriage. Never enjoy grandchildren. He would not see the sunrise gleaming off the white marble of the Roman forum, and he would never again be able to stand in the senate courtyard and gaze out at the eternal city of seven hills. And he would never again see Rachel.

There was one Narcoid closing in on his position, and slightly behind it was the full wave of Narcoid he knew he would have no chance of holding back. He shifted his stance and aimed at the legs of the foremost creature, hoping to disable it since he knew it was too close to kill in time. The vlaser beam could chew through their armor, but the Narcoid seemed to be able to fight on for some time even after they sustained mortal damage.

Valerius was shocked at the ferocity of this battle. No human force would have been able to surge forward into this kind of carnage without slowing down. These creatures didn't care about their own deaths, and seemed unconcerned to use distance weapons, instead preferring to simply swarm forward in a melee. You could kill dozens of them, but once they were on you your only hope was for someone else to shoot them off. Too bad his Roman short sword would prove ineffective against the alien carapace. As he saw his doom looming, he realized that what he really needed was a close combat weapon, maybe some kind of sword with the edge and power of a vlaser. Then an even better thought struck him.

His own weapon was now burning and blistering his hands, making him grimace as he held onto it despite the pain. In the distance he saw Johnson's discarded vlaser, and on a whim he stopped firing at the looming Narcoid that was now only three meters away and instead gave a final blast in the direction of the discarded vlaser. His shot could only have taken a fraction of a second as the Narcoid then filled his view and took his beam full in its torso, but somehow that had been enough.

A huge explosion rocked the tunnels as Johnson's overheated vlaser, hit by Valerius' fire, exploded like a miniature nuclear bomb. The Narcoid in front of Valerius, propelled forward by the explosion, rammed into him and tossed him back like flotsam. Valerius flew backward through the air still holding down the trigger and so spraying the ceiling with vlaser fire. He struck the ground and his world went black as the cavern and tunnel collapsed and sealed the Narcoid and himself in eternal darkness.

CHAPTER 13

The Future has Come to Past

"We have confirmation, sir," said Lt. LeMoray with a grimace. Haarkonan's small defense force had been sniping at smaller Narcoid vessels and trying to avoid the large ones as they raced around *Horizon* to intercept the smaller Narcoid fleet that was coming from the direction of Alpha Centauri. With the human fleet in retreat, two of the Narcoid large ships had engaged *Horizon's* three remaining ground-based vlaser batteries, and so far there was no clear winner.

At first Haarkonan ignored LeMoray as he watched the skirmish with fascination. Each time a large Narcoid craft surged forward to crush a battery all three batteries would concentrate their fire, knocking the Narcoid vessel off course, though not by enough to prevent debris from scoring damage on a battery. The Narcoid vessel would slam into *Horizon*, shudder, then launch back into space for another run. It seemed like both sides were taking a pounding, with the Narcoid vessels getting the worst of it, but Haarkonan knew the tide would turn when the rest of the large Narcoid ships came into range.

He wrestled his attention away from the conflict to focus on the new information. "Confirmation of what?" Haarkonan growled harshly, then softened as he realized LeMoray was not trying to be obtuse but had just been waiting for his commander's full attention.

"The second wave of Narcoid approaching from Alpha Centauri has medium-sized craft that may be assault shuttles. The *Starfire* succeeded in scouting out the new force, and her commander Lieutenant Frida Beroni sent us more intel I'm just now absorbing." LeMoray paused as data flowed into his brain directly from his DataPort at the base of his skull. Information could be assimilated much faster when it was directly interfaced with the brain. "More bad news, sir," he reported a few seconds later.

"Go on. It's not like I was expecting anything to be rosy."

"The second squadron is actually a Mothership followed by medium-sized craft and one larger-sized craft that could be classified as a small battleship or possibly an oversized assault shuttle. For some reason we've not detected any small Narcoid ships as part of this second fleet, even though lidar spotted some a few hours ago."

"Maybe we just can't see them through the Mothership's jamming? asked Haarkonan.

"Could be, sir. We also know that the medium ships started from the Kuiper Belt a bit behind the Mothership, but then they blinked in and out of detection and somehow gained on the Mothership. Now they're clustered into a fairly tight formation and share the same approach vector to *Horizon*. *Starfire's* data suggests we'll make it in time to intercept."

Haarkonan smiled but held back actual laughter. Intercept and do what? His fleet couldn't hurt the large Narcoid craft, and would have no chance against a Mothership. Those ships had crushed entire cities on Earth, and would most likely be set to do the same thing here.

Haarkonan scanned what remained of his fleet. Less than 20 craft were now under his command, and most of them were smaller sizes without vlasers that posed little danger to the Narcoid. *Horizon's* defenses included only two operational batteries, with a third now only able to offer occasional fire. The *Time Raider* itself was a mess, with most of its vlasers overheated and various systems damaged.

The only good news was that his repulsar shields were still operating at full capacity.

As the *Time Raider* streaked around *Horizon*, it simultaneously increased its distance from the planetoid so as to meet the Mothership as far out as possible. As the planet slowly stopped blocking their view, the Mothership appeared on the viz-screen.

It was gigantic. Haarkonan knew they were large, but when last he had encountered the behemoths they were just blips on a screen that he had obliterated with Earth's last remaining ancient nuclear missiles. He had never seen them in a viz-screen like this, looming large. The Mothership was a mix of mottled browns and was not smooth like a human craft but instead had holes and appendages and swirled sinew and cavities everywhere. It looked menacing and deadly, and inspired primal emotions of rage and terror on the command deck.

Haarkonan remembered feeling this kind of fear that provoked mindless aggression when as a boy he had leaped a stream and landed on a rattlesnake. He vaguely wished he could stomp this thing into the dust as he had the snake. The Mothership was unearthly, eerie in a way no Earth-born creation could be, and it was heading to destroy the last vestiges of humanity.

Warning lights flashed into his sight as his DataPort was set to feed data directly to his brain. It was like having a heads-up display on your eyeball rather than on a screen, and while it took some practice to use comfortably, it was by far the best way to get a full picture during battle. Now red lights showed medium-sized craft directly behind the Mothership. Haarkonan speculated that maybe Dr. Plexar was right. Maybe the Narcoid were smart enough to know what temporal transition technology was. It certainly looked like the Narcoid were not going to just mindlessly destroy *Horizon*, but that instead they wanted to raid the place for its technology.

But something was wrong about the medium-sized ships. While they were hidden from direct view by the Mothership, even the scant information on the screen that designated them as blips seemed erroneous. Haarkonan tried to figure out what it was, and called up all available data. There were about 20 of them racing behind the

Mothership in a battle formation wedge, which was unusual for Narcoid but reasonable given their purpose. Then it struck him. The center of the wedge had a larger craft, but all of the rest of the medium ships massed nearly the exact same. Unlike anything they'd previously observed from the Narcoid, the masses of these ships suggested mass production.

Haarkonan didn't have time to consider the consequences of his observation, as he began directing all human fire on the Mothership, concentrating it at one point. Not surprisingly, the Mothership's armor shrugged off even the concentrated vlaser fire and kept barreling toward *Horizon*. The impact of that thing alone would surely damage *Horizon* beyond repair.

Suddenly vlaser fire erupted not from his fleet, but from the medium-sized craft trailing the Mothership. The characteristic full-spectrum light that faded to violet leapt out with searing force. Stranger still, it was not aimed at the human fleet, but at the Mothership. The heat of a dozen suns packed into a few square meters was more than even the huge Narcoid ship could take. The globe-shaped Mothership burst open, its armor ripping like shredded paper before it exploded into a ball of flashing incandescent flame that hurtled chunks of metal and debris in every direction. The blinding fireball grew, then disintegrated into a puff of flaming powder that spewed throughout space. White-hot glowing remains of the Narcoid ship struck *Horizon's* surface, and human repulsars on multiple ships strained to protect people from the burning wreckage.

Lt. LeMoray whooped with joy. Haarkonan and the rest of the command staff aboard the *Time Raider* just stared in disbelief as their eyes readjusted after the blinding explosion. Who were these newcomers, how did they have vlasers, and why did they destroy the Mothership?

Lt. LeMoray broke the stunned reverie. "Incoming message, sir. It's from those medium-sized craft. Patching visual through the main screen—I think you'll want to see this."

The main viz-screen filled with a face that looked vaguely familiar. It was a man in his early thirties with blond hair and sky-blue eyes, dressed in a suit that closely resembled the UE Space navy suit Haarkonan wore.

"Admiral Haarkonan, sir. This is Captain Clint Sorenson, commander of the *Ark of Time* and part of the Alpha Centauri defense force. President Hosheema Cua sends his greetings. We request permission to join your command and engage the rest of the Narcoid fleet."

Haarkonan was stunned. *Ark of Time*? Surely he meant *Ark of Time II*? And Hosheema Cua was the first scientist murdered. Haarkonan had personally spent hundreds of hours trying to find the man's killer. How could he now be president of Alpha Centauri? And why had Alpha Centauri been out of contact for decades if they actually had a thriving colony?

"You're who?" was all Haarkonan managed to get out.

"I'm Captain Sorenson, sir. Son of Dr. Sorenson, with whom you may be acquainted, though you knew him a long time ago. It's a long story. In brief, the *Ark of Time* was not destroyed on its technology-testing mission, but instead launched a decoy detonation and then traveled 40 years into the past so that it had time to reach Alpha Centauri and return here to aid you. When it arrived at Alpha Centauri we cut off all contact with Earth so as to prevent any temporal paradoxes. Sir, we've been preparing for this battle for more than 20 years. Our vlasers are rather advanced compared to yours, and we're capable of engaging those large Narcoid battleships. Permission to engage, sir?"

"Granted," Haarkonan said through an irrepressible smile. "Let's hunt some lobsters!"

As the revitalized human space force returned to reengaged the original Narcoid armada, Haarkonan received a constant stream of information from Capt. Sorenson on the specifications of the Alpha Centauri spacecraft so that he could better deploy them in battle. It seemed that Haarkonan's battered fleet had not merely doubled, but that now it included firepower that could make a difference. His strategic mind quickly plotted the best use of the new assets and sent orders to the fleet.

Plexar's face came up on his DataPort screen projected directly into his mind. It was a strange sensation that seemed to almost redefine the term "mind's eye." The scientist looked pale and frail.

"Admiral, what's happening out there? Did you just destroy a Mothership? I was about to terminate *Horizon*. Now it looks like you're in formation…with enemy craft?"

"They're not enemies. And yes, we destroyed a Mother! Our formation now includes forces from Alpha Centauri, many of whom appear to be descendants of the men and women who we thought perished in the *Ark of Time* disaster."

"What?" Plexar interrupted aghast.

"Look, I don't have time to discuss this right now. You have to hold on a little longer, because the cavalry's on its way!"

"But the paradoxes!" exclaimed the scientist looking even more distraught. "The consequences of paradox—"

"From what I can tell, you don't need to fear paradoxes. These guys are descended from the scientists who were aboard the *Ark of Time*, which didn't explode but instead took a tour of Alpha Centauri before returning to assist us. I don't know the details, but it sounds to me like someone hatched a very careful plan that prevented a doomsday paradox scenario. So just hang on—we're on our way. We can get back to this discussion after we take care of those large Narcoid craft. Haarkonan out."

Haarkonan hated being abrupt with Plexar, but he had a battle to fight. As they approached *Horizon's* battered landing area, Haarkonan's scanner reported that one of the large Narcoid craft he had fled from originally had been destroyed, but there were no longer any functional ground batteries.

Then his heart sunk as he realized his force would be too late. While he would make it back in time to engage the tail end of the Narcoid invasion force that was just now arriving to the battle and included multiple large Narcoid craft, he could not stop the one Narcoid vessel that had survived the battle with the ground batteries.

That enemy craft looked dented and torn, with large chunks of armor missing or hanging off its superstructure, but it nevertheless succeeded in launching itself from the wreckage of the final defensive battery. Its acceleration was erratic as it reached apogee and fired reverse thrusters to propel it in a devastating lunge toward *Horizon's* landing area. Haarkonan knew the impact would cripple the station's ability to receive and repair the now-battered human fleet, and he feared that it would also allow the Narcoid to inject more ground troops that would quickly overcome the defensive team and invade *Horizon's* vulnerable underground habitat.

He wanted to fire on the large vessel, but the Narcoid craft was on the far side of the landing pad and so still sheltered by the planetoid's curve from the human fleet's line of sight. The enemy craft arced toward the landing pad, intent on delivering one last killing blow. Haarkonan's computer counted down the seconds until impact, and all he could do was stare as the Narcoid vessel finished its deadly mission.

Then, less than three seconds before impact, a powerful laser streamed from Plexar's killer satellite. Though the orbital laser could not be moved from its aim at the vulnerable elevator shaft, the shot had been perfectly timed to hit the Narcoid vessel as it crossed its line of fire.

The laser struck off-center and was not enough to destroy the wounded Narcoid craft, but it did succeed in knocking the vessel off course. The large enemy battleship crashed into *Horizon's* surface only a few miles away from the landing pad, but this time it didn't have the ability to rise again.

Haarkonan called up Plexar and gave him a huge grin. "Nice shooting!" he yelled, even as the rest of the command area recovered from the shock and began to cheer. "I thought you were saving that blast to take out *Horizon?*"

"I was," responded Plexar with an uncharacteristically broad smile on his face. "But I found a better use for the satellite. Now aren't you glad we didn't remove it from orbit?"

"Absolutely!" Haarkonan said with conviction as the *Time Raider* came into range of the downed alien attacker. "You timed that perfectly. We'll finish it off." He switched away from Plexar and looked over at his weapons officer. "Fire whatever we have left at that downed craft."

"Yes, sir. We have two vlasers back online. Firing..." said the officer. The two streams of light lanced out at the damaged and downed alien ship which immediately exploded on the planetoid's surface.

"The rest of the Narcoid fleet is now entering weapons range," reported Lt. LeMoray in a professional objective tone of voice. "Alpha Centauri craft are in position and awaiting your orders."

Haarkonan flicked open an all-fleet channel that included the Alpha Centauri force. "I want you all to know you've done well, but we must finish well to be successful. Don't let those lobsters reach *Horizon*, but don't throw away your lives needlessly either. We now have the firepower of the Alpha Centauri fleet. If you don't have operative vlasers you can't play an aggressive role, so your job is to decoy the enemy and bring them within range of the Alpha Centauri ships which will hold the center. God speed, and engage at will. Haarkonan out."

Most of *Horizon's* fleet scurried to the fringes of the battle, as the Alpha Centauri fleet waited in the direct path between the final wave of the Narcoid and *Horizon*. The *Time Raider* waited with the Alpha Centauri fleet, as its damage control had fixed a few more vlaser cannons and its repulsar field was operating at nearly full capacity. The Narcoid looked dangerous as they aggressively decelerated and entered battle-capable speeds.

The first screen of small Narcoid craft raced in at ferocious velocities, seeming to be unconcerned for their own wellbeing and completely without any distinctive formation. The Alpha Centauri fleet was formed up in a tight three-dimensional interlocking triangles formation and waited until the first Narcoid were well within range before unleashing their first salvo of lightning destruction. Multiple vlaser cannons erupted with fire as more than 20 ships sent a wall of destruction into the incoming Narcoid craft. All human fire solutions were networked so that not more than two vlasers hit any single enemy craft. None of the initial wave of small Narcoid craft survived.

Dozens of fireballs lit up the screen as the first Narcoid ships were hammered.

Then the rest of the Narcoid armada arrived, and the human ships were jolted as the sheer number of enemy craft ensured Narcoid aggressors evaded destruction and crashed into the human ships. Haarkonan quickly rewrote the protocols that prevented multiple hits on enemy targets as he noted that the larger Narcoid craft were armored well enough to survive more than just two hits. One large Narcoid craft streaked in below the *Time Raider* and sustained multiple hits before smashing into an Alpha Centauri defender in one of the *Time Raider's* defensive triangles. The Alpha Centauri ship rocked, its repulsar flared then died, and the whole ship disappeared in a ball of fire that quickly turned into an expanding cloud of burning debris and dust.

The explosion hurled multiple fragments of wreckage at the *Time Raider*, and Haarkonan's own repulsar flared a bluish tinge as it absorbed and repulsed the energy and debris. At least five human ships in the vicinity quickly fired upon the large Narcoid ship in a vengeful rage. The alien vessel seemed to shiver, then careened toward another human ship before bursting into flames and wreckage.

The battle was now well underway, with many human ships being rammed by Narcoid attackers. Some human ships erupted in flames immediately, but most remained intact as their repulsar fields screamed into action attempting to prevent hull penetration. The defensive triangle formation was proving effective again, with many human ships scouring enemy vessels from friendly craft in their triangles.

It was soon clear that the Narcoid could not prevail. The human firepower was too great, and the Narcoid fleet was at a huge disadvantage since it lacked distance weapons and had to accept extreme losses before it could engage the human ships. The smaller Narcoid vessels were especially vulnerable, as they could not sustain a single burst of vlaser fire from the improved Alpha Centauri ships. Furthermore, when they rammed a human ship, it took them time to crush through the repulsar and hull armor, and they often would be shot off by a friendly human craft before they could finish their mission of destruction.

"Concentrate on the large craft," ordered Haarkonan confidently over the all-channel. "Only target small craft that are already attached to friendly vessels. If we take out those large battleships we'll secure *Horizon's* future. Then we can mop up the smaller vessels."

Human vlasers lanced out of most of the Alpha Centauri fleet, tracking the remaining half dozen large craft and inflicting severe damage. The Narcoid craft were capable of sustaining multiple hits but started to succumb to the overwhelming human firepower. One or two large craft still reached their targets and destroyed human ships, but even they were quickly incinerated as the human fleet concentrated its fire.

With the larger craft out of the way, the remaining human fleet made short work of the smaller Narcoid craft. As the fleet started its return flight to *Horizon*, Haarkonan simply shook his head in amazement, realizing that what he had thought to be certain defeat had just turned into the first human victory over the Narcoid. Humanity would survive, at least a little longer. And with any luck, it might even be granted the opportunity to retake its mother world.

CHAPTER 14

The End of the Beginning

Haarkonan reached out and smacked his nightstand, silencing his alarm. He had no idea how long it had been bleating before he finally awoke by realizing the noise was a wakeup call and not the final claxons screaming a death dirge as he had been dreaming. He was drenched in sweat and his pulse was racing. He breathed deeply to let the fear subside, then smiled. He was not going to die, and he had not let down the human race. There was now real hope on the *Horizon*.

He swung his feet over the side of his bed and paused before hoisting his large frame up, then shuffled toward the shower. After the battle he had spent another seven hours getting damage reports, ordering repairs, securing billeting for the Alpha Centauri visitors, and visiting the wounded.

There were many wounded. He had held the hands of old friends and strangers alike as they succumbed to their wounds before doctors could staunch the blood or clone and install vital organs that would have saved their lives. While comforting the dying, he had told them of their victory and in return heard many tales of war and heroism. There were far too many heroes who would not be with the living to celebrate their victory. Over 75% of his initial fleet didn't even get a chance to return to *Horizon*, and the ships that were able to limp home hauled back so many wounded that *Horizon's* medical staff had been overwhelmed. Hundreds of brave souls were still being treated in sickbay when Haarkonan had finally reached the point of exhaustion and been forced to bed.

As he showered and quickly dressed, Haarkonan thought of the steep price the battle had exacted. It had been Lt. Col. Staci Minker who had proven the power of the human spirit by making the emergency launch and piloting the *Valkyrie* into the large Narcoid vessel that had nearly destroyed *Horizon*. She had been a friend for nearly a decade and was a good officer and a great person. He would never get a chance to thank her for her sacrifice.

Then there was Lt. Col. Kip Johnson, his former tactical officer, whose charred body he had visited the previous evening. Kip had suffered severe burns to a third of his body, yet he had somehow managed to concentrate long enough to pilot his ship home and even safely land it before passing out from the pain. The doctors had sounded skeptical about saving his life, but Haarkonan knew they were always a bit pessimistic with their estimates so as not to create false hope. Haarkonan wanted to believe that his friend would recover.

Feeling a bit more refreshed from the shower, he pushed the button that turned the space into a full-bodied blow dryer and a few seconds later exited the shower and began to dress for the day's ceremonial events. His dress blacks were kept crisp, tailor-made for his large frame, and boasting silver piping and old-style bullion fringe epaulettes. Haarkonan wasn't really into fancy uniforms and ceremonies, but he knew this was also part of the job, and the human race deserved a moment of celebration and respite before they buckled down and began the arduous task of retaking Earth. With the help of their new technologies and the spaceship support from the Alpha Centauri fleet, they were now just weeks away from being able to launch the war to liberate their home planet.

He flicked on his DataPort and noticed he still had time to make one more visit to the medical bay before the ceremony. He had intentionally curtailed his much-needed sleep so that he had time to check up on Kip and a few others who were not expected to survive.

Haarkonan moved swiftly through the corridors, appreciating them more than ever. Somehow life was more joyous after surviving imminent death, and even the dull blue lit hallways radiated a new energy after the space victory. He shortened his stride as he entered the medical bay and passed into the long rooms that housed the patients in critical care. Kip was still there, which at least meant he was alive. Haarkonan went over and took his friend's hand, said a brief prayer under his breath, and then pressed on to other beds when he was sure his friend was not about to come out of his coma.

The room smelled like death despite the efficient air recycling system. A faintly ferruginous smell of fresh blood mixed with whiffs of urine and fecal matter was surrounded by a sickly sweet smell of airborne antiseptic. A few people moaned or whimpered, but most were sleeping. One patient near Kip was awake and talking in quiet tones with a chaplain. Glancing around, Haarkonan recognized a large man who was stooping over a patient in the far corner of the room. The patient seemed to be awake, but was covered in so many bandages that he looked more like a mummy than a man.

Haarkonan smiled as he hurried over to the far corner. The mountain-sized man grinned. "Haarkonan! How nice of you to visit, sir!" greeted Otho with a broad smile.

Haarkonan shook his hand. "Good to see you too. How is he?"

"Oh him? He'll live. I'm the one who lost an arm." Otho held up his left arm with obvious pride. "They gave me this nice shiny machine arm to replace it. I think this one works even better."

Haarkonan smiled at the big man and then looked back at Valerius. "So he's OK?"

"Ah yah, he may be small, but he's tough enough. Sadly, he probably won't learn anything from firing weapons in enclosed areas making rocks rain on him in an avalanche and nearly destroying our fragile planetoid. That one's proof that you don't have to be smart to survive. You just have to be lucky."

"That'll do, Otho," said Valerius from the bed a bit hoarsely with a wan smile. "I might be in bed, but I'm still your commanding officer. And the only luck I needed was a friend like you to come back and pull me out of the rubble. That's another one I owe you."

"We all pitched in, sir. Even the wee Chinaman pulled out rocks to uncover your hide. And you were lucky. That Narcoid body shielded you from the blast and protected you from the avalanche."

Haarkonan reached the bedside and grasped Valerius' upper arm in the traditional Roman style greeting, but when Valerius didn't return the grasp he realized the arm was probably broken and that he was causing pain so he quickly released it. "You live, my friend! I was so concerned yesterday about my fleet that I didn't have time to seek you out."

"Aye, he lives," interjected Otho. "But not by much. The fool decided to create a miniature nuclear explosion in the tunnels to seal them off from the Narcoid. That was a close one. We were only seconds away from having the buggers overrun the place."

"It was close," agreed Valerius. "But our defensive strike team performed admirably, as your fleet must have done, 'else we'd not still be here."

Valerius tried to lean forward, gave up on the attempt, and slumped back in bed with a small sigh before continuing. "What happened out there? My friend here visits me before getting any information, so we're both in the dark. How did you convince that Narcoid invasion fleet to hold its sting?"

"We defeated them," Haarkonan bragged with some satisfaction. "Complete victory. We sent every last one of them to Hell, or wherever aliens go when they die. But we had a little help."

"Help?" asked Valerius.

"A lot of help. It turns out that Entwater and some other scientists decided to take a paradox-risking trip to the past. The *Ark of Time* didn't explode but instead went back in time 40 years, traveled to Alpha Centauri, and joined humanity there to prepare to defend our present day *Horizon*. They covered their move with a time-delayed explosive and tampered with the computers that recorded it all. Alpha Centauri didn't cut contact with us because it was wiped out by the Narcoid but because they had to go silent so as to prevent any temporal paradoxes."

"What about the murders?" asked Valerius.

"The murders were not murders at all. Dr. Entwater planned the mission and realized that some of the best scientists needed to be on the *Ark of Time*, but he didn't know exactly who they were. He therefore watched the research and when scientists proved themselves capable he replaced them with a cloned dead body and arranged for them to go back in time to board the *Ark of Time*."

"But Dr. Cua could have been on the second flight and didn't need to be cloned," said Valerius with a puzzled expression.

"I asked about that," said Haarkonan. "Dr. Entwater said that Dr. Cua actually got off the ship and missed the second takeoff, so he had to transport him back just a few minutes and use the clone due to the room occupancy sensors. It was that initial required time jump that gave Entwater the idea to transport all the best scientists back to board *The Ark of Time*.

"But how?" asked Otho, relieving Valerius of the strain of asking the obvious question. "If the *Ark of Time* was gone, how did Dr. Entwater make time transitions?"

"I have to give it to the weasel—that took real genius. He stole the original time transportation device from the museum, then modified it with our present day knowledge and hid it in some outer tunnels. I had just discovered its energy signatures before the Narcoid arrived, but then I was busy with our defensive plan. Evidently Entwater has one of the highest temporal transition potentials, and somehow he was able to take people back despite the presence of so many other people on *Horizon*. I guess it was possible because rather than hauling a ship load of people he just did temporal transitions with single individuals."

"That also explains why the bodies were no help at all in solving the murders," said Otho contemplatively. "They weren't wiped clean, they were made clean. And since Entwater was the primary operator of the clone machine, he could easily make clones without anyone knowing something was amiss."

"Indeed. I would be upset at all the wasted time and frustration chasing a non-existent murderer, but I must admit that in the end their plan worked. Without the Alpha Centauri fleet and their weapons that were decades ahead of us, we would never have been able to defend *Horizon*."

"So what's next?" asked Valerius weakly.

"'Next' is you getting some sleep. Hasn't anyone told you? You look terrible. 'Next' for me is Plexar's little celebration ceremony. 'Next' for all of us? I believe we're very close to switching into the second phase of this war and contesting the Narcoid's grasp on our planet."

"Valerius?"

Haarkonan turned around to see Rachel jogging toward the bed. She didn't even seem to see Haarkonan or Otho, but went straight to Valerius and hugged him, eliciting a wince from the Roman that was partially veiled by a look of joy.

"You're OK?" she asked with clear concern in her voice. "You will recover?"

"I'll make it. They'll be transferring me out of critical condition today. I was lucky that Otho got me here before the fleet returned and swamped our resources. It took some doing, but I have a few new organs and many bones mending."

"Come on, Otho," Haarkonan said with a smile. "Let's leave these two alone. We've a victory celebration ceremony to attend."

***

The large hanger bay was packed with people facing a make-shift central stage that nuzzled up against the main door into the *Ark of Time*. Hundreds of chairs full of smiling people fanned out from the platform, and behind them thousands of people stood to watch the victory ceremony. Many wore uniforms, many more wore civilian attire, and scattered throughout could be seen lab coats, utility coveralls, and even some time-specific traditional clothing. It was indeed a motley crew, thought Haarkonan, but they had been able to keep it together and repel the Narcoid fleet.

Haarkonan had a seat on the stage near the *Ark of Time* and watched as Dr. Plexar stood up and strolled in his measured gait to the center of the platform. The lanky scientist raised his hands to get the room's attention and switched to broadcast mode on his DataPort. Plexar's voice sounded clearly in Haarkonan's head via his DataPort.

"Welcome to the victory celebration!" The room erupted in cheers before he could continue. Despite the pain and loss of friends and all the grueling effort leading up to the battle, these people were excited to be alive and proud to have come to this point in time.

"I want to congratulate every one of you for our victory," said Plexar when the noise started to ebb. "You repelled the Narcoid invasion, destroyed their fleet, and have earned humanity a future. I hereby declare this day to be a permanent holiday for the human race, commemorating the day the war turned and the human race won its first victory against the Narcoid. We have earned the right to survive!" The crowd again reacted with cheers and clapping. Some of the more exuberant types gave out whoops of joy. Haarkonan couldn't stop smiling, as the huge gathering somehow felt more like a family than what it really was: a collection of humanity that spread across 6,000 years and six continents.

Plexar scanned the crowd and continued. "We could never have done it without this ship," he said, waving at the monstrosity behind him. "The *Ark of Time* was christened with the realization that time would be the saving ark for the human race. We didn't realize how prescient that naming was. Just as we are told in ancient history that an ark saved humanity from a flood, so the *Ark of Time* has ensured that the human race is not doomed to drown from this alien invasion."

"Humanity will not give up hope. We will not give up faith in the human spirit. And we will not surrender our home planet to an invading alien force. We've survived the depths of space, we've survived a Narcoid attack, and now we'll bring survival to our loved ones as we take this fight back to Earth.

"So celebrate this day, rest and enjoy victory, but do not forget there is much work to be done. We must repair this station, repair our spaceships, and most importantly, repair our people. We must continue to search for volunteers from the past to help us in the present. And we must launch the ground war to retake our earth. It must be done soon, for our planet and our people are suffering. Enjoy today, for as one great man of history has said: this is not the end, this is not even the beginning of the end. But this is the end of the beginning."

Haarkonan smiled as the crowd applauded the inspiring quote from Sir Winston Churchill. Winston himself had suggested using it. They had gathered to this distant *Horizon* the best minds and technology humanity had to offer, and he could tell this ebullient crowd didn't think anything could stop them.

As he looked deeply into their faces he saw many friends and many strangers, but no one seemed too strange. They were no longer a discordant bunch but had somehow been changed by adversity and forged into a real united force. Haarkonan was surprised to realize that something had changed in his own heart as well. He was no longer just in this to avenge his wife, without really caring about a future. Humanity deserved a chance to live, and for the first time in what seemed like forever, Haarkonan felt a strange feeling. He didn't recognize it at first, but then it came to him: he felt hope.

THE FOLLOWING IS A FREE PREVIEW FROM *The Ark of Earth*, **WHICH IS BOOK TWO IN THE ARK TRILOGY, EXPECTED TO RELEASE IN DECEMBER 2015 BUT STAY TUNED TO TheArkTrilogy.com FOR DETAILS.**

CHAPTER 1

Valerius the Viking

":*We have suffered loss,*" The Mission Overlord allowed his mental tone to radiate anger.

":*Yes, Great Lord,*" his understudy's mental tone was neutral. "*The squishy bipeds on the dark asteroid have destroyed more of the Host than we lost in the entire invasion of Earth.*"

":*How did they manage to destroy a third of the Host? They were not supposed to even have the means to take down a Battleship. Yet we now know that they murdered a Mothership.*"

":*We're not certain how it was done, Great Lord. We believe they had help. A fleet with superior armaments arrived.*"

The subordinate's mental stream was met with silence, so he continued. ":*It is indeed shocking that they would murder a Mothership.*"

":*From whence did this new fleet originate?*" Now the Overlord's tone was cold and calculating.

":*We do not know. The humans may have a distant colony, on another living planet.*"

":*Let us find this second living planet. Then we can send greetings to the Most High Overlord of Hosts, may he live forever, that tempers our setback here with the good news of another living world to assimilate."*

":Yes, Great Lord," the subordinate said, attempting to keep his cringing feelings out of the mind stream. He took the further silence as dismissal, and withdrew to contemplate how best to discover the second planet the human race had contaminated with its presence.

"The last thing we need is more of those Vikings on *Horizon*!" Otho said between mouthfuls of grayish mash that tasted like potatoes and mutton with a hint of mint. A small globule stuck to the outside of his lip and had just begun to slide into his beard when his meaty backhand smeared it off his face and flicked it to the floor.

Valerius smiled, not so much amused by Otho's lack of table manners as by the truth behind his words. The few hundred Vikings who had been taken forward in time and housed at the asteroid base *Horizon* had been rather unruly, raiding food storage areas and on one occasion staging a nonviolent protest to demand an immediate ground war to retake Earth from the Narcoid invaders.

"My friend, I understand your sentiment, but in truth we can use anyone who is willing to fight, and I've never known a Viking who didn't want to fight."

"Aye," said Otho with his mouth still full. "They like to fight, and they like to drink, don't be forgetting that."

"I haven't forgotten," said Valerius with a smile. "That mead of theirs packs a punch. But I don't understand you. I'd think you'd get along with them."

"Me?" said Otho indignantly.

"Yes you. You have a lot in common. For instance, most of them are graced with large physical size and a small sense of responsibility."

"They like to have fun, and so do I, so there is that," said Otho, his large brown eyes twinkling. "And they average a bit bigger than the typical wee Romans of noble blood like yourself, though that's not so very hard, is it. But that's where the similarity ends," said Otho petulantly.

"I think your problem is that you have too much in common with the Vikings," said Valerius, enjoying the chance to goad his friend and former senior noncommissioned officer in the Roman army. "You just don't like the competition they give you."

"Blah," said Otho in disgust while stuffing a second bread roll into his mouth.

"There's that too. You and the Vikings are always so eloquent."

This time all he got was a good-natured glare from his friend. Otho was seldom in a bad mood while eating.

"In any case," continued Valerius. "This should be an interesting mission, complete with a real mystery. I'm told the Vikings made an establishment in the Americas, but the settlement was lost and there're no record of what happened. We might have the chance to solve the mystery, and if we're lucky we'll rescue an entire town or two from some calamitous fate. That would be a nice addition of troops for our imminent war with the Narcoid."

"I don't care about solving mysteries," said Otho with a big grin. "But I like the sound of having a whole village. *Horizon* has good food, but it could use more good women."

"So you like Viking women, just not their men?" Valerius accused with a smile.

"I'm just saying we snatch far too many men. We need more of a balance, that's all."

"You're sure that's all? I saw you flirting with that Viking chieftain's daughter the other day. You know, the big blonde one. Be honest—you like Viking women."

"What's there not to like?" asked Otho with an innocent grin that would make a Cheshire cat envious. "Viking women have lots to love and hips to survive child-bearing. You pure-blooded Romans follow the silly Greek ideal, preferring women with figures that resemble girls before puberty. The Vikings appreciate real women with mature figures."

"I think you appreciate any woman who pays attention to you," Valerius said good-naturedly. In truth, Otho got along well with the fairer sex, who found his rugged looks and teddy-bear nature endearing.

Valerius finished his food and politely wiped his mouth with his napkin as he stood up. At 5 foot 10 inches he was above average height for a Roman, with a slender build, olive-colored skin, and an aristocratic nose. His bright blue eyes contrasted with his dark hair and skin, and while they could be piercing when he turned his gaze on a misbehaving subordinate, his eyes often sparkled with good humor and a generally optimistic outlook.

Otho finished wolfing down his meal and rose as well. In contrast to his commanding officer, Otho towered head and shoulders above most men and was broad-shouldered. His Germanic ancestors were also evident by his pale-white skin and full beard. As Valerius surveyed his friend he thought that while Otho may not want to be associated with the Vikings, he certainly *looked* like one of them.

The two men cleaned up their area, carrying the plates to the conveyor that scraped off all food materials for recycling. They then strode toward the temporal mission briefing room for their final discussion about the upcoming mission.

Valerius kept quiet during the short walk, contemplating the mission. There was a lot to prepare. This wouldn't be a simple temporal grab. Instead of showing up and rescuing people in the midst of a storm or other natural catastrophe, this time the *Time Raider* had made a series of jumps to determine when the Viking settlements in North America vanished, and now they would send Valerius and his team in to be ready to call in the insertion team at the right moment. The key was to allow history to play out and only intervene at the last second when the intervention itself would not really change history. Living people would be rescued from certain death, and then clone bodies would replace them, so that posterity never knew the future had come to the past. It was called a "seamless temporal insertion," and Valerius already had dozens of successes to his credit.

The two men rounded a corner and entered the briefing room. "Atten-shun!" demanded an orderly near the door. Chairs slammed back as people quickly rose to honor their senior-ranking officer.

"At ease," said Valerius as he went to the head of the table and took his seat. The others then sat down too, with Otho sitting a few chairs further down the table from Valerius.

The lights dimmed and historian Dr. Barry Bernard ambled up to the stage. Behind him the screen switched from a beautiful live picture of the earth slowly rotating to a scene filled with brutal snow and ice.

"According to the *Sagas of Icelanders*," began Dr. Bernard without preamble, "The Vikings settled Greenland in the 980s. They called it 'Greenland' so that other Vikings would settle there as well, just like they named Iceland with the intent of dissuading heavy influxes of settlers." The room chuckled at the dark-ages propaganda.

"The attractive name succeeded in bringing in waves of Vikings from Denmark, Norway, and Sweden, but when the settlers discovered exactly how harsh the conditions were, some of them decided to try to sail southwest toward friendlier climes. One such Viking was called Eric the Red."

The picture behind Dr. Bernard switched to show an artist's rendering of Eric the Red. He was dressed in furs, and had a large sword in a leather scabbard. His skin color seemed a bit too red. Valerius decided that the artist had guessed the color moniker was due to a ruddy complexion. Knowing some Vikings first hand from living with them on the dark planetoid *Horizon* for the past year, Valerius would have guessed the color choice was somehow associated with bloodshed.

"Eric the Red was expelled from Iceland for manslaughter," continued Dr. Bernard, making Valerius smile as his suspicion was confirmed. "By 985 he was leading expeditions to scout the North American waters and was a landowner who granted large tracks of land on Greenland. Trade flourished, as Greenland exported walrus ivory, furs, rope, sheep, whale, and seal blubber for candles. We even have records of them exporting live animals such as polar bears, which fetched a sizable price in Norway.

"In 1000 AD, Eric the Red's son Leif Ericson sailed 1,800 miles with a crew of 35, reaching down into what would become Canada and possibly even the United States of America. Behind me is a copy of the Skálholt map, possibly showing what the Vikings knew of the geography. Unfortunately, a mini-ice-age ensued in the 14th century, and by the 15th century the settlements in Greenland were effectively cut off from Europe. When Norwegian missionary Hans Egede was finally sent to reestablish contact with the Greenlanders in 1721, he discovered no one of European decent was left alive. All of the settlements had vanished."

"What do you mean by 'vanished'?" asked Valerius. "Did they die off or leave?"

"We didn't know until this very mission," said Dr. Bernard, clearly unwilling to skip part of his lecture. "Until now we had not had a chance to go back and see what happened to them. Most historians guessed that the Vikings lost a war with the indigenous peoples, as the Viking tales speak of skirmishes. They called the indigenous populations 'skraelings,' which was a derogatory term, probably meaning 'weak barbarians.' Eventually the term entered more modern Danish to mean "weakling," and may even be where our modern Angelsk gets the word "scrawny."

"You can skip the etymology lesson," said Valerius. Modern academics seemed to love going off on tangents.

"Right," continued Dr. Bernard amiably. "The important thing I was getting at is that the Vikings were very formidable, and they were not at all afraid of the skraelings. In fact, Leif's sister Freydis is said to have scared a whole tribe of them away while being pregnant simply by beating her bare breast with a sword."

"Aye, that's the Vikings alright," interjected Otho with sincere admiration. Dr. Bernard ignored the comment and continued.

"From our recent temporal transitions we now know that the thousands of Vikings in Greenland were forced to migrate south, and that they ended up in Nova Scotia and Maine. I had suspected as much, because in the 20th century we discovered the Maine Penny, which was a Norwegian coin from King Olaf Kyrre's reign at the end of the 11th century."

"So what happened here," broke in Valerius, a little impatient with all the history. "What's my team getting into?"

"This is an interesting situation," said Dr. Bernard thoughtfully. "The *Time Raider* and *The Ark of Time* have each made dozens of temporal transitions to map out what happened to the Vikings here in the new world. Basically, it's a classic situation of slow demise. The

Vikings suffered numerous small wars with the natives at first, but the skraelings pulled back because they lost every confrontation. The Vikings then endured disease, freezing winters, hurricanes, and even a few rebellions and splits before their civilization crumbled. Within a century of being in the New World the Viking settlements had completely disintegrated. A few boats were launched to carry the last Vikings back to Europe, but none of them made it."

"So what we have here is a completely isolated civilization that will eventually die?" asked Valerius.

"Exactly. The settlement below is never to be heard from again, and is effectively lost without ever affecting anyone else. It has been deemed an acceptable situation for a time snatch."

"But there's a difference here," said Valerius contemplatively. "To date, we only snatched people whose death was imminent. Many of these people have their whole lives ahead of them. Is it right to take people who have many years left without their consent?"

"'Course it's right," said Vinney Walscot who sat to Otho's left. Vinny had been a British naval officer and then a notorious pirate before he was time-snatched and recruited into the military of the future. He wore his blond hair long and had far fewer scruples than most men. Surprisingly, Valerius liked the man anyway, and knew there were few men in any time period who could match his nautical skills.

Vinny tugged at the corner of his mustache and continued. "We need 'em to 'elp us retake Earth of the future. No sense gettin' all philosophical 'bout it."

"I know *why* we want to take them," said Valerius patiently. "But I think they deserve a say in the decision. The last thing we need are a bunch of disgruntled Vikings aboard *Horizon*."

"Yah," interjected Otho with a smile. "The happy ones are trouble enough!"

"So what are ya supposing to do?" asked Vinny. "Ya can't just go down there and ask 'em to take a vote. Even if they was a democracy, which they ain't, they'd never really know what it was they was votin' about."

"That's a fair point," said Valerius. "But I still think they need at least some say in this. Maybe they won't understand exactly what we're proposing, but if we can at least put some of it into their words it would be worth doing."

"Are you really saying that you want some of us to go down there and reason with Vikings?" asked Otho incredulously. "And these aren't just normal Vikings. These are the crazy ones who settled in Greenland, migrated to the 'warm' climes of Maine, and will fight each other into oblivion in the coming decades."

"Exactly right," said Valerius with a mischievous smile. "I have an idea, and you, Otho, are the real key to it all."

***

He was colder than he had ever been. Having grown up and lived around the Mediterranean Sea most of his life, Valerius had never had to acclimate to subzero temperatures. He and Otho were now trudging through snow drifts toward a Viking settlement, and even with the modern thermal fabrics he felt his bones freezing and all his exposed skin tingling, possibly on the verge of frostbite. His idea to reason with the Vikings had seemed wise when he was aboard the *Time Raider*, but now that he and Otho were actually putting the plan in action, he was having some doubts.

Wouldn't it have been easier to simply fly over the Viking settlements and beam them with knock-out sonics, then abduct them as they had countless others who were doomed throughout history? And what if his plan failed and the Vikings refused to volunteer to be a part of the future military force that would retake Earth from the invading aliens? Would he accept their answer and fail in his mission, or would he abduct them anyway against their will?

Valerius glanced over at Otho and noticed that the big man looked comfortable in his bear-skin pelts, Viking chain mail, and iron helmet. In fact, in all the 15 years they had served together in the Roman army, Valerius was hard-pressed to remember a single instance where the man had looked uncomfortable. Not only was he sauntering through the snow as if it were a warm July, but he also had a look of blissful confidence on his face. The big man flashed him a grin he could not return, so he just went back to looking down at his feet as they plodded through the snow drifts.

Sometimes he envied Otho's personality and station in life. It would be so much easier to just accept orders rather than be the one responsible for giving them, thought Valerius. Noble blood was a blessing, and command brought rank and privilege, but it was times like these where he wished the burden of decision could be shared or wholesale given to another. Otho simply trusted that Valerius knew what he was doing. Valerius wished he had that much trust in himself for this escapade.

He felt especially uncomfortable in the Viking attire. Everything felt baggy, his chain mail felt wrong, and his embossed shield hung heavy on his back. He longed for his snug-fitting Roman armor. At least the Viking long sword hanging at his side closely resembled his beloved *spatha* Roman cavalry sword. What he especially despised was the long tresses of blond hair that had been sealed onto his head, as well as his scraggly new beard. Why the Vikings preferred to have blond hair, and even went so far as bleaching it with strong lye-based soap, was beyond him. Romans were not meant to have beards, but at least this one gave him an added measure of warmth.

"Hey commander!" bellowed Otho over the howling wind. "Guess what? This new arm feels the cold even better than my real arm!" Otho chuckled, clearly pleased that the mechanical arm's temperature sensors were functioning. Otho had lost his left arm battling alien invaders, but had been pleased to discover that the 24th century had excellent mechanical replacements for all limbs.

As it had been explained to Valerius, Otho's new arm was much more powerful and could be more or less sensitive than a real arm, depending on the preference of the user. The arm communicated wirelessly to the user's brain via the DataPort interface that had been surgically implanted at the base of their skulls. The DataPort was originally designed to access the Internet and plug into vehicles, but its uses had quickly expanded and now it served many purposes. Not only was it delivering sensory data to Otho's brain, but its outstanding language program was set to deliver all the vocabulary they would need for this mission. Valerius and Otho were now fluent in Old Norse, having spent only a few hours practicing the language. Practice was essential to train the tongue and develop an intelligible accent.

They were now emerging from a forest that opened up to a small plain where a cold river slowly winded its way toward the nearby ocean. Less than a Roman mile away Valerius could see log buildings circled around a center great hall and nestled against the river's mouth. The heart of the town was clearly the huge hall at its center, though other large longhouses were pressed up near the docks at the far side of the town. Most of the longhouses were medium-sized, built to protect about 20 people each, and had the characteristic steep thatched roofs that reached almost all the way to the ground. While most of the dwellings seemed to be without heat, a small cloud of smoke arose from the great hall. The billowing smoke chugged out of a chimney only to be quickly whisked away and dissipated by the frigid arctic winds.

Valerius knew the Vikings were great warriors. While they lacked many of the finer points of civilization that he cherished, he had seen these people in action in the vidz and he knew that no civilization of this time period could match their battle ferocity, warfare cunning, or weapons technology. As he and Otho emerged from the woods and approached the outskirts of the small village, a man in thick furs with a large round shield spotted them. He growled wordlessly and then started running toward the town hall shouting an alarm. Evidently the Vikings didn't rely on the cold to keep foreigners out but had developed a very functional system of sentries. This particular sentry didn't think it wise to try to take on the two wanderers by himself.

Valerius was impressed with the speed of the Viking village's reaction. Although it only took them a few minutes to reach the village outskirts and pass by the first few houses, already he saw many men running out of their homes while strapping on baldrics and slamming helmets on their heads. The oldest men looked to be in their thirties, while the youngest ones were probably not yet through puberty. Rather than running toward Valerius and his huge companion, they were all running toward the great hall at the town's center, most likely in order to form up a shield wall and receive instructions from their chieftain. Valerius guessed that these were some sort of standard orders, which suggested that this town had been attacked before. As they passed houses he heard scrapping noises as bolts and door bars were set in place.

As they reached the clearing before the great hall Valerius said a quick prayer to Athena, the goddess of wisdom. Standing in front of him were at least 40 Vikings, most of them clad in thick furs and wielding all kinds of weapons ranging from axes and adzes to thrusting spears and swords. Most of them also had circular or triangle-shaped shields, already held up at the ready position in case he and Otho had projectile weapons. Valerius had elected not to include bows and arrows in their arsenal because he wanted to make a strong first impression and he knew that many Vikings considered those weapons cowardly.

It was clear who was in charge. At the center of the Viking formation stood a giant red-bearded man who was almost as large as Otho. He had an iron helmet with gold embellishments and wore a full iron chain-mail tunic. Despite the cold, he had bare arms that were well-muscled and encircled with many gold and silver arm rings. Valerius knew those suggested the man was a well-honored warrior. Even his shield suggested wealth, as it was embossed with a dragon head. The large man's drawn long sword glinted wickedly.

Valerius held up a hand to show it was empty and strode forward toward the man he guessed was the chieftain. He knew this situation could easily go awry, and he started to doubt the wisdom of his decision to only bring Otho. He needed the Vikings to trust him, and he wasn't looking for a bloodbath. He took some comfort from knowing that the *Time Raider* was hovering somewhere above the cloud cover. While the ship could come to his rescue if something went wrong while they were outdoors, once they were inside things would get trickier.

Valerius turned both of his hands palms up, showing the big Viking that he approached unarmed. "I come to speak, not to fight," he said in what he hoped would be understandable Old Norse.

A large man on the chieftain's right screamed a war cry and burst forward, raising his sword high above his head. Valerius' war-trained reflexes reacted in an instant, as he swiftly took a step back and desperately grabbed at his sword that was still sheathed in its scabbard. He didn't have time to unsling his shield, and he was several paces ahead of Otho who could only watch is dismay as his friend and leader was attacked.

The large warrior erupted from the Viking line up, but then tripped and splayed onto the frozen ground, sprawling at Valerius' feet with a painful grunt. Valerius drew his sword as quick as lightning and was about to thrust it down at his assailant's neck when he heard the Viking chieftain roar "Nej!"

Valerius glanced up and noticed that the chieftain's foot had moved forward, and that it was he who had tripped the aggressive warrior. Looking up now he noticed that the chieftain's command had not been to tell him to refrain from striking the man on the ground, but had been directed at his own men to keep them from charging forward. The chieftain held out both arms, one with a shield and the other with a sword, symbolically holding back the flood of his warriors.

Valerius checked his downward death swing, and stood upright. He slowly sheathed his sword. The large man on the ground had clearly been humiliated, and crawled back a few feet before standing.

"Into the great hall, Olaf!" commanded the chieftain in a tone of scorn and rebuke. The big man snorted and pressed through the Viking line toward the hall.

"We do not want killing," starting Valerius again. "We are friends."

"We have no friends in this land," the chieftain said cautiously. "I am Jarl Erondel the Fierce. Who are you and how have you come to my village over the winter land?"

"I am Valerius, a messenger of Odin, and I have come to give you a warning--"

"Do not threaten me here, in my own village, strange one," interrupted Erondel with iron in his voice. "And do not make claims of identity that you cannot prove. You are no Valkyrie sent from Odin to collect the dead."

"You misunderstand," said Valerius. "My warning is not a

threat, and I do speak for Odin. Grant us the right of visitors, and we can enter your hall where it is warm and there discuss these things."

"You speak the true tongue, and these are times with trouble enough. I do not believe your claims, but I'm willing to hear you out. Do you also pledge to uphold your duties as guest?"

"We do," said Valerius with an inward sigh of relief. He rolled his shoulders slightly to try to relax his coiled muscles.

The chieftain also visibly relaxed. "Then I grant you the rights of guest for this evening. You will leave your weapons here, as it is our custom not to bring them into a place of festivities and drinking. Come and tell me what you must, and tell also of how you came to my threshold and what you know of the homeland."

Erondel lowered his weapons, giving his shield to a shield bearer. "Jens, Sven, go throughout the village and announce that the danger is over. Tell them also to double the sentries, in case there are more 'friends' in the woods. Clause Nygaard, see that the women are told that tonight we feast on pig flesh and the good mead, and have them prepare lodging for our guests." He then abruptly turned his back on the foreigners and strode back to the warmth of his great hall.

Valerius signaled to Otho to approach and begin removing his weapons. He set down his own sword and took out his boot knife, placing it beside his sword on a wooden pallet that was just outside the great mead hall. He noticed that two of the armed Vikings entered the hall behind their chieftain with their weapons, but that the rest of the men who started entering the hall had removed their weapons. Most of the Vikings stood back and watched wearily, looking at the newcomers with suspicion as they disarmed. Valerius was a little concerned that these armed Vikings might make trouble, but then they started melting back into the village, most likely planning to reassure their families that all was well.

Valerius cautiously walked through the large doors and into the great hall, but before he could look around a thick arm with multiple silver arm rings of honor shot out to bar his passage. It was one of the men who had entered the hall with his weapons, and he clearly was a guard who enforced the no weapons rule.

"What is that?" asked the guard indicating Valerius' holster. The man's breath reeked of onions and his skin smelled of pig fat that Valerius knew was slathered on to seal out the winter cold.

"This?" asked Valerius, indicating his holster. "It's just a hammer."

"Why do you carry a small hammer? Are you a leader or a carpenter?" demanded the Viking, chuckling as if he had made a witty jest.

"I'm both," said Valerius with more confidence than her felt. "A real warrior builds his own dwelling and his own ship. This is both a tool and a symbol of leadership. Are you afraid of my hammer going into the great hall?"

"I fear no hammer, just as I fear no carpenter," said the Viking with newfound disdain. "You can take it inside," he said, waving his hand to shepherd Valerius further into the building.

Valerius stepped further in and looked around. The large hall was impressive, and doubly so for being in such an otherwise primitive setting. No doubt it was made to impress visitors. Valerius marveled at the skill that had built the wooden rafter beams which stretched to a point at least four man-lengths above his head. The room was mostly open, except that in the center of the huge hall were four square wooden pillars supporting an elevated square-shaped structure that held up the roof. Each of the pillars was wider than Otho's broad shoulders. The center area of the hall was flat, but there were two broad tiers or benches to the right and left of the hall, and a raised tier at the far end of the hall. It reminded Valerius of a mini-amphitheater, as the horseshoe of flooring was clearly meant to afford many people a good view of whatever entertainment was being played out on the lower center stage. Some tables were already placed in front of the right and left tiers, and the entire far end boasted sturdy tables covered in embroidered cloth of fine white flax.

Valerius knew that white cloth was often favored for things that frequently got dirty because it was easy to bleach, whereas colored cloth required much more work to clean without ruining the colors. The far wall was also lined with two rich red tapestries, and the side walls had scattered animal pelts of various kinds to assist the sturdy wooden walls in holding off the winter chill. Torches lined the side walls, making the place seem cheerful and warm.

Valerius spotted Erondel at the center of the table on the far wall, and started walking toward him. The Jarl sat behind a table that was elevated above all of the other tables, and that table alone had its own chairs rather than being complemented by the natural benches like the other tables. The big man seemed to be arguing good-naturedly with a skinny old man who had a shock of white hair covered by a skullcap that might have been made from snake skin.

Beneath the Jarl's feet was a marvelous carpet of thick pelts. Intrigued, Valerius looked around and discovered that the hall had no other carpeting, but he did discover that the floor was well-constructed, with carefully laid interlocking pine boards and some sort of hardened tar filling in the natural gaps.

Then Valerius spotted a very welcome sight. On the right side of the hall near the far end was a huge stone hearth with a blazing fire and some food dangling over the flames. Cooking implements hung near the fire place, and a large iron spit was being pulled out and made ready to begin roasting a pig. Altogether it seemed a rather cheerful place, if a bit below what a Roman would expect in the way of cleanliness standards.The whole place smelled of sour mead, animal greases, and smoke. There was also a faint sweet smell of grasses that probably originated from the thatch roofing.

As Valerius reached the head table, Jarl Erondel waved him up to sit in the place of honor to the chief's immediate right. Turning around, Valerius noted that Otho had successfully unarmed himself and passed by the door guards. He seemed to be mulling about aimlessly until a cute young Viking teenager with platinum-blond pigtails approached him and kindly escorted him to a table on the right side of the large room. Other Vikings were also being directed by young ladies, suggesting that the Vikings followed a protocol when it came to seating arrangements. Otho got a good seat near the head table, but was clearly more interested in the full-figured young blonde than the seating arrangement. Valerius chuckled as he watched the big man stare with great interest at the maiden.

"So you claim to speak for Odin," boomed Erondel good-naturedly. "My wise counselor Kvasir here says I should kill you and see if you indeed are immortal, but I say we first hear you out."

The skinny little old man seated to Erondel's left leaned forward to stare at Valerius over his lord's shoulder, then sat back and grunted his dissatisfaction for having his counsel ignored.

"You are wise to do so," said Valerius.

"Kvasir is more often right than wrong," Erondel said to placate his advisor. "But I think even if you do not speak truth, what you say will amuse us. So, let us begin to test your story. Look at my hall! Does your master Odin have a great hall as magnificent as mine?"

"Valhalla is the greatest of halls, as you well know," said Valerius diplomatically. "But yours is truly one of the greatest I have seen on Midgard."

"So you also claim to have been to other worlds?" asked Erondel with a smirk, clearly more amused than persuaded. "Why not just claim yourself to be Thor, eh?" the big man chuckled.

Valerius smiled quietly. That was pretty close to what he intended to do. That was why he had donned a silly blond wig and brought his "hammer."

Erondel sobered some at his guest's silence. "Stranger, I do not wish to offend you, as it is our custom never to mock or insult a guest. But you must admit that your words are amusing, and we don't get many visitors to amuse us with claims of grandeur. All we get are skraelings who are little barbarians hardly more worth fighting than children, yet they rove in gangs and commit atrocities."

"You see Oda there?" He pointed at the blonde maiden who had helped seat Otho. "Just last week the coward skraelings trapped her by the river and forced themselves upon her. She wounded more than one of them before they overwhelmed her. When our warriors noticed and charged forward for battle, the puny skraelings just ran away into the woods. That girl is my niece, and I have sworn vengeance for her being violated!"

Valerius was startled by the frankness of the story and the raw ferocity that had entered his host's voice. He tried to keep his face blank, but he could see from Erondel's face that the big man had noticed his reaction of surprise and anger.

The great hall was quickly filling with people and noises. Dinner was getting started, tables were being prepared, and ladies were bringing in baskets of food. Many of the Vikings who had previously been outside in armor were now entering in more casual clothing. Everyone seemed to be in good spirits, glad for the warmth of the hall and the chance to celebrate the newcomers' visit. The warm atmosphere must also have melted some of Erondel's wrathful mood, as his angry ardor evaporated as fast as it had appeared.

The Jarl drank deeply of his mead and then slammed his cup onto the table, getting Valerius' attention again. "You say you are a Valkyrie, yes?" he asked mockingly.

"No great Jarl, not a Valkyrie. I said I was called Valerius."

"Valerius then. I have never known one called Valerius. It's not a proper name, is it? Regardless, you also said you were a messenger from Odin?"

"Yes, Jarl."

"Then deliver your message, and I will weigh your words carefully."

Valerius drew a quick breath and launched into his tale. His oratory-trained voice carried throughout the hall, and men everywhere quieted down to hear his story. "Odin, the one-eyed seer of the future, who wrestled the mighty Yggdrasil tree and tore from its roots the wisdom of runes, has foreseen your future here in the new world. He has seen the threads the three Norns intend to weave to create your wyrd and was displeased. Since he has accepted your sacrifices and knows of your piety, he sent me to warn you of a slow death unworthy of warriors, and to give you an honorable and glorious alternative."

"A man's fate cannot be altered," protested Kvasir, but he was quickly silenced by a wave of Erondel's hand.

Valerius continued. "While a man's fate is inexorable, the great Odin decrees for you a choice of two fates. Most men only have one fate, and wyrd is wyrd for most men. Yet you stand at a fork in the road of fate. If you continue on your current path, you and your people with suffer disease and death, fires and infighting, skraeling raids and natural disasters. You will slowly be erased from memory—

no sagas will remain of your lives and great deeds—and your people will die out slowly and painfully like a man with a shallow stomach sword wound."

Valerius paused for dramatic effect and scanned his audience. He had the whole hall's attention now. "Because you are favored, Odin has sent me to give you this option: you may choose to take all of the people of your village to the final battle of Ragnorok! Odin seeks faithful allies who will fight in the final battle for Midgard, against creatures from the other nine worlds. You will have a chance for glory, a chance to die clutching your swords and so be taken by the Valkyries into Valhalla! And there is also a chance for life, more full and rewarding than you are ever fated to have here. Will you join the gods for a final battle that will be retold as the greatest story of all time? Or will you accept a slow and pitiful death in this frozen country?"

"Do you take us for fools?" asked Kvasir angrily, spitting with rage. "This is just a ruse to make us leave these lands so that you may have them. And how will you take us to Ragnorok? Is there a boat that sails the sea of time?"

"There is indeed just such a ship," replied Valerius, a little shaken by Kvasir's prescience.

"Bah!" erupted Kvasir, leaping to his feet so that he could stare down at Valerius and project his voice throughout the room. "You are just a man, and men make many claims with their mouths. Gods need not make boastful claims. They get what they want by actions. Our stories of old speak of Odin's messenger crows, but not of messenger men. Are you prepared to back your identity claims with action? I say you are a liar, and to save your honor you must prove yourself through personal combat!"

"Calm down Kvasir," said Erondel, waving his advisor to be seated before turning back to Valerius. "Our sagas tell us of Odin disguising himself and of gods walking among men, yet we have never experienced this thing. I do not wish to anger you who have the right of guests, but I also will not be taken for a fool. You have been challenged as a liar. Do you wish to apologize or are you prepared to accept a challenger?"

"I am prepared," said Valerius calmly, thinking he might actually have a good chance against the skinny wise man.

Erondel looked up to address the whole assembly. "And who here will test this man's words through battle?" Valerius cringed inside, realizing he would have to face someone other than the skinny old man. He presented a stoic face even as he looked around the room at the many fierce potential opponents.

"I will!" cried a big man who sat at the head table on the far side of Kvasir. Valerius recognized the man as the impetuous Viking who had wanted to attack him outside the hall but who had been tripped.

"It is fitting," said Erondel. "Olaf, son of Kvasir, you will be the challenger. In this way you may regain my favor. Let us have the match now, so that we do not waste food on the loser. Contestants, prepare yourselves for personal combat!" The Viking Jarl then sat back, a slight smile spreading across his face.

So much for oratory skill, thought Valerius. He had hoped that his sophist-trained powerful rhetoric would win the day. Now his muscles would have to do what his mouth could not accomplish. He stood and moved around the head table and jumped down into the middle arena area. The hall broke out in cheers as Olaf also entered the arena and raised both arms, playing to the crowd. Valerius took a deep breath and then looked up at his foe. Unfortunately, he had to really look *up*, as the Viking towered over him by at least four inches. What was that modern saying he had heard? Something about the bigger they are the harder they fall? He hoped that saying would come true, and that it was not just more worthless modern prattle.

"Let this be a wrestling match without weapons," directed Erondel from his chair. "He is, after all, a guest. As the *Gragas* law states, you may at any time leave the arena and forfeit the fight. However, that also means any injury you sustain in the arena is your own fault. The winner is the last man alive in the arena. Bring out the *fanghella* stone!"

Three large men grabbed a jagged black rock that was about two feet in length and width and maybe a half foot high. They bent over it and strained to place it in the center of the arena between the two contestants, then withdrew back into the crowd. Olaf took off his shirt, showing mountains of rippling muscle.

Valerius desperately accessed his DataPort to understand what the rock was for. His mental commands were immediately answered as the data flashed into his conscious thought. "The *fanghella* stone was used in wrestling contests to hurt the opponent more severely than would a flat floor. Stories describe contestants being thrown on the stone to break their backs and ribs, or tugged across it to inflict cuts and bruises…"

"*Beegynde at kæmpe!*" yelled Erondel over the roar of the crowd. Fortunately the command to begin gave Valerius just enough warning so that he succeeded in ducking as Olaf leaped over the stone and swung a meaty fist at his head. Valerius was now bent over and off balance, but so was the Viking after his blow only met air. Valerius didn't have time to straighten up and deliver a counter-punch, so instead he continued his downward motion, resulting in an awkward forward roll to the side of the ominous black stone.

Valerius sprung to his feet as Olaf turned toward him with an oafish grin. "Maybe you'll last longer and give us more pleasure than my last opponent," he taunted.

"I hope to do just that," replied Valerius calmly.

"Shouldn't be too hard," said Olaf, crouching into a fighter's stance. "Eric the Blue was already dead by this time in my last *kæmpe!*" Olaf then roared as he rushed forward.

Valerius had learned Greek wrestling in his own time period, and had learned some martial arts while aboard the *Horizon*. He knew the manly thing to do would be to close with his opponent, each man grasping the other's shoulders and attempting to take the other down. He also knew that was a sure way to death, as the Viking outweighed him and was clearly no stranger to unarmed combat.

Olaf ran forward reaching out to grasp Valerius, and Valerius also reached up for Olaf's shoulders. Just as Olaf's fingertips reached Valerius' shoulders, instead of resisting the force Valerius rolled onto his back, stuck his foot in Olaf's stomach, and used the man's own motion against him to fling him through the air. The big Viking careened out of control before crashing in an ungainly manner a few meters beyond where Valerius lay. Valerius quickly rolled over and stood up. Olaf got up a bit slower, but not slow enough that Valerius could follow up the throw with a stronger offense.

Olaf was no fool. Having missed his target twice due to attacking with too much haste, this time he advanced slowly in a fighter's crouch. Valerius noted that the Viking had a dull red foot mark on his stomach, but the man's rippling muscles there told Valerius that the throw had probably done no significant damage.

This time Olaf swung his right fist at Valerius' midsection, but Valerius anticipated the blow and skipped backward toward the *fanghella*. Olaf's swing stopped in mid motion. It had only been a feint! The Viking stepped forward and quick as lightning delivered a left uppercut to Valerius' chin, lifting him off the ground and throwing him backward. He crashed to the ground dazed, his head barely missing the sharp edges of the *fanghella*.

The crowd yelled its approval as Valerius fought for consciousness and tried to gather his wits. His head ached, and his vision was blurred, but he could just make out Olaf's huge figure waving to the crowd. As his vision cleared a bit further he saw in the distance that his friend Otho had stood up and was watching him with great concern. He motioned with his hand to tell his friend to sit back down. This was something he had to do on his own, or he'd have no chance convincing the Vikings to come with him willingly into the future.

Olaf must have noticed that Valerius had begun to recover, as he turned back toward his prey and started forward. Valerius was still on the ground and had to think fast to avoid being stomped to death. As Olaf stalked forward ominously, instead of creeping backward Valerius scrambled forward using his heels and elbows, and pushed his left foot against Olaf's shin while hooking his right foot around the back of the Viking's knee. Valerius then rolled, pushing with his left foot and pulling with his right. Olaf crashed forward, face-planting on the *fanghella*. The big man thrust out his arms, but they were on either side of the stone and failed to hit the floor before his face rammed into the rock. Olaf hit so hard that his head bounced off the stone only to come crashing back onto it a second time.

Valerius quickly arose and tried to press his advantage by

grabbing the man's back, thinking that he'd try to toss him to the floor. Valerius' hands slid clean off Olaf's skin due to the slippery pig-fat. It briefly reminded Valerius of the oils the Greek and Roman wrestlers used to make themselves harder to manhandle. Olaf started to recover, pushing himself upright. His face had been shredded by the sharp rock, with blood dripping from the man's chin, nose, cheek, and eyebrow. A look of sheer rage filled his face as he tried to push back from the rock and stand up.

Valerius felt exhausted and wondered if he had a concussion. He knew he had to finish this quickly or else he would make a mistake and the big man would have a brutal revenge. Since he couldn't grab Olaf in order to throw him, he stepped forward and kicked Olaf in the kidney, forcing the big man back to hugging the rock. He then stepped to the far side of the *fanghella* while grabbing Olaf's hair with both hands and smashed the big man's face back into the rock. The crowd let out a sympathetic grunt of pain as Valerius rocked the man's head back and forth into *fanghella* a few times.

When Valerius finally released his head, Olaf seemed to be only semi-conscious. The crowd was roaring. At first he thought they were mad that he had won, but then he saw their lewd gestures and realized that they wanted him to continue slamming Olaf's face into the rock until he died. That may have been standard procedure for the Vikings, but Valerius was already appalled at his own brutality and had no intention of killing the man if he could help it. He grabbed one of Olaf's arms and hauled the brute to the side of the center ring, giving him a final push to ensure he was well outside the arena and therefore forfeited the match. Olaf let out a grunt when he was pushed, letting Valerius know that the big man still lived and would probably recover from his wounds.

Some of the Vikings booed at his merciful treatment of Olaf, but most of them roared their approval of his victory. Valerius accepted the congratulations by raising his hands into the air, and the Vikings increased the din by banging their mead steins on the tables. Valerius was surprised that they were not concerned that one of their own had lost. Maybe Olaf wasn't well-liked? Or maybe the Vikings valued entertainment too much to worry about who paid for it with pain.

As the battle-lust drained from his body, Valerius noticed that he was breathing hard and that he had a few new pains and bruises. His head pulsed with pain at each heartbeat, but he was glad to be alive. He decide it was time to get back to dinner and so staggered toward his seat at the front of the hall. Erondel was still sitting there. A slight smile formed on his lips, and he made a small head nod to recognize Valerius' victory. Beside him, Valerius noticed that Kvasir didn't look concerned for his son so much as disgusted by the loss.

"Watch out!" cried Otho suddenly. Valerius whirled around but stumbled to the ground because his balance was still being affected by his head injury. Olaf leapt back into the arena area, but now he was brandishing one of the door guard's long swords. His face was bloodied and filled with insane rage as he rushed forward, both hands raising the double-edged sword high over his head. Valerius scrambled on the ground but knew he didn't have time to rise as the Viking bore down on him with the huge sword and crazed eyes filled with hatred and a lust for revenge.

ABOUT THE AUTHOR

Peter A. Kerr is a graduate of the U.S. Air Force Academy and veteran of the wars in Bosnia and Iraq. He finished his military career at the Pentagon leading media relations for the Ronald Reagan State Funeral. Since then he has taught communications at a university, founded his own consulting business (KerrCommunications), served as Chief Media Liaison Officer for all Outdoor Games in Beijing for the 2008 Olympics, and started a writing career. Peter speaks various languages, has traveled to more than 60 countries on six continents, and brings a wealth of experience and two masters degrees to fortify his writing passion.

For book signings or author presentations email peter@kerrcommunications.com. Also be sure to visit www.ArkTrilogy.com to read about the latest book, to see if there will be a signing near you, or to contribute your thoughts to the debate about who the future most needs from the past.

Coming soon from A Deo Lumen...

Want more of Haarkonan and Valerius in the Ark Trilogy? Tell your friends about the Ark of Time, visit and share your ideas at ArkTrilogy.com, and be ready for the next books that are coming soon!

Book 2: The Ark of Earth

Horizon continues its plan to time snatch valuable people, starting with Vikings in the New World at the turn of the first millennia. The invasion of Earth, space battles, and a detour to Mars to meet the Narcoid make this a sequel you won't want to miss!

Book 3: The Ark of Revenge

This stunning series conclusion is one you won't want to miss (and we don't want to reveal anything about until you've read Book 2)!

THE SCIENCE & THEOLOGY BEHIND LASTING RELATIONSHIPS

Adam Meets Eve draws on current scientific research, insightful and often humorous stories, and timeless wisdom to illuminate the process of building romantic relationships. It will help you navigate every aspect of relationships, from initiating conversations to recognizing mature love to finally enjoying an engagement that properly lays the foundation for love that lasts a lifetime. **You'll find out:**

- Why did Adam need Eve?
- What are men/women really looking for in a mate?
- What should you do to attract the person of your dreams?
- How do you know when you're in love?
- How does one be romantic?
- How does current scientific research reinforce the wisdom of Biblical dating principles?
- How do you build a loving relationship that lasts a lifetime?

Adam Meets Eve won a "Top 3" Award at the Tyndale ReWrite contest and a "Book of Merit" certificate form Deep River Books. For more information please visit **AdamMeetsEve.com.**

Available in print and Kindle formats at Amazon.com